Shattered Trust

Mary Rivera

Contents

1. Chapter 1 — 1
2. Chapter 2 — 3
3. Chapter 3 — 9
4. Chapter 4 — 17
5. Chapter 5 — 25
6. Chapter 6 — 33
7. Chapter 7 — 42
8. Chapter 8 — 51
9. Chapter 9 — 61
10. Chapter 10 — 69
11. Chapter 11 — 76
12. Chapter 12 — 83
13. Chapter 13 — 90
14. Chapter 14 — 98
15. Chapter 15 — 105

16.	Chapter 16	118
17.	Chapter 17	129
18.	Chapter 18	139
19.	Chapter 19	149
20.	Chapter 20	158
21.	Chapter 21	167
22.	Chapter 22	174
23.	Chapter 23	184
24.	Chapter 24	193
25.	Chapter 25	203
26.	Chapter 26	212
27.	Chapter 27	221
28.	Chapter 28	231
29.	Chapter 29	242
30.	Chapter 30	251
31.	Epilogue	260

CHAPTER 1

I was always different from most girls, and I knew it.

During my years of middle school, I only had one friend who accepted who I was. Clarice Adams was just like me. The both of us spent most of our middle school years together, watching horror movies instead of going shopping, reading novels instead of painting nails, and arguing over music instead of shoes. We both didn't care too much about our looks and what people thought of us. That was what made us so compatible.

It completely broke my heart when Clarice decided to try out for the cheerleading team in the beginning of freshman year in high school. I knew personally that Clarice was never too interested in school spirit. Clarice only wanted to make the cheerleading team to become known in Woodrow Wilson High School.

Clarice eventually did make the team. You can thank the three years of gymnastics she took in elementary school. She had new friends by the time football season started. The more she cheered, the less I got to see her. And when I did see her, it

was during passing in the school hallways. She was always sur-
rounded by a group of girls with matching red and white cheer
uniforms, giggling about the football quarterback, or squealing
about a pair of sparkly heels.

I guess what hurt the most was when she left me. She decided
to leave me when I needed her the most, and she knew it. I would
never forget the look of guilt that flashed across her face when
my father told her dad that my mother died.

Anyway, she ignored me for a few months after she joined
the cheerleading team. But, naturally, the popular and most
respected people in our school would do their best to bring
down the loners.

I was one of the loners.

Before I knew it, Clarice would gather around me with her
group of bubble gum popping bitches. They were verbally abuse
me, while everyone stood around to watch and laugh. I knew
Clarice felt bad for bullying me, because I could see the glint
of sorrow in her eyes every time I was called a bitch by one of
her friends. But, she had to go along with it, just to keep up her
reputation.

CHAPTER 2

The house was dead quiet when I woke up the next morning.

I wasn't surprised, though. My father was probably gone, and would return some time in the middle of the night, hopelessly drunk.

I went downstairs to the kitchen, where the sink was overflowing with a scattered stack of dirty dishes. I opened the refrigerator door to find nothing in it but a jug of expired milk and a carton filled with two broken eggs. Groaning, I slammed the door shut, clenching my fists into a tight ball as I made my way out the door to go to school.

Walking on the sidewalk, I noticed a cotton candy pink Bentley driving by me. In the Bentley was a group of giggling girls, with Clarice being one of them. The driver was Clarice's best friend, Aubrey Small. Aubrey's fire red hair tossed behind her effortlessly, as she drove by me.

"Loser!" I heard one call after me as they drove away.

I dropped my head low, as I made my way towards school, while they were probably already halfway there in Aubrey's stupid, pink Bentley.

When I got the school, I walked by the parking lot. I couldn't help but notice Aubrey's pink Bentley standing out from all the other cars. I had to claw my fingers into my palms to resist myself from keying her car.

The hallways were empty when I got to school, signaling that I was probably late. Again.

Pushing open the doors to my first period class, history, I grudgingly made my way towards my desk. Before I even got to sit down, Mr. Lieberman called me out.

"Aerial Mason, care to explain why you're late for the second time this week?" Mr. Lieberman asked, tapping his fingers impatiently on his desk.

"I drove by Aerial while going to school today, and I saw her smoking weed!" Aubrey Small answered before I got to say a word. She batted her eyelashes innocently, pouting out her lower lip. Was she actually that delusional to think that she looked cute batting those spider legs that hung on the edge of her eyelids?

"Is she telling the truth, Miss Mason?" Mr. Lieberman asked, raising a bushy eyebrow at me.

"Of course I'm telling the truth! I have five girls as witnesses!" Aubrey exclaimed, pointing to her row of friends. One of them included Clarice.

Four out of the five girls immediately nodded. Clarice was hesitating, but after a while, she finally dropped her head low, nodding weakly.

I took in a deep breath of air, feeling my cheeks flush with embarrassment. "Mr. Lieberman, I was not." I quietly said, digging my nails into my flesh.

Mr. Lieberman didn't look convinced. "Are you really telling me that six girls are lying?" his voice low and dangerous, looking at me with disappointment.

I hated this feeling; this feeling of weakness and powerless.

"No." I mumbled.

Mr. Lieberman was already writing down a detention slip for me, shooting out his hand for me to collect. Clutching the end of the detention slip, I took it out of his hands as I shoved it into my back pocket.

"Go to your seat before you get into further trouble." He spat.

Sighing, I trudged my way towards my seat. Passing by Clarice, she looked up at me with a concerned frown. Rolling my eyes, I glared at her as I sulked down in my seat.

The hallways were empty during lunch. I was by my locker, stuffing in my textbooks from morning classes, while taking out the rest of my books for my afternoon classes. Just as I was about to close my locker, a voice called out.

"Aerial!" someone squealed.

Turning around, I spotted Clarice, all by herself. She was smiling at me like we were still best friends, but I stared at her as if I didn't recognize her.

She used to be like me, a jeans and t-shirt kind of girl. But, standing in front of me now, she was wearing a short skirt that wrapped around her hips, a hot pink blazer, and six inch stilettos. Her face was covered with various colors, and I could easily tell that she had her hair bleached into a piss blonde color.

"What?" I gritted through my teeth, too angry to stare at her in the eye.

She gave me a sympathetic smile, shifting her green eyes down. "I wanted to say sorry, about this morning."

I snorted, shaking my head. I reached into my back pocket, waving my detention slip in her face. "It's a little too late for that."

Her smile faded, as she knitted her perfectly plucked eyebrows together. "I know. I just feel really bad."

"You should." I glared at her. "Because of you, Mr. Lieberman probably thinks I'm high every time I'm in class."

I never had the guts to say this to Clarice in front of her friends. I knew that they would gang up on me. But, seeing Clarice standing in front of me, completely alone, I felt like I was in charge. I felt as if I had to power to bring her down, the way she did to me for two years.

"I did it to keep up my-"

"Reputation." I finished for her, the word rolling off the tip of my tongue as I stared at her with disgust. "I know."

After all classes were over that afternoon, I walked up a few flights of stairs to get to the fourth floor detention room, which was specialized for juniors.

Entering the room, I watched as Mrs. Fletcher, one of the oldest staff members in this school, lay her head flat on top of the surface of her desk. I heard a short snort from her, as I scrunched my nose with disgust, finding myself a seat at the desk in the back row.

The room was extremely quiet, making even the clock that hung up on the wall sound loud when each handle ticked.

In the room with me was only one other person. I recognized the guy as Hayden Durant, who was in my biology and economics class. It wasn't hard to remember who he was, anyway. He was my lab partner in biology, but he barely ever showed up to that class. I was always stuck doing the labs by myself, while he was probably cutting class with his delinquent friends.

"What are you looking at, sweet pea?" he suddenly spoke up, as his eyes met mine from across the classroom.

I gave him a glare, rolling my eyes. "Don't call me that."

He shrugged, as he slouched down in his seat, kicking his legs up as they rested on the desk. "I'll call you whatever I want, sweet pea." He emphasized.

I gagged, flipping him my finger. I knew this guy was a delinquent, but he had to be annoying, too?

He must've noticed my royally pissed off expression, because the smirk on his face fell. It was replaced with a soft smile. Hayden placed his legs down from the desk, sitting up straighter. "Listen, let's just start over, alright? I'm Hayden."

I narrowed my eyes at him, nodding. "I know." I paused. "You're the asshole that never shows up to lab, leaving me without a partner."

He chuckled, shaking the blonde hair away from his face. "It's not like I'd be any help, anyway. So, you're that Aria girl?"

"Aerial." I corrected, crossing my arms.

He nodded. "Right. So, what are you in detention for? I've never seen you around here."

I sighed. "Aubrey Small snitched on me, lying to Mr. Lieberman that I was smoking weed before class."

Hayden smirked, shaking his head. "And that dick believed her?"

"Her," I nodded, "and her five other minions."

Hayden shrugged, giving me a lop-sided smile. "I kind-of feel bad for you."

I frowned. "Kind-of?"

"Yeah. I would feel entirely bad for you, except, I really want some weed right now." He grumbled.

Glaring at him, I groaned. "You're completely hopeless."

He smirked, lifting his head up as his eyes met with mine. "That's what everyone tells me."

CHAPTER 3

"Hey, Aerial, wait up!" a voice called behind me, as I walked out of the school after detention.

Turning around, I found Hayden jogging up behind me. He came to me in short breaths, as I crossed my arms. "Yes, Hayden?" I urged for him to speak.

"Do you want to come over to my friend's house? A few of my other friends are going to be there, too." He asked me, grinning.

I frowned, as my eyebrows knit together. "I just met you."

Hayden shrugged. "I know. But, you seem interesting."

I stared at the time on my phone, noticing that it was a little bit past four. My father won't even be home until midnight- or maybe he won't even come home, at all. He's become such an workaholic, and stayed up most nights at the bar drinking to get his mind off of-

"So, are you in or not?" Hayden cut off my thoughts, giving me a curious smile.

I sighed, nodding with defeat. "I'll come- on one condition."

"What is that?" he asked.

"You aren't allowed to do drugs."

Hayden choked on his saliva, staring at me with disbelief. "What makes you think I do drugs?"

I rolled my eyes, poking my hand against his chest. "You're a delinquent, aren't you? And I'm pretty damn sure your friends are, too."

Hayden groaned, smacking his palm against his forehead. "Aerial, just because we get into a few fights-"

I coughed, giving him a bland look.

"-a lot of fights, doesn't mean we snort on cocaine during our spare time."

I pursed my lips together, looking over to the side. "Okay. Maybe, I was a bit judgmental." I admitted.

"Alright then." Hayden nodded. "Let's go. The guys are probably there already."

"Hayden, who's the chick?" one asked, eyeing me up in down.

I rolled my eyes at the douche, crossing my arms protectively. How could he check someone out when he didn't even met them yet?

"Guys, this is Aerial. I met her in detention today." Hayden explained, pushing me forward.

I frowned at Hayden, nudging his elbow, as he gave me an assuring smile. "They'll like you, don't worry." He whispered.

"H-Hi." I muttered, dropping my gaze to the floor.

There were five guys here, and I've witness them all in at least one fight in school.

"Man, you got detention, again?" one asked Hayden, shaking his head. "You should've just ditched, like us."

Hayden grumbled something under his head, before popping open a can of beer. "I couldn't. Hallie made sure I went to school today."

"Your sister is such a pain in the ass. But, she's so hot. Remember the time she wore that little skirt that made her ass look-"

I sat up from my seat, shaking my head as I raised my hands up in exasperation. "Tell me why I'm here again?"

Hayden tugged on my arm, signaling for me to sit down. "Calm down, Aerial. The guys are just messing around."

"Yeah, we're just kidding." One smirked. "If you're getting bored, you can come sit right here." He patted on his lap.

I could feel my face morphing into an expression of disgust.

"Leave her alone, Damian." Someone suddenly said, entering from the bottom of the staircase.

My breath got caught in my throat at the way his blue eyes shined with fury. I've definitely seen him around in school before, but I've never actually encountered him, up until now.

"Road kill." Damian cursed under his breath, glaring at the blue eyed God as he made his way towards us, taking a seat across from me.

"Who are you?" he asked me, blue eyes burning into mine.

I tried to speak, but all I could utter out was, "U-Uh…"

"Alex, why do you always have this effect on women?" Hayden teased, punching his friend in the shoulder.

I finally regained consciousness, shaking my head as I threw Hayden a look. "Shut up." I snapped.

Hayden smirked, rolling his eyes. He threw an arm around my shoulder, as he pulled me in close. My head was tightly compacted in his chest, as he grinned at Alex. "This is Aerial."

Alex gave me a short nod, before turning his attention away from me. "Who wants to take me next?" Alex asked the guys, grabbing an Xbox controller from the ground.

"That's what she said!" Hayden burst into a misfit of uncontrollable laughter.

Damian took the second controller off the ground, pressing a few buttons, as the levels of difficulty for the game appeared on the television screen. "Alex, do you me to go hard or easy on you?" Damian continued the joke.

"Click hard. You know Alex likes it real hard." Another guy pitched in.

Alex glared at the three guys, as he selected the level of difficulty as hard. Everyone chuckled at the lame joke, as I tried to bite back a smile by gnawing on my lower lip.

"Laugh, I know you want to." Hayden encouraged. "Let loose."

I smiled up at him, as I watched Damian and Alex start a game of Call of Duty.

I was in the kitchen of Alex's house, rummaging through his fridge for a drink. I grunted with irritation when the only thing I came across was beer and alcohol.

"What are you looking for?" a voice suddenly startled me.

Jumping with surprise, I bumped the top of my head against the fridge. I let out a groan of pain, as I rubbed my head with my palms. "Shit." I muttered, feeling a bump already in the process of formation. "I'm just looking for a drink."

Alex gave me a small grin of amusement, as he signaled for me to step aside. He opened his freezer, taking out some ice for me to put on my bump.

"Do you drink?" he asked me, peering in his own fridge himself.

"No- well, not necessarily." I mumbled.

He stuck his hand in the fridge, as he pulled out a bottle for me. "It's lemonade."

I stared the bottle hesitantly, before popping open the cap. I pressed the tip of the bottle to my lips, letting the cool liquid slowly make its way down my throat. As soon as I felt a burning sensation in my lungs, I coughed, placing the bottle down. "What is this?!" I sputtered.

Alex smirked. "Mike's Hard Lemonade."

I glared at him, slapping his chest. "Are you insane? I told you that I didn't drink!"

Alex shrugged, taking the bottle from me, and indulging it himself. "Sorry, I didn't know you were that weak."

"W-weak?!" I uttered, staring at Alex with disbelief. "You're-"

Suddenly, a head popped into the kitchen. "I heard some really bad coughing." Hayden frowned, staring between Alex and I. "What's going on?"

I glared at Alex, as Hayden stared at the bottle in Alex's hands. "Oh, Alex. Did you trick this innocent girl?"

"Can't help it." Alex shrugged. "Either she's too gullible, or she didn't bother to read the label of the drink."

I shook my head, tossing the pack of ice in the sink. "It's getting late. I'm going home." I muttered under my breath, brushing past Alex and Hayden.

"Late? It's only nine." Hayden whined.

"I didn't ask you to leave with me, did I?" I snapped, feeling angry for being tricked so easily into taking my first sip of alcohol. I didn't want to become an alcoholic like my dad. I didn't want to be violent and hopeless like him.

Hayden's face softened. "I could take you home."

I suddenly felt bad for being so harsh to him, when he did nothing wrong. I gave Hayden a small smile, shaking my head. "It's fine. Have fun."

As I passed through Alex's living room, Damian and the others turned to look at me. "You're leaving already?"

I nodded, giving them all a small wave. "I'll see you guys around." I paused, giving them a smirk. "If you show up to school."

Damian winked at me. "I'll show up, just for you."

As I exited the house, I heard footsteps behind me as I was near the end of Alex's driveway.

"You should stop walking now if you want a ride home." A voice, that I recognized as Alex's, said.

Without turning around, I flipped him my finger, as I kept walking.

"Aerial, don't be stubborn. The streets are dangerous at night." Alex said, suddenly with seriousness.

I stopped in my tracks, feeling my breathing become heavy. I turned around, staring at the devil himself straight in the eye.

"Are you getting in the car or not?" he asked, opening the driver's seat of his black BMW.

Groaning, I trudged my way up the driveway. I placed my hands on the handle of the door, swinging it open, as I obnoxiously got in Alex's fancy car.

"Where do you live?" he asked me.

"None of your business." I said immediately, as if it was a reflex.

Alex smirked at me with amusement. "I'm going to need your address if you want me to bring you home."

Oh, right.

"19 Riverhead Drive." I muttered, turning my head away from him, so I was staring out the window.

Five minutes into pure torture of silence, Alex spoke up. "So, do you have any pets?"

"No."

"What's your favorite color?"

"Green."

"When's your birthday?"

"December 23rd."

"What's your favorite food?"

I turned to him, raising an eyebrow. "Do you really even care?"

He opened his mouth to speak, but he immediately snapped it close. "Are you still pissed about the lemonade thing?"

"Yes." I snapped.

Alex rolled his eyes, shaking his head. "I don't get it. It was just a tiny sip."

I laughed bitterly, shaking my head. "Of course you don't get it. You never will."

Alex pulled up to the driveway of my house, as I got out, slamming the door closed behind me.

When I got inside my house, I noticed that Alex didn't leave until he saw me turn the lights on. I also noticed that my father wasn't home tonight, again.

Before I went to take a shower, I made my dad some dinner. I wrapped it up with plastic wrap, placing the pasta on the dinner table that was rarely used.

I heard my dad coming home during the middle of the night.

The next morning, he was gone, again.

But, so was the dinner.

CHAPTER 4

The hallways were deadly quiet this morning.

I liked the peace and quiet. For once, there were no girls squealing about pointless things, or guys hollering down the school corridor. I was glad that my ear drums wouldn't be bleeding today.

I completely jinxed it.

Right when Clarice Adams came through the school doors, the silence was completely gone. It was replaced with a misfit of chatter. Everyone wanted to get a glimpse of Clarice Adams, and her boyfriend, Daniel Reynolds.

The only reason why the entire student population- excluding me, supported Clarice and Daniel so much was because they were pretty much the definition of Barbie and Ken.

Clarice was the golden blonde, sun kissed tanned Barbie, who was the captain of the cheerleading squad. Then, you have Daniel, who was pretty much the human version of Ken. He was the shaggy blonde with crystal clear eyes, who was the school's quarterback.

I could tell Clarice was so in love with Daniel. The way her face goes red every time Daniel holds her hand, and the way she always has a dazed look in her eye gives it away immediately. I've known Clarice way too long to know that she had strong feelings for him.

Even though Clarice pretty much took a knife, stabbed it in my back, took it out, and stabbed me in the chest as well, I still cared if she got hurt or not.

And I knew pretty damn well that Daniel Reynolds was going to hurt Clarice sooner or later.

"Hey, I found you!" Hayden's cheery voice suddenly greeted me.

I stared up at Hayden's pair of hazel eyes, before giving him a small smile. "Hi, Hayden."

A few girls brushed by Hayden and I, looking at us with curious expressions. "What the hell is Hayden doing with that loser?" a girl hissed, glaring at me.

"We have biology first period today." He smiled proudly. "See? I remembered."

I chuckled, shaking my head. "We have biology seventh period today. We usually have biology first periods on Thursdays."

Hayden's face suddenly fell, as he turned pink. "O-Oh. I knew that."

"But, I'm pretty sure we have study hall together right now." I smiled, pointing at my schedule.

Hayden's face lit up again, as he tossed his arm around my shoulder, leading me towards the east wing of the second floor.

"Hayden, where are you going?" I asked, muffling back a laugh.

He stared at me with a blank expression. "Study hall?"

Sighing, I adverted our positions back towards the opposite direction. "Our study hall class is on the west wing." I shook my head. "How often do you go to class?"

Hayden shrugged, his face in complete concentration. "I just skip all the boring ones. Physics, Biology, Calculus, French, Global, Economics, English-"

"Basically everything?" I cut in, as we entered the study hall classroom.

Hayden grinned. "Don't say it like that. It makes me seem like a bad student."

"And you aren't?" I teased, poking his shoulder.

Hayden laughed, shaking his head. "So, Alex gave you a ride home yesterday?"

I scratched the back of my neck. "I guess so."

"I'm sorry for what he did, by the way. I completely beat the shit out of him last night- in an intense match of thumb wrestling." I could tell Hayden was trying to keep a straight face, but he eventually cracked a smile.

I rolled my eyes playfully, punching his shoulder gently. "Thanks, Hayden."

"It's funny, though." Hayden suddenly muttered.

"What?" I asked.

"Alex. Alex never offers to drive a girl home." Hayden pointed out.

I felt my throat get tighter, as I licked my lips. What in God's name is Hayden trying to prove to me? And, how many girls have Alex actually been with? I mentally slapped myself before my thoughts went on further.

"So? I don't care." I crossed my arms.

Hayden frowned with curiosity, but he quickly dropped it once he saw the expression on my face.

"Well, class is going to be over soon." He paused, taking a look at the time from his phone. "Do you want to sit with us at lunch today?"

I bit my lip, shaking my head. "Sorry, I don't think that's the best idea."

"Why not? The guys really like you." He offered me a smile.

"I like them, too." The thought of the guys accepting me made me happy. "But, I never go to lunch. I always stay in the library."

Hayden smirked. "Library? There's no fun in that cramped place."

"Well, I'd rather be in the library for an hour than be constantly tormented by Aubrey Small and her minions." I shuddered.

"Don't worry about her." Hayden assured. "We'll defend you if she tries anything on you."

"Thanks." I smiled.

Should I even do this?

I haven't stepped foot in the cafeteria for two years.

I knew it sounded ridiculous that I was stressing over something stupid like this, but it was so nerve wrecking for me.

I took in a deep breath, as I placed my right foot in the cafeteria, entering an environment where there were different cliques at each table.

I immediately noticed Clarice's group. It wasn't too hard to notice, either. It was the biggest group out of all of them, and everyone there was either wearing cheerleading outfits, or football jerseys.

"Aerial! This way!" a voice suddenly called from across the cafeteria, creating an echo.

Everyone silenced, as they stared at me. My face turned bright red, as my palms began to sweat. I noticed Aubrey Small's vicious green eyes shooting poison ivy at me. I quietly made my way towards the left of the cafeteria, where I spotted Hayden.

"Do people always stare at you like that?" Damian asked, as I took a seat across from him.

I chuckled, shaking my head. "No." I paused. "I think the only reason why they stared at me for that long was because Hayden decided to scream my name out loud."

Hayden grinned, as he stuffed a fry in his mouth. "At least everyone knows who you are now!"

"Are you hungry?" Damian asked, offering my half of his sandwich.

I smiled thankfully at him, taking his other half. I bit into my sandwich, as the guys started to talk.

"Do you need a drink with that?" a voice suddenly sent chills down my spine.

I stared up at a pair of blue eyes. Alex was grinning smugly down at me, holding out a bottle of apple juice for me. I eyed the drink suspiciously, as Alex's eyes twinkled with amusement. "It's alcohol free." He assured.

I glared at him, before snatching the bottle from his hands. "Thanks." I mumbled, slamming the bottle down on the lunch table.

After five minutes, I turned around, noticing that Alex was still standing behind me. "What?" I asked him.

"You're in my seat." Alex explained.

I knit my eyebrows together, staring at Alex with distaste. "Do I see your name on it?"

Alex shrugged, weighing his opinions. "Well, it's not on the seat, but it's written under the table."

I stared up at Alex with disbelief, as he hovered over me. Was he expecting me to check for verification?

"Alex, quit teasing her. Sit down next to your best friend." Hayden said, patting the empty seat beside him.

Alex smirked down at me, before taking his fingers, and flicking my nose. I gasped, and just as I was about to whirl around to give him a nice black eye, he was already beside Hayden, across from me.

We all resumed to speaking terms after that, and the guys started to crack a few jokes, making me nearly choke on the apple juice Alex gave me.

"Hey, Aerial." Damian suddenly interrupted.

"Yeah?" I muffled, chewing on the sandwich he gave me.

"Why does that red head cheerleader keep staring at you? She's been for a good thirty minutes now." He questioned, peering his eyes over to Aubrey.

I opened my mouth to speak, but before I could utter anything out, Damian cut me off. "Wait, she's coming over this way!" he hushed.

Hayden, being the idiot he was, turned his head around, locking eyes with her.

Aubrey gave Hayden a wink in return, as she swayed her hips to the front and center of our lunch table. "Hey, guys." She smiled flirtatiously, twirling the ends of her red hair with her fingertips. "Aerial." She said bitterly, looking at me up and down with disgust.

"So, what are you guys up to?" she asked, plastering on a fake smile across her lips, making it look painful. "You look really hot today, Hayden."

Hayden looked at me uncomfortably, before giving Aubrey a weak smile. "Thanks." He mumbled.

"Actually," she paused, darting her eyes at me. "You all look really hot. What I don't get is, why are you ruining your good looks by hanging out with this, nobody?"

Aubrey Small was giving all of her attention to me, glaring at me through her dark green eyes.

"She's not making us look bad." Alex said suddenly, with a hint of amusement in his eyes. "If anything, she's making us look better."

I watched as Aubrey's smile morphed into a scowl. "Oh, Alex, honey." She grit through her teeth, seething at me. "You don't have to lie just because fragile Aerial is here."

"Fragile? She's one of the strongest girls I know." Hayden joked. "She can really give me a punch."

I bit back a smile, incredibly ecstatic that the guys were actually defending me.

"Strong?" Aubrey scrunched her nose with disgust. "That's not a word to describe little Aerial here. You see, she's been weak ever since her-"

Before Aubrey was about to spill my secret and completely ruin everything I ever had to friendship in high school, a mouth clamped over her glossy lips. I stared up, noticing that Clarice was the one who stopped Aubrey from babbling on.

"Aubs! The girls and I have to show you the Prada bag they just released!" Clarice squealed with false excitement, dragging Aubrey away from us.

Why was Clarice helping me?

Or did she really have to show Aubrey some stupid bag?

As soon as Aubrey was out of earshot, Damian spoke up first. "She's crazy." He muttered, shaking his head.

"Amen to that." Hayden said, raising a can of soda in the air, taking a large sip.

Everyone continued on with their previous conversations, completely forgetting what Aubrey had to say.

Well, everyone except Alex.

He knew I was hiding something.

And I knew he knew, because he wouldn't stop looking at me for the rest of the lunch period.

CHAPTER 5

I was walking to the bookstore after school that day when a bright pink Bentley pulled up to the sidewalk that I was walking on. The window rolled down, revealing a blonde figure, as she stared at me with a light smile.

"Aerial, let me give you a ride." Clarice's glossy lips stretched into a smile.

I didn't even spare her a glance, as I kept walking. "I don't need one."

From the corner of my eye, I saw Clarice's smile drop. She sighed, as she followed me, driving up slowly beside me. "Please, Aerial." She begged with eyes full of desperation. "Can we talk?"

Clarice's pupils only grew large when she needed help, badly. I knew that from the time when we were in the seventh grade, and Clarice stared at me while we were taking a test. She barely studied for that one, and I knew by the look in her eye that she needed help from me. I ended up helping her by giving her hand signals while the teacher wasn't looking. She passed with a ninety- four on that test.

I raised an eyebrow at the stupid pink Bentley that Clarice was driving in. I can't believe I was going to get into that thing. I approached the car, as I opened the door to the passenger seat. When I got inside, Clarice looked pleasantly surprised, but she gave me a smile. "I'm so glad you're here." Clarice's voice came out with relief.

I rolled my eyes, refusing to meet her eye. I stared out the window, crossing my arms. "Take me to the bookstore on Fairview Avenue." I mumbled, eyes concentrated on a small pile of dog droppings that were on the edge of the sidewalk.

"I haven't been to that bookstore since the eighth grade." Clarice suddenly said, starting up the car. "I remember we went there for a book signing with Lois Duncan."

I bit back a smile from the memory. "She was our favorite author in middle school."

Clarice let out a short laugh. "I remember I cried when she signed my book. I have a picture of us outside the signing. My face was all red from crying, and you were laughing next to me. It's still next to my nightstand."

I licked my lips, feeling my heart pang with pain at the old memories that Clarice and I used to share, before she left me.

"I didn't come here to talk about books with you." I suddenly snapped, cutting to the chase. "What did you want me here for?"

Clarice's grin fell from her face, as she kept her eyes on the road. "I'm sorry for what Aubrey almost told everyone earlier today."

I crossed my arms. "Whatever. Is that it?"

I saw Clarice's hand shaking as she gripped the steering wheel. Her face became white and pale, even under all of that makeup she had caked on. "There's actually something I need to tell you."

"What is it then?" I snapped, growing impatient.

Clarice licked her lips, pulling up the parking lot of the bookstore. "Can we go grab a coffee in the bookstore and talk?"

I pursed my lips. I answered hesitantly, "Fine."

We got out of Clarice's pink Bentley, as we made our way in the bookstore. Heads turned towards us, but I couldn't blame anyone that was staring. Any human being could be able to tell the difference between Clarice and I, appearance wise. I was dressed in a simple university sweatshirt and a pair of jeans, while Clarice was wearing a pair of neon yellow stripper stilettos, a bright pink pair of hot pants, and an eye blinding orange top that hugged her chest.

Needless to say, it was like the rainbow puked on a runway model, walking side by side with a no body like me.

"Is the hot chocolate still good here or what?" Clarice asked me with a smile, as she sat down at a stool across from me.

Clarice and I used to get a cup hot chocolate whenever we came by here. It was like a tradition for us, and this was a reunion, except, everything between the two of us is completely different now.

Perry, the waitress that's been working at the café in the bookstore here since I was a toddler, approached the two of us. "Aerial, it's good to see you again, sweetheart." She paused, taking a minute to eye Clarice. "Who's your friend?"

Clarice smiled brightly at Perry. "Perry! You don't remember me?" Clarice squealed.

Perry squinted her aged eyes at Clarice, before a smile began to spread across her lips. "Clarice Adams, aren't you? The little girl who used to come here with Aerial after soccer practices?"

"That's me!" Clarice giggled.

Perry eyed Clarice's outfit of choice, forcing a smile. "I must say, you've changed quite a bit. I couldn't even recognize you."

"I guess I've grown up a bit." Clarice smiled.

Perry raised her eyebrows, nodding. "Or a lot." She whispered under her breath, just loud enough for me to hear. "So, the usual for you, Aerial?"

I nodded. "Make that two, actually. Clarice wants one, too."

Perry nodded, as she jotted down our orders down on a notepad. "Do you girls want to try some new fried cake pops? It's on the house." Perry winked.

I smiled. "I'll take one, thanks."

Perry looked at Clarice. "What about you, darling?"

Clarice shook her head, giving Perry a thankful smile. "That sounds nice, thanks.

Perry returned back to the back of the café, as I stared at Clarice with an impatient expression. I finally realized now that I shouldn't even be here with Clarice, after everything she did to me, let alone get hot chocolate and cake with her. I only wanted to hear what she had to say, and nothing more.

"Are you planning to tell me anytime soon?" I pressured.

Clarice stared down at the white and black checkered table-top, licking her lips. "Before anything, Aerial, I wanted to say sorry to you."

My eyes snapped up to her, giving her an accusing glare. "For what?" I asked bitterly.

"For throwing our friendship out, and for not being there for you when your mother passed away." She said softly.

I swallowed the lump in my throat, biting the insides of my cheeks. "I don't need your sympathy."

"It's not pity, honestly." Clarice said quickly.

Perry came back with a tray in one hand, settling down our steaming hot drinks and cake pops on a plate in front of us. She left without asking a question as another customer entered the café.

"Can you forgive me?" Clarice asked suddenly, voice so quiet and weak.

I clenched my jaw, as I stirred the marshmallows that were already dissolving in my cup of hot chocolate. "Why do you need my forgiveness? Especially after so long?"

Clarice hands trembled as she pressed the cup of hot chocolate against her lips. As she took a drink, a small smile appeared on the corner of her lips. "Because I need your help." She said.

I snorted, rolling my eyes. "Of course, Clare Bear," I referred to the old nickname I gave her when we were friends, "always crawling back to me when you need something. What is it?" I asked coldly, taking a drink from my mug.

"I-I think I'm pregnant."

I choked on the lukewarm liquid that was caught in my throat, coughing loudly. I leaned over my chair, as I coughed, clutching my stomach.

What did she just say?

"Are you okay? Do you need me to get you some water from Perry?" Clarice asked, frowning.

I coughed one last time, shaking my head. I blinked a few times, before staring back at the blonde. "Did you just say what I thought you said?" I asked, feeling my heart beat against my chest.

Clarice's face paled, as she stared down at the neon pink painted nails. "Yeah, Aerial." She paused, sighing. "I haven't gotten my period this month, and I forgot to take my birth control when I was with Daniel."

My heart sank to my stomach. This couldn't be real. This couldn't be happening.

"D-Did he use a condom?" I asked cautiously, hoping the answer would be yes.

"No. He never does. He just assumes I'm on the pill." Clarice admitted, feeling ashamed.

I sank back in my seat, trying to process all of the information. Sure, Clarice became a complete different person from what she used to be, but I always thought she was smarter than that. Clarice had always been the responsible one in our friendship when we were little. How could she be knocked up now? Oh God, she was going to be one of those teen moms that are on television.

"Why are you coming to me about this anyways?" I asked. "I mean, there's always Aubrey, you're best friend."

Clarice pressed her lips together. "Aubrey will never get it. She'll judge me." She paused, staring at me in the eye. "Aerial, you're the only real friend I ever had. I regret losing you, but I need your help, now."

I shouldn't care that Clarice could possibly be pregnant.

I shouldn't care that she needs me.

I shouldn't care about her.

But, I do.

I pushed myself off of the stool, taking my hot chocolate to-go.

Clarice stared at me with a confused and blank face.

"Well, are you coming or not?" I asked, crossing my arms.

"Where?" she frowned.

"To the drugstore. We need to get you a pregnancy test." I said.

A smile stretched across her face, as she nodded. She took her hot chocolate in one hand, and her Chanel bag in the other. "Coming!" she chirped, following me behind.

We walked in Clarice's house with a bag from Walgreens, which contained four different pregnancy tests. The cashier stared at us curiously as he scanned our products, but we had to buy a couple extra just to be safe.

"My parents aren't home, so we don't have to worry about them catching us." Clarice said, as we headed up to the bathroom in her room.

Clarice's room was the exact same as it was in the eighth grade. Four red painted walls with a plushy white carpet. She even had a couple of soccer trophies that she won when we joined the soccer team together in middle school. The only thing different about it had to be her wardrobe.

I took out the four tests that were in the plastic bag, handing them to her.

"So, do I just pee on these?" she asked, reading the instructions that were imprinted on the bottom of the boxes.

"Guess so." I shrugged.

Clarice took in a deep breath, before making her way to the bathroom. "Alright." She breathed heavily. "Thanks for helping, again."

I bit my lip, nodding. "It's fine."

She gave me a gentle smile, before closing the bathroom.

She came back out after, with four tests in her hand. "It says you have to wait a few minutes before the results come up." Clarice muttered, staring at the tests with a white face.

"You're okay, right?" I asked.

Clarice nodded robotically, putting the tests down on her desk. She walked over to her bed, sitting down. She buried her head in her hands. "What if I'm really pregnant, Aerial? My life will be over." She muffled.

"We don't know for sure, yet." I said, sitting down next to her.

We sat in silence, until the couple minutes were up. "Oh my God, I can't look." Clarice said, her face filled with horror. "Check for me, will you?"

Nodding, I made my way over to her desk, anxiously. I read each of the four pregnancy tests one by one, feeling myself unable to breath. Positive, positive, positive, positive.

"Well, what is it?" Clarice suddenly asked, licking her lips.

"Clarice, you're fucking pregnant."

CHAPTER 6

Clarice's face was blank and pale. Her usual glowing hazel eyes were dull and lifeless.

"Clarice?" I asked cautiously, dropping the tests that were in my palms.

I made my way over to Clarice, as she stared down at her fingers. He pale pink lips began to quiver, as she took in a deep breath. "It's really happening, isn't it?" she asked, voice cracking.

She dropped her head low, as a trail of black tears rolled down from her corner of her eyes, down her cheeks. I wiped the smudged mascara below her eyes, rubbing her back gently. "Clarice, it's going to be okay. You know that, right?"

Clarice sobbed, shaking her head. "Don't lie to me, Aerial. I'm pregnant, and you know it." She cried, hiccupping.

"I swear Clarice. Even if everybody leaves, I'll still be here. I promise." I assured.

Clarice sucked in a deep breath of air, giving me a weak smile. "I really don't deserve your help, Aerial. After everything I've done to you for the past two years, I really don't."

A returned her a small smile. "It's fine."

Clarice laughed, smiling suddenly with hope. "Daniel's going to be happy, at least. He loves me." She leaned her head against my shoulder.

I wasn't too sure of what Clarice said. I personally didn't think Daniel was going to be happy with the fact that he was going to be a father. He would never be able to give up his freedom and lifestyle.

"Yeah, I'm sure he will." I muttered.

I went to the doctors with Clarice the next week after she took the pregnancy tests. We wanted to make sure that Clarice was for sure pregnant. And not surprisingly, she was. I mean, what can you expect before you go to the doctors to confirm your pregnancy after you got four positive test results?

I came home later that night, completely tired and groggily from visiting the doctors with Clarice. So, I was startled when I saw my father in the living room.

But, I wasn't surprised to find his head hanging over the couch, legs all sprawled out. He was hopelessly hung over from wherever he went last night.

"Dad, get up." I said, shaking his shoulder.

He let out a grunt, unwilling to open his eyes.

Getting frustrated, I spoke up louder this time. "Dad, go sleep in your room."

"Why won't you just leave me alone?!" my father suddenly shouted at me, swatting my hand away from his shoulder.

I took a step back, feeling my heart sink with emotional pain. "Dad, please get up." I begged.

His eyes suddenly snapped open, completely red and blood-shot. "Get away from me!" he raised his voice even higher, giving me a threatening glare.

I stood exactly where I was, not taking the shortest inch of a step. My shoulders were stiff, and my breathing was slow and tense.

When dad figured that I wasn't leaving anytime soon, he grumbled. He stood up, inching closer to my face. Under his eyes were evident bags, and his breath reeked of alcohol. He was so dangerously close to me, that my hand was trembling with fear. It didn't help that he was sober and hung over, either.

"I told you to leave." He whispered, incredibly sharp, yet low. "Why don't you leave me? Just like your mother did?"

I clenched my jaw, feeling my throat tighten up, as my eyes became moist with tears. "She didn't have a choice." I grit through my teeth, my voice cracking.

His hand suddenly snatched out to grab my wrists, as he clutched on them tightly. I could feel my blood circulation being cut off, as I winced in pain.

"She could've chosen chemo! But she was too fucking stubborn to!" Dad screamed, his face becoming red with anger.

A tear trickled down my cheek, as my hands shook in his grip. "She didn't want to suffer." I croaked.

My father's hung over face softened for a split second, before it became hard again. He glared at me, dropping my wrists. Immediately, I felt blood rushing through my veins, again.

"I need a drink." He muttered under his breath, heading towards the kitchen.

As soon as he disappeared in the kitchen, I ran out of the house. I dashed down the driveway, running as fast as I could away. It wasn't like dad cared enough to come after me, anyway. I ran as far as my legs could take me. My lungs were burning, as my heart pounded against my chest aggressively. Tears streamed down my face as I ran through the wind.

I finally collapsed on the sidewalk many blocks away from home, as I panted roughly.

Taking out my phone, I dialed the number that Hayden had given me a couple days earlier at school. After a couple of rings, a voice finally spoke through the phone. "This is Hayden!" he chirped.

My breathing was still a bit ragged, so it took a while for me to catch my breath.

"Hello?" Hayden asked with a slight edge in his voice after I didn't speak.

"Hayden? It's Aerial." I said, clutching the phone against my ear.

"Aerial! What's up?" he asked, his voice instantly lightened.

"Can you come pick me up? I have no where to stay." I admitted, feeling a tear roll down my cheek.

After thirty minutes of sitting on the edge of the sidewalk in the cold dark, a car pulled up beside me.

The windows rolled down, revealing a dark haired figure. "Hayden said you needed urgent help?" Alex asked, raising an eyebrow.

I gulped, pushing myself up, as I got into the passenger seat of his car. Alex studied me for a minute, noticing my knotted hair and tear stained cheeks. He didn't say anything, as he started to drive.

"I'm taking you to my house." He paused, licking his lips. "Hayden said he couldn't have anyone over right now."

I nodded, leaning against the window. "Whatever." I muttered.

Alex didn't pester me for the rest of the car ride. He sensed that something was wrong, but he decided not to pressure me about it. And, I was thankful for that.

"My mom's out on some business meeting for the week." Alex said, rummaging through his dresser. He pulled out one of his oversized t-shirts, and a pair of boxers. "Do you mind sleeping in my clothes, or do you want me to find something of my mom's?"

I shrugged, taking the clothes he got for me out from his hands. "I'll take it."

He nodded, as he pointed to the bathroom that was across the hallway from his room. "If you aren't tired yet, I ordered pizza a few minutes ago."

I didn't say anything, as I turned around, heading towards his bathroom.

"Just come down if you're hungry." He grunted.

I locked the door, as I stripped out of my dirty clothes. I turned on the shower, stepping in, as the warm water shot down, massaging my skin. I closed my eyes, as tears streamed down my face.

I had a father that didn't want me anymore, and a knocked up ex-best friend who decides to make amends with me now.

I got out the shower, and patted myself dry with a soft white towel Alex gave me. I threw his t-shirt over my head, as the hem reached my mid-thigh. I couldn't help but notice how clean and fresh his shirt smelt like. I continued to sniff his shirt, but stopped before I realized how wrong it was for me to smell his shirt. Shaking my head, I pulled his boxers up to my hips, getting out of his bathroom.

I debated on whether to go downstairs or not, but my growling stomach eventually psyched me out.

I skipped down the stairs, following the trail of light that was coming from the television that Alex had turned on.

Alex was slouching on his leather couch, a box of pizza on the coffee table. He didn't say a word to me, as I sat down to the seat opposite from him. His eyes glanced over at me briefly, before returning back to the television screen.

I lifted up the pizza box, noticing that there were only three slices left in the box. "You ate five slices?" I asked, taking one on a paper plate.

Alex smirked. "It wasn't like you were going to eat that much."

Rolling my eyes, I stuffed the pizza in my mouth, ripping out a rather large bite. "How would you know?" I muffled, while chewing on the cold pizza.

"Because, you're a girl." He snorted, as if it were the most obvious thing in the world.

I glared at him, swallowing down the pizza. "That's a bit sexist, don't you think?" I snapped.

"Whatever." He groaned. "I'll be impressed if you finish two slices."

I scoffed. "I'll be able to finish the rest of that box. Challenge accepted."

From the corner of my eyes, I could see Alex smiling with a glint of amusement in his clear blue eyes.

My father's hand struck against my cheek, as I flew to the ground, clutching my stinging cheek. "You're nothing to me!" he shouted, with his eyes bloodshot and red.

I sobbed, as I backed away from him. A drunken smile spread across his face, as he raised a broken glass beer bottle to the air, aiming it towards me. "You deserve to be with your mother." He slurred, aiming the broken glass bottle towards my throat.

Clarice leapt in front of me. She crashed to the floor, as the glass made a deep cut across her cheek. Her very evident baby bump hit the floor with an impact, as Clarice started to cry in pain. Blood started to bleed through her bottoms, as she squeezed her eyes shut tightly.

"M-my baby!" she panted, as I stared at her with wide and panicked eyes. "It's gone!"

My father stared at the two of us with a startled expression, as his hands trembled. "You did this to yourself!" he shouted, making a run for it.

"It's dead, Aerial." Clarice breathed. "Holy shit, my baby's dead!"

I let out a scream, as I shot up from my bed, sitting straight up. My forehead was dampened with a thick coat of sweat, as I breathed heavily with ragged pants.

The bedroom door flew open, as Alex appeared in my room with a metal baseball bat in one hand. He scanned around the room, but his eyes landed on me.

"I heard screaming." He said, looking around one last time, before settling down the bat. "What happened?"

I tear slid down my cheek, as I shook my head pathetically. "He killed the baby, Alex." I whispered, vision becoming blurry. "He killed the baby."

Alex sat down beside me, rubbing my back soothingly. "It was just a dream, Aerial."

I can't believe Alex was witnessing me crying my eyes out over a dream. I felt so weak and fragile. "Look away." I demanded, wiping away the tears that were trailing down my cheek.

Alex frowned. "What?"

"I said, look away!" I demanded.

Alex was hesitant, but he turned his head away from mine. I wiped away all the evidence of me crying, as I sighed. "You can look now." I muttered, crawling back into the comforter.

Alex stared at me with his blue eyes, probably thinking of how stupid I was. "Are you going to be okay for the rest of the night?"

I laughed bitterly. "I probably won't be able to fall back asleep, but yeah, I'll be fine."

Alex stood quiet for a minute, before walking towards the opposite side of his mother's bed. I gasped as he slid in the empty spot beside me.

"What are you doing?" I asked, feeling a faint blush appear on my cheeks.

"I'm staying with you for the night." He paused, raising an eyebrow. "Problem?"

"Yes!" I hissed.

Alex smirked, shrugging. "I don't care. It's my house."

I opened my mouth to speak, but reluctantly closed it. I sighed, feeling my body tense up as I struggled to go back to sleep.

After two hours of not being able to fall back asleep, I gave up. I kept seeing the pain in Clarice's eyes, and the evil in my father's.

"Quit moving." Alex groggily mumbled without opening his eyes.

I glared at his sleeping figure, but my features softened up when I saw how relaxed he was. He didn't have that scowl on his face. He almost looked peaceful and innocent.

"Didn't I say to stop moving?" Alex snapped angrily.

Note, do not make interrupt Alex's sleep. He gets cranky.

Alex let out a grunt when I accidently moved my leg. With one hand out, he wrapped his muscular arms around my waist, as my eyes widened. He pulled me towards him, making my back press against his toned chest. "Uh, Al-"

"Shut up, Aerial. Just shut up." He muttered.

I fell asleep after that.

CHAPTER 7

"Did you have a good sleep last night?" Alex asked, as I entered the kitchen the next morning.

Alex had a blue bowl out that was filled with milk and some kind of sugary cereal.

"Yeah, I did." I muttered, pouring myself a glass of orange juice from his fridge.

"Of course, you were all cuddled in my arms." Alex smirked, stuffing a spoonful of cereal in his mouth.

I choked on the tangy orange juice, as I stared at him with disbelief. "Excuse me? You came on to me!"

Alex rolled his eyes. "Yeah, whatever." He muttered sarcastically. "A few of the guy's are coming over soon."

"Alright." I said, staring down at the baggy clothes Alex lent me. "Do I have to get dressed or something?"

"No." Alex scoffed. "Who are you trying to impress?"

I glared at him, as Alex poured the rest of his unfinished cereal in the sink. "No one." I muttered, setting down my empty glass in the sink.

An hour later, the door was pushed open, as Hayden rummaged through the door with Damian, Ashton, and two girls whom I've never met.

"Aerial!" Hayden grinned when he saw me, coming over to give me a tight bear hug.

I choked as I patted Hayden's back. "Hayden- can't breathe!" I coughed.

Hayden immediately let go, giving me an apologetic smile. "Sorry, I just haven't seen you around in a while." He paused, remembering my phone call to him last night. "Did something happen last night? You sounded kind of upset when you called me."

I shook my head, giving him a forced smile. "I'm fine now, I swear." I lied, tearing my gaze away from him.

Hayden bought my lie, as he nodded. "Oh! And sorry I couldn't give you a place to stay last night. My parents were over, and they still wouldn't forgive me for getting suspended a few weeks ago."

I frowned, giving him a smile. "I don't even want to know about it."

Hayden chuckled, as my eyes wandered over to where the two girls, whom I've never met before, were. "Who are they?" I asked, keeping my eyes on the one who had messy dyed, red hair. She had black eyeliner covering her entire lid, and had pouty lipstick red lips. She was wearing leather tights, and a top that exposed the tattoo on her stomach. If that didn't scream 'badass', then I didn't know what did.

Her eyes locked into mine, as she raised an eyebrow at me. "What are you looking at?" she snarled at me, eyeing my outfit up and down. "Why the fuck are you wearing Alex's shirt?"

She was exactly like Aubrey Small. They both had the same, catty attitude. The only thing that sets them apart was their appearances. Aubrey liked to wear bright clothing, and always had a clean look. But, this bitch clearly had trashy stamped on her forehead.

"Natalia, don't be a bitch." Damian said, as he appeared from the kitchen with Alex, holding a few bottles of beer in their hands.

I flinched when I saw the alcohol in their hands, but I tried to hide any signs of discomfort.

"Don't be calling me names!" Natalia snapped at Damian, raising her hands to the air. She turned her attention back to me, giving me a disgusted glance. "Are you some slut that Alex banged last night?"

The words made me flinch, as I stayed close to Hayden. "Fuck off, Natalia." Hayden spat at her, as she rolled her eyes. She ignored Hayden, as she continued to pester me. "Do you have some kind of stripper name, too?"

I stayed quiet, as Hayden laced his fingers through mine protectively. It wasn't in a romantic way, but more of a brotherly perspective.

"Let me guess," Natalia rambled on, "Tit whore Tracy? Crack head Cindy? Butt-"

"Shut up." A voice suddenly said coldly, making everyone's head turn.

We all stared at Alex, before Natalia growled at him. "What?"

"I said, shut up, Nat." Alex snapped, glaring at Natalia with harsh eyes.

Natalia pursed her lips together with anger, as her cheeks flamed up into a spicy red color. She scoffed, reaching in her black purse. She pulled out a small zip-loc bag that had some small, crushed green leaves in it. "I need to get stoned right now." She said, staring at everyone. "Who wants a blunt?"

Damian and Ashton grinned, as they followed Natalia to Alex's back porch, along with the other girl that was beside her.

"Alex! You better come if you want some, babe!" Natalia called out from the back porch.

Alex looked hesitant to go, but he shot me a quick look before he left to where the others were.

When he left, I noticed that Hayden was still beside me, still holding onto my hand. "You can go, if you want." I smiled, not wanting him to hold back because of me.

Hayden chuckled shaking his head. "I don't do weed." He paused, before giving me a small smile. "Sorry about Natalia. She's a bit tough and gets jealous easily."

We let go of each other's hands, as we took a seat on the couch next to each other. "Jealous? Of what?"

"You, of course." He said, as I stared at him with a confused expression.

Something clicked inside Hayden's head, as he muttered something under his breath. "Oh, right. You don't know yet."

I frowned. "Know what?"

"Natalia is Alex's ex." He said.

My eyes widened, as I stared down at the clothes that Alex gave me to wear. No wonder! She hated me for wearing her ex-boyfriend's clothes. "Oh." I muttered. "It makes sense now. What happened between the two of them?"

Hayden smirked, leaning back on the couch. "They have a lot of history." He paused. "They met each other a year ago at some club we snuck in to. They hooked up after they both got drunk, and Natalia kind of stuck to Alex ever since. Alex gave Natalia a shot, and he actually ended up liking her. But, Natalia cheated on Alex last month with some guy, and Alex literally got in jail for breaking the guy's nose. They broke up after that. We all kind of thought that Natalia and her friend would just fade and leave, but they still stuck by us, as much as we didn't like them. I think the only reason why Damian and Ashton don't mind them is because she gives them free weed."

"Oh." I muttered, my gaze falling to my fingers. "Does Alex mind that she's still hanging around?"

Hayden shrugged. "He never admits it, but I know he does. I think it's because he still has feelings for her."

I don't know why, but my heart sank when Hayden said that Alex still had feelings for Natalia. It was almost supernatural for me to feel that way.

Suddenly, the strong gas of burnt weed hit my nose, as I coughed. Hayden stared at me with concern, as he pulled me up. "Are you okay? Do you need some air?" he asked.

I nodded, shielding my nose from the heavy scent. Hayden led me outside to his car, as he opened the passenger door for me. He slid in the driver's seat next to me, starting up the car. "Do you want to get some breakfast?"

I nodded, staring down at Alex's clothes. "I can't go wearing this." I pointed to Alex's boxers.

Hayden smirked. "Of course. I'll take you home to change."

My heart picked up its beat, as I nodded cautiously. I didn't know whether my father was home or not. I didn't want to risk bumping into him, and having him slaughter me for running away.

I told Hayden to park a street away from my house, just to be safe. When I walked up my front steps to my house, I noticed that my father's car wasn't in the driveway, which was a sign that he wasn't home. Sighing with relief, I opened the front door, hurrying to my room.

I grabbed a large duffel bag out from my closet, as I began to stuff it with as many clothes as I can. I quickly ran to my father's room to grab a wad of money to keep me safe for now. Zipping up the duffel bag, I didn't realize how heavy it would be. I threw it over my shoulder, as I staggered my way out of the house, and pulled it to Hayden's car. I tossed the duffel bag in Hayden's back seat, as he stared at me curiously.

"Why do you have a duffel bag?" he asked me, eyeing it suspiciously.

I should come forth to Hayden now, since he trusted me so much. I sighed, as I turned on the radio that was in his car. "I'll tell you over breakfast."

A plate of bacon, sausages, pancakes, eggs and fruits were set in front of me, along with a tall glass of apple juice.

I drizzled a pool of maple syrup of my pancakes, as I began to poke into them.

"So, are you going to tell me why it seems like you're running away?" he asked me, eyebrows raised.

Hayden just had to ruin my moment with my pancakes and I.

"I'm not technically running away. I'm going to have to go home eventually, maybe when I run out of money or whatever, but-"

"The point?" Hayden reminded me, stopping me from rambling about pointless things.

I sighed, giving him a look. "I'm getting there." I paused. "I can't stay with my dad anymore."

Hayden frowned, not getting it. "What?"

"My dad- he's changed ever since my mom, " I took in a deep breath of air, "died, from cancer. He turned to drinking, and he comes home every night completely cranky and... violent."

Hayden's eyes widened, as his face hardened. "Did he ever hurt you?"

I cleared my throat, as I stared at my pancakes. They suddenly didn't look so delicious anymore. "He's hit me a few times, but-"

"Shit." Hayden glowered, as his eyes darkened. His eyes traveled to my wrists, as he finally noticed bruises around them. "He did that to you, didn't he?" Hayden asked, his angry brown eyes piercing into mine.

I begged to myself to not break down and cry in front of Hayden. I was scared that I would scare him away.

"That's why you got so pissed at Alex for giving you a drink, right? Because-"

"I didn't want to become like my father if I got drunk." I finished, taking in a deep breath of air, as I poked at my untouched pancakes.

Hayden sighed, biting his lips. "If only there was a way to help you."

I shook my head, giving Hayden a reassuring smile. "You don't need to help me, Hayden. Trust me, you've done enough, just by being my friend."

Hayden smiled, staring down at me. "That's a bit sappy."

Rolling my eyes, I let out a deep breath of air. "Whatever." I muffled, taking a bacon strip, and stuffing it in my mouth.

Hayden took a sip out of his drink. "So, where are you going to stay?"

I licked my lips, wiping the grease off of my lips with a napkin. "I haven't figured that out yet. I was hoping I could find a place to crash at before the weekends over."

Hayden suddenly looked guilty. "If it weren't for my royally pissed off parents, I would let you stay over at my place."

I chuckled lightly, shaking my head. "It's fine, really."

"Just stay over Alex's for the week! His mom's not going to be home." Hayden beamed. "It wasn't so bad staying over at his house yesterday, was it?"

I blushed at the memory of the two of us sleeping together last night, my back pressed against his chest and all. "I-I guess not." I hesitated. "But, he wouldn't let me stay for that long."

"He would! He let me stay over at his place for a month when my mom kicked me out." Hayden said.

I frowned. "Kicked you out for month? What the hell did you do?"

"That's not the point." Hayden rolled his eyes. "Anyway, I'll talk to him."

I shook my head, staring at him with pleading eyes. "No, it's okay, really!" I remarked.

Hayden's face suddenly turned serious, as he gave me a look. "I don't want you camping out on the streets, Aerial. Just trust me with this, okay?"

I opened my mouth to speak, but Hayden's eyes bored into mine, making my mouth go dry. I sighed with defeat, leaning back in my chair. "Okay, fine." I muttered, crossing my arms.

Hayden laughed, as he nodded. "Alex was right when he said you were stubborn." He mumbled under his breath.

CHAPTER 8

Hayden dropped me off at Alex's front steps after we spent the day together in town. I pulled my duffel bag from his backseat, as I gave him a smile before he drove off.

I took in a deep breath, as I walked up to Alex's front door, clicking the doorbell. I waited a good two minutes before the door opened, revealing Alex. I couldn't help but noticed how messy his hair was, and how tired his eyes looked.

I licked my lips, wondering what I was supposed to say to him.

Was I supposed to just invite myself in?

Was I supposed to say that Hayden allowed me to stay at your house for the week?

"You look like shit." I finally said, feeling my cheeks flame up with embarrassment right after the words escaped my mouth.

Alex rolled his eyes, as he stepped aside, letting me inside. The place no longer reeked of weed, which I was glad of. But, the living room was completely trashed with beer cans, shattered bottles, and basically- trash. There was even a hot pink thong lying on floor.

"What the hell happened in between the hours that I left?" I asked, kicking over the thong with disgust.

Alex shrugged, as he flopped himself down on the couch, closing his eyes. "I don't know." He muttered. "I was fucking high."

I shuddered as I thought of all the possible things that they could've done while they were stoned and high. "Whatever." I sighed, taking a look again at the mess. "I'm taking a shower."

Alex grumbled something under his breath, as I disappeared upstairs. I laid my duffel bag in his mother's room, where the bed was still messy and unmade from when I slept in it. I unzipped my bag, taking out a pair of plaid pajama shorts, and a plain black tank top.

I took a warm shower, lathering my hair in the sweet strawberry shampoo that I was assuming was used by Alex's mother. I used the same white towel as I used last night to dry myself off, as I got dressed in my soft sleeping clothing.

When I came out of the bathroom, I noticed that Alex was no longer in the living room. I heard the shower that was downstairs start to run, and I assumed that he went to take a shower.

My stomach began to rumble, remembering that I had forgotten to get dinner with Hayden tonight. I made my way over to Alex's kitchen, flickering on the lights, as I began to rummage through his fridge. I took a carton of half eaten vanilla ice cream out of the freezer, grabbing a spoon out of the dishwasher.

I took a seat on the stool that faced the counter in the kitchen, lifting the cover off. I dug my spoon in the ice cream, as I let the sweet flavor melt in my tongue.

The ice cream brought back memories from when I was a child, where I was still innocent, and things were perfect. My mother and father took me out to the boardwalk two hours away from home for my birthday. We spent the entire day there, and my mother said she would buy me whatever I wanted at the amusement park. I ended up asking for an ice cream cone every hour, each time asking for a vanilla with chocolate fudge. It got to the point that whenever I came to the same ice cream parlor each hour, the worker there didn't even have to ask me for my order anymore.

"Are you enjoying my ice cream?" a voice suddenly startled me, making me jump from my seat.

I turned around to see Alex standing behind me with an amused expression. My heart beat calmed down from the sudden surprise, as I handed the carton over to him. "Do you want some?" I asked.

Alex stared down at the carton, before back up at me with an unimpressed expression. "You ate all of my ice cream?" he asked, irritated.

I shrugged, throwing out the empty carton, and quickly washing the spoon I used. "There was only half left before I ate it."

Alex rolled his eyes, as I muttered something under his breath.

I upstairs to sleep after I brushed my teeth from eating all that ice cream. After an hour, when I was finally actually getting some sleep, I felt weight being pushed down on the mattress.

I opened my eyes, and found Alex's eyes staring back at mine. "What are you doing here?" I hissed, rubbing my eyes.

"I'm sleeping here, duh." He grunted.

"I'm not having any nightmares." I mumbled, pulling the covers tighter to my chest.

"That doesn't mean I can't sleep here, does it?" he asked me. Even in the dark, I could see that stupid smirk that was plastered on his face.

"Yes, actually. It does." I snapped.

Alex closed his eyes, ignoring me. "Just shut up and go to sleep." He grumbled.

I glared at his sleeping figure, cursing under my breath, as I turned my back to him. With one arm, he pulled me into him, just like he did last night. Only this time, my back was pressed against something warm and bumpy.

I frowned, as I pulled his arm away from me. Alex stirred in his sleep, as I turned to face him. Hands shaking, I held them up under the covers, pressing them against his chest. A gasp escaped my lips when I realized that he wasn't wearing a God damn shirt. Immediately, my hand jerked away, as Alex flinched in his sleep.

"Alex!" I hissed, shaking his shoulder.

Alex groaned. "What the fuck do you want now, Aerial? Just go back to feeling me up."

My mouth dropped, as I punched his shoulder. Alex winced, as his eyes finally snapped open. He sat up, as he stared at me with a glare.

"I wasn't feeling you up, bastard!" I spat.

Alex rolled his eyes. "Oh really? What do you call your hands roaming all over my chest?"

I balled my hands up in a fist, lashing it out on his shoulder. "I was feeling to see if you were wearing a shirt!" I paused, glaring at him accusingly. "Which, you were not!"

Alex shrugged. "Who cares? I always sleep shirtless."

I bit my lip, refusing to stare at the way his pale skin looked against the moonlight that was coming from the window.

"I-it's weird." I admitted.

Alex groaned, falling back, as his head hit against his pillow softly. "Just go back to sleep. I'm tired."

I hesitated before going back to sleep with a shirtless man.

Alex probably thought I was so pathetic for not being able to sleep with him shirtless. He probably thought I was some low-life virgin- which I guess I was.

Again, Alex's arm snaked around my waist, pulling me in to his chest.

This time, I didn't oblige.

There was just one stray hair that my fingers were itching to brush.

Alex was still sleeping, but I'd been awake for a good fifteen minutes now. I stared at Alex's sleeping figure, and couldn't help but notice a stray hair that was hanging over his forehead. I was debating on whether or not to brush it out of his face, or leave it there.

I licked my lips, as my fingers finally pushed the strand of hair away. It made Alex stir in his sleep, as his eyes opened gently, still looking tired. He rubbed his eyes, as he stared at me before clearing his throat. "How long have you been awake?" he asked.

I couldn't help but notice how deep his voice sounded in the morning. It made shivers go down my spine, as I bit my lip. "Around fifteen minutes ago." I said.

Alex turned over to me, smirking. "Have you been staring at me since?"

I blushed, as I glared at him. "Of course not, idiot."

Alex chuckled, a small grin spreading across his face. "I'm just teasing you, Aerial." He flicked my nose with his fingertips. "No need to be so defensive."

I swatted his hand away, mumbling something under my breath about how irrational Alex was being.

The both of us lay back on the same comforter together in silence for a little while longer. I suddenly turned to him, licking my lips. His eyes traveled down to my lips, before slowly making their way back to my eyes. I cleared my throat, as Alex reached out to twirl a piece of my dark hair.

"You never told me that Natalia was your ex-girlfriend." I said suddenly, surprised at my boldness.

I felt Alex's entire body tense up, as he closed his eyes for a brief second. "I didn't tell you, because it wasn't really any of your business." He said, nothing at all nice in his tone.

I narrowed my eyes away, as I let his cold and harsh tone sink in. Suddenly, his fingers that were playing with my hair stopped, as I felt a hand gently tracing my left cheek. I glanced over at Alex, who looked guilty and regretful. "I didn't mean it like that." His soft fingers stroked my cheek.

I sighed, pushing his hand away from my face. "Whatever." I mumbled, tossing the covers off of me, as I got up from the bed. "It wasn't my place to ask you, anyways. So, sorry."

I grabbed a change of clothing from my duffel bag. I could feel Alex's eyes following my back, as I exited the room.

When I finished taking a quick morning shower, I went downstairs, where Alex was nowhere to be found. I assumed he went back to sleep or something after I left.

Taking my phone out of my bag for once since I ran away, I noticed many missed phone calls and voicemails from my father, and my home phone.

I bit my lip, and reluctantly opened one of the voicemails he left me. The date that it was left was two nights ago, the night when I ran out of the house.

"It's midnight, Aerial. Where the fuck are you?" my dad's drunken voice angrily slurred.

I gulped, as I licked my chapped lips, opening another message; one from yesterday morning.

"You didn't come home last night. You're going to be in so much fucking trouble once you get back!" he shouted through the phone.

My hands trembled, as I clicked the last voice message; one from late last night.

"Baby," my dad croaked on the other line of the phone, "I just got home from the bar, and I found half of your stuff missing. Please don't tell me you're actually leaving me. Please don't go."

I felt my heart crack at how desperate my father sounded on the other line. I understood the way he felt, being left and abandoned. He lost my mother, and now he was losing me. But, I couldn't go back home; not just yet.

I was too afraid to.

My phone suddenly buzzed in the palm of my hand, and I thought it was going to be another call from my father. But, I was both relieved and disappointed that it wasn't. It was just Clarice.

"Clarice? Why are you calling me so early today?" I asked, glancing over at the clock that hung in the kitchen.

I could hear Clarice's voice trembling on the other line. I knew something was wrong. "Aerial, c-can you please come over?"

I sighed, biting my lip. "I don't exactly have a car, Clarice."

Clarice sobbed on the other line. "Fine, then I'll come pick you up. Are you home?"

"No," I paused, taking in a deep breath of air, "I'm actually over at a friend's house."

"Give me the address." Clarice said, voice breaking. "I just need to see you, now."

I told Clarice the address to Alex's house, and she said she was coming immediately. Whatever she needed me for, I knew it wasn't going to be good, judging by the way she was bawling on the other line over the phone.

Moments later, the doorbell rang, alarming the entire house. I jumped from the couch, as I ran over to the door. I swung it open, revealing Clarice, who looked distressed and tired. Her hair was a complete mess, her eyes were bloodshot red, and she didn't have the 'happy' aura around her like she usually did.

"Aerial, who's at the door?" Alex came down the stairs, in nothing but the same pair of boxers he wore last night.

I watched as Clarice's red eyes flickered to Alex, and back to me. She raised an eyebrow, before introducing herself with a hoarse voice. "I'm Clarice. I'm just going to borrow Aerial for a few hours."

Alex frowned. "Aren't you one of Aubrey's friends, though?"

Clarice shrugged. "So what?"

"Well, if you haven't noticed, Aubrey is a major bitch who seems to be on her period every fucking day." He paused, looking angry; as he came down to hold my arm protectively. "What the hell do you want with Aerial?"

I rolled my eyes, ripping my arm away from Alex's grip. "Alex, you don't know what you're talking about. I'll be back in a couple hours."

"Wait, Aerial-"

I closed the door on his face, following Clarice out to her pink Bentley.

"He seems to be protective of you." Clarice said, as we got in her car.

I shrugged, putting on a seatbelt as Clarice began to drive. "It's no big deal."

Clarice gave me a weak smile. "I'm not so sure about that. I think he likes you."

I gave Clarice a bland look, shaking my head. "No fucking way. Alex wouldn't like me, never."

Clarice shook her blonde head of hair, pulling up to an empty parking lot outside of a local coffee shop. "I see your stubbornness hasn't changed over the years."

I rolled my eyes, following Clarice into the coffee shop. Immediately, the fresh scent of brewed coffee beans filled my nose, waking me up instantly. "That's not what you took me out here to talk about." I paused, sitting us down at a booth.

A waiter came by our booth to get our order, as Clarice ordered two mocha lattes for the both of us.

"Now tell me, what's wrong? Because you didn't sound too happy over the phone earlier." I said, frowning with concern.

Clarice sniffled, as she stared out the window. "It's Daniel."

I already knew what she was going to say. She was going to tell me that Daniel didn't want the baby.

"I-I told him that I was pregnant with his baby." She paused, struggling to keep her voice from breaking. "He told me that he didn't want to deal with me anymore, or the baby."

I was right.

A tear slid down from Clarice's eyes, as she took in a deep breath of air. "He left me, Aerial. He didn't even care."

I reached over to the other side of the table, cupping my hand over hers. "Clarice, God, I'm so-"

"I'm going to raise a fucking kid by myself." She cried.

I shook my head, giving her a small, reassuring smile. "Trust me, Clarice. I'll be here for you."

Clarice remained silent, as the waiter set down our drinks.

"You know, I thought he was the one." She whispered softly.

"There's going to be someone out there, who would love to raise that child with you." I smiled.

Clarice gave me a small smile, sighing. "What if it's him that I want?"

I laughed bitterly, shaking my head. "Honey, you want him, but you actually don't need him."

CHAPTER 9

Clarice offered me and Alex a ride to school the next morning. I took her up on the offer, but Alex simply shook his head, and told us that he was going to go to school late today.

I walked beside Clarice as we entered the school together, heads of our fellow classmates turning towards us. I didn't know whether everyone was whispering about the fact that Daniel told everyone that Clarice was pregnant, or that I was actually side by side with her.

We ignored all the whispers and stares, as Clarice dropped her head low. "This is horrible." Clarice whispered beside me. "I just want to go home."

I gave her a look. "Be strong, Clarice, for you and your baby."

Clarice sighed, as we walked down the hallway, making our way to our first period class that we had together.

"So, it's really true, isn't it?" a voice snarled from us behind.

Clarice and I stopped in our tracks, as we turned around to face Aubrey Small and her followers. Aubrey snickered at the both of us, rolling her eyes. "Oh, isn't this sweet? Aerial Mason and Clarice Adams are having a reunion!"

"Aubrey, leave us alone." Clarice said boldly to the red head.

Aubrey rolled her eyes, holding up her perfectly manicured fingers to Clarice's face. "Shut up, Clarice." She snapped, glaring at her. "You know, all this time, I thought we were best friends. But, no. The first person you go running to when you're knocked up is some bitch who you left."

Clarice's face was full of pain, as she stared at Aubrey with a frown. I could tell that Clarice was beginning to crack under the pressure. "Aubs-"

"Don't call me that, you slut!" Aubrey spat at Clarice.

I bit my lip, as I held onto Clarice's arm protectively. "Don't be hypocritical here, Aubrey." I finally set off, snapping at Aubrey. "Aren't you the one who sleeps around with every guy in this school?"

Aubrey looked startled at my sudden outburst, as she bit her lip, staring down at me as if she was better than me. "Mason, you have no place here. Got it?" She raised an eyebrow at me. "I suggest you leave this to Clarice and I, before things get ugly."

I clenched my fists by my side, as Clarice whispered in my ear. "Leave her, Aerial. She's not worth it."

I ignored Clarice, feeling all of the anger that I've kept in for Aubrey suddenly starting to explode like a firecracker. "You actually think you're better than me, don't you?" I asked, clenching my jaw.

Aubrey rolled her eyes. "That's because I am, honey." She examined her fingernails, before darting her poison ivy green eyes back up to me. "I'm actually known at this school. You're nothing here."

"I'd rather be known as nothing, than be known as the school slut like you." I spat, making everyone that was gathered around us gasp.

Aubrey's face went blank, as she opened her mouth to speak. She couldn't have looked more of a bigger idiot when nothing came out of her mouth.

"Nothing to say?" I asked, taunting her. "Good, because my business is done here."

Pulling Clarice's arm with me, we strutted out of the crowd, pushing past anyone that was in our way. As soon as we escaped to our classroom, Clarice burst into a misfit of laughter. "You totally won that one, Aerial!" Clarice paused, taking a break as she gasped for air. "Holy, you should've seen her face! It was priceless!"

I blushed. "Shut up, Clarice."

Clarice shook her head, still giggling, as the teacher entered the class.

"I'm so proud of my little Aerial." Hayden chuckled, throwing an arm around me, as we all gathered in Alex's house later that night. "You completely embarrassed the shit out of Aubrey this morning."

Alex's head turned towards me, as his face turned into a frown. He ended up just skipping school today. His excuse to us was that he was just too tired and slept in for the entire morning. "You did what?"

Hayden laughed, taking a beer, and gulping it down. "Man, you should've seen the whole thing. Aerial was on a roll, and Aubrey was fucking fuming, steam coming out of her ears and all."

I let out a soft laugh, staring up at Hayden with an amused expression across my face. "Whatever, Hayden, it was no big deal." I shrugged.

Hayden ruffled my hair, as Alex stared at the two of us with his eyebrows raised. "Why did you suddenly flip your shit out on Aubrey anyway?" Alex asked. "You've always been the quiet girl who stayed out of crap like this."

I blushed, shrugging. "Someone had to stick up for Clarice."

Hayden choked on his beer, as he sat up straight. "Wait, isn't she pregnant now?"

I nodded, feeling a bit of guilt for telling Hayden and Alex behind Clarice's back. But, it wasn't a big deal, I guess, because Aubrey and Daniel pretty much told everyone they knew.

"Damn. What's the history between you two, anyway?" Hayden asked, as Alex took a seat on the couch, stuffing his face with some chips.

"Shut up, Hayden." Alex muffled, munching on chips. He swallowed, as his eyes turned to me. "She doesn't have to tell you about her past if she doesn't want to."

Hayden rolled his eyes at his best friend. "She already has."

Immediately, Hayden's eyes widened, as he slowly stared at me with regret and guilt in his eyes. I clenched my jaw, as I turned away from Hayden, cursing under my breath.

Alex stared between Hayden and I with a curious frown. "What the hell does that mean?" he asked.

Hayden cleared his throat, as he took a sip from his can of beer. "S-she told me about the time she was eight." Hayden paused, looking nervous and sweaty. "And she got on a tree and fell. Like really, really badly and all."

I wanted to smack him for his beyond horrible attempt of lying. I didn't know if it was possible for anyone to be worse than that.

Alex glared at Hayden, knowing that everything that just spilled out of his mouth was a bunch of utter bullshit.

He turned back to me with a blank stare in his eyes, as if he was trying to read my face for any clues.

When he couldn't find what he was looking for, he let out an obnoxious groan. "Whatever." He mumbled, turning away from me, as he turned on the television.

As Alex's eyes were glued to the television, I turned to Hayden with a glare. "What the hell?" I mouthed to him.

His eyes were apologetic, as he mouthed, "I'm sorry."

I sighed, nodding. Hayden's lips stretched into a wide grin, as he pulled me in, arm around my shoulder.

An hour later, the doorbell rang, as Alex got up to get the door. Immediately, I heard a loud rumble of hoots, as Damian and Ashton huddled in the living room with us. I noticed Chinese takeout bags in Ashton's hand, while Damian had three stacks of pizza boxes in his arms.

"Why are you guys here?" Alex asked with a low grunt, crossing his arms.

Hayden jolted up from the couch, running over to where Damian sat down the pizza. "Who gives a shit, Alex?" Hayden beamed, grinning like a child. "They bought food for us!"

Ashton and Damian gave Alex a smirk, before they started ripping open the boxes of food. Damian turned to me with a smile, offering me a plate. "Come on, help yourself."

I took the plate, giving him a smile, as I got up from my seat. "Thanks." I said, pulling a cheesy slice of pizza onto my plate.

"You better hurry if you want some of those noodles, though." Damian said, gesturing over to the box of Chinese noodles that were already half gone. "Hayden and Alex fight over them like animals."

I chuckled, as I took a fork, pulling up a good amount of the noodles onto my plate. Alex came back from the kitchen, holding four beers in his hands, and a can of soda. He tossed everyone a can of alcohol, but me. His eyes lingered on me, before throwing me the can of soda.

"So, when are you planning to invite Natalia and Phoebe over?" Ashton asked Alex.

Alex grumbled something under his breath, sticking some fried rice in his mouth. "Never."

I bit back a smile from his response, as I poked at my noodles that were scattered all over my paper plate.

"Dude, seriously? She gives us free weed." Damian huffed, slouching back in his seat.

Alex glared at Damian. "If you want her weed so badly, why don't you just date her?" Alex snapped at Damian. Alex sounded challenging, but everyone in the room knew that Alex didn't mean it. Everyone knew that Alex would beat the crap out of Damian for going for his ex-girlfriend, who he might still have feelings for.

The tension was thick, and no one dared to say a word.

It was finally Hayden who broke the ice.

"Let's watch a movie." Hayden said, getting up, and searching over Alex's rack of DVD's. "The Ring, anyone?"

"I've seen that already." Ashton said, popping open his can of beer.

"Same here." Damian asked, frowning at Ashton. "Didn't we watch it together, when we were double dating with those hot Fletcher twins?"

Ashton smirked, nodding his blonde head of hair proudly. "Damn, I still remember the good old times with Emily Fletcher. She was sweet and innocent on the outside, but she's a feisty one in-"

"Okay!" I said, cutting Ashton off from finishing his statement. "We get it."

"The Grudge?" Hayden asked, pulling out a DVD out of the rack.

"I'm fine with it." Alex said, kicking his feet up on the coffee table, as Ashton and Damian nodded.

Hayden turned to me, raising an eyebrow. "Aerial? You alright with the Grudge?"

I gulped, nodding quickly. I wasn't going to tell them that horror movies made me piss my pants. They would think my skin wasn't thick enough or that I was too weak to hang around them.

"Poke her." Someone chuckled lightly, as I felt a finger being jabbed against my cheek.

"Is she a heavy sleeper or not?" a different voice asked, as I felt someone pulling on my hair. "Alex? Yes or no?"

I heard an irritated grumble above me, assuming it was Alex. "Move." I heard Alex's deep voice command everyone. I felt who arms pick me up from the couch, as my eyes attempted to open. "A-Alex?" I mumbled, feeling my eyes close.

"Go back to sleep, Aerial." Alex said, placing me on a bed, throwing a blanket over my body.

CHAPTER 10

"You look horrible." I said directly, as I slid in the booth across from Clarice.

It was early the next Saturday morning, and Clarice called me up, asking me to meet her at the coffee shop near the gas station. I spotted her in the back, head hanging low, palms around a steaming hot mug of coffee. It wasn't until I saw her face that I sensed something was wrong. Her lips and cheeks had no color, absolutely white and pale. She looked like the complete opposite of what she usually is- or was.

Her dull blue eyes met mine, as she sulked down in her seat. "Thanks." She muttered, voice hoarse.

I frowned. "Did something happen?"

She took in a deep breath, releasing it out slowly, as she shook her head. "I've just been throwing up lately, a lot."

I nodded my head, giving her a small smile. "That's normal, right?"

"Yeah." She paused. "I'm just wondering how long it'll take before my parents catch up to all of this."

My eyes widened. "You haven't told your parents?"

She shot me a look, shaking her head. "No. They'll kill me if they find out."

I scoffed at her. "The entire school population knows already, and your parents don't?"

Clarice rolled her eyes at me, slamming her fists down on the table, making the salt and pepper shakers shake. "What the fuck do you want me to say to them, Aerial?" she snapped, biting down on her lips. "Hey mom, dad, I'm pregnant with a guy who just left me." She imitated, shooting me an annoyed look.

Throwing up, check.

Mood swings, check.

Clarice Adams was most definitely pregnant.

I sighed, leaning back in my seat. I didn't want to argue with a pregnant woman, not now. "I'm just saying," I paused, looking her in the eye to calm her down, "its better if your parents find out sooner than later."

Clarice clenched her jaw, releasing a deep breath of air. Licking her lips, she nodded reluctantly. "Your right." She said. "Sorry."

"So, are you going to tell them, or what?" I asked.

Clarice laughed bitterly, stirring her black coffee that was getting cold in front of her. "I guess I don't have a choice."

Nodding with approval, I smiled. "Good. If anything, you can stay over at Alex's place with me if they kick you out." I said teasingly, earning a grin from Clarice.

"Oh, shut up." She bit back a smile. "What's the deal with you and Alex, anyway?"

I frowned. "What do you mean?"

Clarice laughed half-heartedly, shaking her head, as messy blonde strands fell in her face. "Come on, Aerial. You pushed away this subject last time, but I'm not letting you leave without an explanation." She took a sip of her coffee. "Are you guys like dating, or something? You're always sleeping over at his house."

I choked, staring at the blonde with disbelief. "It's not like that!" I sputtered, feeling my cheeks become warm.

Clarice chuckled. "Really? Then are you guys like friend are with benefits?"

I closed my eyes together tightly, smacking my palm to my forehead. "Alex and I have no special relationship. We're just friends- or even acquaintances."

"That makes no sense." Clarice smirked. "Why do you keep staying over at his house, anyways?"

I gulped nervously, playing with one of the salt shakers on the table. She's one of the only people who know that my mother passed, but she doesn't know anything about how my father comes home completely wasted and violent every night. I can't tell her I ran away. I told Hayden, and he almost blew up my spot in front of Alex.

"My dad's out of town for a few weeks, business meetings and all." I explained, lying right to Clarice's face.

Clarice studied my face for a long moment. I didn't dare to meet her eyes, because if I did, then she would find out. She would know about my lies, and everything. But, her stare was so intense, as if she was a magnet, trying to pull my eyes towards hers. And eventually, I did finally look up to her.

"So, you're still a complete and utter shit liar, aren't you?" Clarice raised an eyebrow, shaking her head at my horrible attempts of lying.

I pursed my lips, giving her a glare. "Can we just drop it Clarice?"

Clarice scoffed, shaking her head. "No, Aerial. We can't." she stopped talking, waiting for me to continue. When I sat silently with my arms crossed, Clarice spoke up, again. "Just tell me, Aerial. You're making this harder by-"

I was getting extremely aggravated by Clarice's constant pressuring now. I didn't have to tell her anything I didn't want to. She left me for two years. She would've known what my problems were with my father, if she didn't decide to ditch me and leave me when I needed her the most. "Stop, Clarice. Just stop." I grit through my teeth, nothing nice in the tone of my voice at all.

Clarice blinked, looking shocked at my cold tone. "Did I say something wrong? I just wanted to help." She snapped, angry clearly expressed on her face.

I sighed, letting out a deep breath of air. "I don't need your help, especially since you suddenly start caring two years after."

Clarice gasped with surprise, as she licked her lips. She stayed silent for a moment, before she sat up straighter, clearing her throat. "Listen, I didn't come here to make things worse with you, Aerial." Clarice rummaged through her purse, slapping down a creased ten dollar bill on the café table. "Talk to me when you stop holding a grudge."

Clarice got up from her booth, looking back at me for a moment to see if I was going to call after her. When I didn't, Clarice huffed, heading out of the café. I watched from the glass windows, as she slid in her car angrily, starting it up, and driving away.

Clarice was being incredibly unreasonable, and having pregnant mood swings wouldn't pass off as an excuse for me. If she thought that I would open up to her again just because I decide to help and care about her baby, then she was dead wrong.

I don't know if I could trust Clarice Adams ever again.

"Why are you packing your stuff up?" a voice startled me, as I was putting away a pair of skinny jeans in my duffel bag.

I turned around to face the doorway, where Alex was standing. His cheeks were pink, and he had a white towel wrapped around his neck. I also couldn't help but notice how he was shirtless. His biceps were just the right size, and his six pack abs was hard not to notice.

"Did you just come back from the gym?" I asked, tearing my gaze away from him, as I secretly blushed for checking him out.

I heard his footsteps getting closer to me, as I continued to pack my clothes away. I could feel the warmth of his skin brushing against mine, as Alex stood next to me. I tried my best to ignore the sweaty shirtless guy beside me, but it wasn't easy.

"Mind putting on a shirt?" I muttered, trying not to glance over at him.

Alex didn't answer me, but instead, his hand covered over mine, holding me tightly. My breath hitched, as I gulped. I could feel my heart rate pick up when Alex wouldn't let go.

"What are you doing?" I managed to ask without stuttering.

Alex's blue eyes bored into mine with intensity. "You never answered me." He said lowly, moving his head closer to mine. "Why are you packing?"

I licked my lips, noticing how our noses were so close from touching. If I moved my head an inch closer, then our lips would be touching. We would be kissing.

"I have to leave." I said.

Alex's hand tightened around mine, as he asked, "Why?"

I adverted my eyes away from his, not trusting myself any longer if I looked into those blue eyes again. "It's been a week." I paused, biting my lip. "Your mom should be back from her business trip."

"It won't be a few hours before she leaves again." Alex said. "Stay."

I frowned. Why wouldn't Alex's mother come home? And why did he want me to stay so badly? His house wasn't a free hotel, and I can't just take advantage of him like that.

"But-"

Alex pressed his forehead against mine, making my eyes go wide.

Was he insane?

"Please, stay." His warm breath tickled my lips. "Everyone leaves me."

I closed my eyes, taking in a deep breath of air. Did Alex actually want me to stay? He sounded so genuine when he told me to. It was a side I've never seen of him before. He always had this tough exterior, and now he was practically begging for me to stay? Unbelievable.

I pulled away from his grip, creating a distance between us.

"I'll stay," I paused, a small smirk forming across my lips, "if you go take a shower, right now."

Alex bit his lower lip, trying to bite back a grin that was threatening to spread across his rosy red lips. "What are you trying to say, Mason?"

I chuckled, flicking his nose teasingly, the same way he usually does it to me. "I'm saying that you smell." I said, which was a complete lie. Even though it was evident that he spent the afternoon at the gym, he didn't smell of odor or sweat, at all.

Alex rolled his eyes, giving me a small smile. "Whatever, Mason. I'll go shower, if it bothers you."

Smirking, I turned my back on him. "Thank you." I sarcastically remarked.

I heard Alex laughing from behind. The sound of footsteps disappeared down the hall, and soon, the sound of running water was audible.

And all I could think was, what have I gotten myself into?

CHAPTER 11

"Thanks for being here the day the teacher decides to not show up." I sarcastically said to Hayden, as he took a seat next to me in the biology lab.

Hayden chuckled, running a hair through his messy brown hair. "Hey, be happy that I even came today."

"Then what about all of the other days? When I actually need a lab partner?" I asked, raising an eyebrow.

Hayden shrugged, leaning back in his seat, kicking his legs up to the table. "I don't think you would need help from me, anyway."

"And why is that?"

"Because the highest grade I ever got in biology was a C," he paused, giving me a serious look, "minus."

I rolled my eyes, but I couldn't help but let a grin slip across my face. "Touché."

Hayden rummaged through his book bag for a moment before taking out a flattened bagel with cream cheese oozing from the sides. "Want a bite?" he asked me, taking a rather large bite out of the bagel himself.

I shook my head. "I'm fine."

Hayden shrugged, chewing on his sandwich. "So," he paused, swallowing his food, "you're staying over at Alex's for longer than expected, huh?"

I felt my cheeks get warm, as I bit on my lower lip. "How do you know?"

Hayden rolled his eyes, munching away on his bagel obnoxiously. "He's been by my side since the first grade. He tells me everything."

I nodded, taking out a math assignment I didn't get to finish last night. "Oh, right." I paused, jotting down some answers to my home work.

"I don't know if it's just me, but I'm sensing some romantic activity between the two of you." Hayden suddenly said, making me break the tip of my pencil.

My hand shook, as I went through my bag for a new pen.

Why was my heart beating against my chest so hard?

Why did my cheeks feel so hot?

I cleared my throat, licking my dry lips. "Please, Hayden." I paused, erasing the stray mark that I made on my homework. "Cut the bullshit out."

Hayden threw the wrapper of his bagel in his bag, as he kicked his feet down. He leaned closer to me, elbows resting against his kneecaps. "I'm serious," he paused, letting out a chuckle, "for once."

I glared at him, pressing down on my pencil harder than intended. "Alex and I-"

"What about us?" a new voice suddenly spoke, making me jump from my chair.

Hayden looked up before I did, a nervous grin slipping across his face. "Oh, hey Alex." His voice staggered, making me want to punch him for being so obvious.

"No one's going to answer my question?" Alex asked, raising an eyebrow. When neither of us spoke up, Alex shook his head, scoffing. "Whatever."

Alex pulled up a chair from an empty desk, planting it beside Hayden's desk.

"You're in school, for once." I sarcastically commented.

I watched as a smile began to stretch across Alex's lips. Alex opened his mouth to speak, but Hayden beat him to it. "You're in the wrong class, though."

"Right, you never have biology with us." I added.

Alex let out a deep breath of air, rolling his eyes. "I don't give a shit what class I'm in or not."

It wasn't hard to notice that Clarice was being shut down by the entire student body today. Everywhere she went, people stayed out of her path, and stared at her if she were some kind of unknown creature.

I watched from behind my locker as Clarice walked down the halls, head stooped low, books pressed against her chest. Her hair was a frizzy mess, and her lips were white.

"She just threw up all over the toilet seat in the girl's bathroom." A brunette whispered to her group of friends when Clarice walked by them. "It reeks in there."

I opened my mouth to say something, but my throat was completely dry.

I promised Clarice that I was going to be by her side throughout her entire pregnancy. Not for her, but for the baby that was growing inside her stomach. Was I being an utter liar by not walking by her side and not sticking up for her? I should've been in that bathroom with her, holding up her blonde hair as she puked her guts out.

I watched from my locker, as Clarice escaped into the library for lunch.

As the hallways cleared up, I slowly made my way into the library, the place where I used to spend every lunch hour at.

I found Clarice at the back computers of the library, dabbling away on the keyboard. It took her a while to notice that I was standing in front of her. She hazel eyes met mine, as she pressed her lips together tightly. "Is there something wrong?" she asked me, voice cold and unforgiving.

I took in a deep breath, as I pulled her up from her seat.

"What do you think you're doing?" she hissed, pulling her wrist away from my grip.

"I'm trying to drag you to the cafeteria to bring you out of your misery." I snapped.

She glared at me, eyes full of frustration. "Why? Because you feel bad for me?"

I scoffed. Clarice has pitied me for the last two years since my mother's death, and now she is the one who is accusing me of giving her sympathy? "Oh please, Clarice. Don't even go there." I spat in a low voice.

Clarice licked her lips, as she crossed her arms. She remained silent, as she followed me out of the library, into the noisy cafeteria.

As I walked across the cafeteria with Clarice following behind me, I couldn't help but catch the attention of Aubrey, who was burning her eyes into mine.

I slid into a seat across from Hayden, as Clarice stopped by the front of the table. "Sit." I said to her, as I began to unwrap a sandwich I bought at the bakery this morning.

Clarice looked nervous, as she bit her lips. "I don't think that's a good idea." I whispered, as Hayden's eyes stared up to her.

"Is this your friend, Aerial?" he asked, as I nodded. "The one that's preg-"

I shot him a glare, as Clarice's cheeks turned red.

"Yes." I hissed at Hayden, making him smile at me weakly.

Clarice looked extremely uncomfortable, as she wobbled on the balls of her feet. "Maybe I should just sit at another table." She muttered, turning around.

I rolled my eyes. "No, Clarice." I snapped, making her turn back my way. "Sit."

Clarice sagged her shoulders with defeat, as she slid in the only empty spot at our table, next to Damian.

After a moment of silence, Damian was the one who was brave enough to spark up a conversation with Clarice. "Don't look so nervous. We aren't that scary, are we?" he teased, flexing his arms.

Clarice giggled, as she shook her head. "No, not really."

Damian grinned, as he offered Clarice some of his fries. "Are you hungry?"

Clarice shook her head, as she took out a plastic bag of celery and carrots. I thought it was perfectly normal, until I saw her dip a green celery stick in some kind of suspicious brown sauce.

"Clarice, what are you eating?" I asked, making everyone's head turn.

Clarice blushed at the attention that she was receiving. "Some veggies." She paused, holding up a cup of brown dip. "With barbecue sauce."

I raised my eyebrows, as Hayden bit back a laugh across from me. Everyone began to chuckle, as Clarice lowered her head, biting her lips from smiling too wide.

"The appetite of a pregnant woman." Damian joked.

After school, I headed back to Alex's house. He gave me my own key to the front door yesterday, even though I tried to protest against it.

I wasn't sure if Alex himself was home yet, since I couldn't find him anywhere after classes were over.

"Alex?" I called out, creating an echo in the house.

I climbed up the stairs, turning to the left hallway to the last right door. I opened the door to Alex's room, noticing for the first time that I've ever seen or been in it. So, I was pleasantly surprised when I saw that his room wasn't a complete mess. His bed was made neatly, and his clothes weren't scattered all over the floor, like I had expected them to be.

I was about to turn away and head out from Alex's room once I noticed he wasn't there, but a picture frame that was on his dresser caught my eye.

I bit my lip, debating on whether or not to snoop through his stuff. I eventually gave in, and grabbed the frame off of the dresser, holding it in my palms.

My breathing stopped once I realized that the picture was of Alex and Natalia. Her lips were pressed against his right cheek, and he had his arms snaked around her waist.

The picture was a bit dark, but not dark enough to cover their faces. Natalia was wearing a tight red dress that showed off every curve, and Alex was in a dress shirt with a tie that wasn't tucked in his jeans.

Taking the picture out of the frame, I saw that there was a message scribbled on the back with a loopy cursive handwriting.

Happy seventeenth birthday, baby! You're the best thing that's ever happened to me. We have out ups and downs, but I still love you with everything I have.

Natalia.

"Are you done snooping through my son's stuff?"

CHAPTER 12

"Are you done snooping through my son's stuff?"

The sudden voice startled me, as the frame of the picture slipped out of my hands. I watched with widened eyes as the glass shattered in a messy pile by my feet, the picture laying face down on the floor.

"Look what you did! Who the hell are you?" an angry voice shouted at me, making me jump as the shards of glass went into the balls of my feet.

I let out a whimper, as I stared up weakly at the woman standing by Alex's doorway. She had a cold scowl across her face, a neat and tight bun on the top of her head, and a wrinkled pencil skirt.

"I-I'm sorry." I stuttered, trying to ignore the pain in my left foot. "I'm Aerial, Alex's-"

She raised an eyebrow, snorting. "Girlfriend?" she finished for me.

My cheeks flushed up, as I shook my head quickly. "No, no! I'm just a friend of his." I said, his mother looking unconvinced.

"That's his girlfriend." I told her, pointing to the picture that was lying lifelessly on the ground.

My foot gave up by now, as I limped towards Alex's bed, taking a seat. I lifted my foot up to my thighs, examining the sharp glass that was pressing against my skin. My hands shook as I pulled it out slowly, wincing every so often at the pain.

"Just hold on for a minute." His mother said to me, letting out a deep sigh. "I'll go get the first aid kit."

I nodded, as Alex's mother disappeared from Alex's room. She returned momentarily, kneeling down on the floor, as she began to take out some disinfectant. "Don't cry. This might sting a little." She muttered, dabbing some cold liquid on my foot.

I bit back on my lip, closing my eyes, as the disinfectant stung my cut. Soon, the pain disappeared, as I watched Alex's mother wrap my foot up in a tight bandage.

"I'll tell Alex that I broke his frame." His mother said, kicking over the glass into one pile.

I sighed with relief, giving her a small smile. "Thanks."

She studied the picture, as I watched her eyes focus on Natalia. She wiped the sweat on her forehead with the back of her hand, as she licked her lips. "I'm sorry about being so harsh when I thought you were the girl that gave Alex marijuana."

My eyes widened, as I bit my lip. "O-oh." I muttered, scratching the top of my head. "It's fine."

"So," she said, placing the picture without a frame back on Alex's dresser, "why are you staying over at my house?"

I blushed, as I stared on the floor. "I'm having issues with my dad at home."

Alex's mother stayed silent for a moment, and I could feel her eyes roaming across my face. "Is he a single parent?"

I nodded, suddenly feeling insecure talking about my father to a woman whom I've just met minutes ago. Plus, it didn't help that I gave her a bad first impression as well. I was going through Alex's stuff, for crying out loud.

"That must be hard. I'm a single mother, as well." She said, letting out a sigh. "My husband and I got a divorce when Alex was ten. He took it pretty damn hard. The boy locked himself in this very room for weeks. When he finally came out, he was a completely different person. He wasn't the playful, innocent Alex he used to be. He was cold, always had his guard up."

Then, I realized that Alex had only ever mentioned his mother to me. He never once brought up his father. I swallowed the lump in my throat, and suddenly, I could no longer feel the pain in my foot.

All I could feel was the aching pain in my chest.

"That," I paused, letting out a deep breath of air, "really sucks."

Alex's mother let out a bitter laugh. "I'm never home for that boy anymore. Being a single parent is hard." she gave me a weak smile. "Maybe it's a good thing that you're staying here. You could keep Alex from being lonely. You're good, Aerial, you're good for him."

Alex's mother stayed with me for a bit longer before she had to leave for a flight to Canada.

She helped me down the stairs with my cut foot, even though I told her I could walk perfectly fine. She shot back at me, saying how I couldn't go a step without limping, and that it was bad for me to put pressure on the ball of my foot while it was cut.

His mother even went as far as making dinner for Alex and I, leaving some leftovers on a platter for him on the kitchen counter. She told me that her homemade spaghetti and meatball pasta was Alex's all time favorite food.

"Alex can't get enough of this stuff." She muttered, as I watched her stir the tomato sauce. "I haven't made this in years."

And after I had the first bite, I understood why Alex loved it so much.

When Alex came home later that night, his mother was long gone.

I was sitting on the couch, watching some an old episode of Family Guy, almost falling asleep when the door bustled opened. I sat up straight from the couch, as I watched Alex walk in, looking exhausted.

"Where have you been?" I asked him, as he took a seat on the couch across from me, resting his head in his hands.

"Out." He mumbled under his breath, making me roll my eyes.

"There's some dinner on the counter for you." I told him. Alex raised his eyebrows at me, as he got up from his seat. He came back seconds later, holding the platter of cold spaghetti as he planked himself down back on the couch.

"I didn't know you could cook." He smirked, taking off the plastic wrap, as he shoved his fork into the pasta.

I cleared my throat, shaking my head. "I didn't make it. Actually-"

"My mother was here?" he cut me off, swallowing his first bite.

I licked my dry lips, nodding. "Yeah, she left a few hours ago."

Alex pressed his lips together tightly, as he sat up straighter. "You met her?"

I nodded, trying to hide my bandaged foot under some decorative pillows Alex had scattered all over the couch. "She's a nice woman."

Alex scoffed, rolling his eyes. He placed the plate on the coffee table, pushing it away. "You must've met the wrong woman, then."

"You're not going to eat that?" I asked, frowning at the barely touched food. "She told me it was your favorite."

Alex glared at me with annoyance. "Oh, so now you and my mother are best friends?" he asked, voice cold and harsh, making me flinch. "What else did that bitch tell you?"

I bit my lower lip. What the hell was wrong with Alex? His mother was a nice and posh woman, and I couldn't understand why he didn't respect that. "What's your problem with her?" I snapped.

"My problem is with her shit parenting." He flipped me off. "She barely even knows she has a son because she's always out."

I was getting aggravated at him now. He was being so unappreciative. He was lucky he had a mother that actually cares about him. "She's out because she has to work to raise a kid herself!" I snapped at him.

Alex's eyes widened, as he remained silent. I could tell he was fuming by the way he was scowling at me. "Oh, so the bitch told you that my dad left us, too?"

I clenched my fists by my side, as I stood up straight, ignoring the pain that was shooting up my leg. "Quit calling her that! She's your mother!" I spat.

Alex rolled his eyes, slouching back in his seat. "You don't know anything, Aerial. Stay out of my business." He said firmly, giving me an intense glare. "Why do you even care so much, anyways?"

I clenched my jaw, as I felt the lump forming in my throat.

No, I couldn't.

"I care," I started, feeling my voice breaking already, "because you're lucky enough to have a mother that's not dead."

Immediately, I could feel the thick tension in the room.

Alex's face full of hate dropped, being replaced with a blank expression.

Great, this was the part where he starts to tell me how he's sorry, because he pities me.

I don't need any more sympathy.

I didn't want any more sympathy.

"Aerial-" His voice called out for me, much more controlled and softer this time.

I shook my head, as I turned around, not wanting him to see the way my tears fell down my cheeks. "Don't, Alex." I muttered, lips trembling.

I could hear him getting up from the couch, as I felt a strong hand grip around my wrists. "Aerial, listen, I-"

"Just shut up!" I snapped, showing my red and teary eyes to him for the first time. I ripped my wrists away from him grip, as his face crumbled. His blue eyes stared at me with so much guilt and regret, it was making my stomach twist into a tight knot. "Leave me alone."

As I run up the stairs, I almost forget the pain in my foot. I almost forget that I shouldn't be putting so much pressure on it. I almost forget everything- until I trip on my way to Alex's mother's room. I trip, and all I could feel was the pain becoming worse, and the stinging becoming stronger.

I crawled up to the bed, as I buried myself under the comforter.

Make the pain go away, I begged my mother.

Make the pain go away in my foot, and my chest.

I broke down into tears, as I gripped tightly onto the sheets.

If my mother was here, she would cradle me into her arms, and hold me tightly.

"Everything's going to be alright." I could almost hear her voice tell me. "Everything's going to be alright."

Chapter 13

I arrived at Clarice's house early a few mornings later, upon her requests. I walked up the front steps, ringing the doorbell that had a nice tune to it. I waited, staring at the maroon red door. I remember it used to be a creamy white back when Clarice and I were in middle school, but I guess a lot changes in two years.

The door swung open, revealing Clarice's father. He seemed to recognize me immediately, but it took me a while to process in his newly, aged look. He used to have a full head of golden blonde hair, but most of it has disappeared, leaving a noticeable bald spot in the middle. "Mr. Adams, good morning." I forced a smile.

Mr. Adams still seemed a bit shocked, but he settled down his morning newspaper, giving me a pat on the back. "Aerial Mason, it's good to see you after so long." He smiled down at me.

I laughed briefly. "You too, Mr. Adams."

He cupped his hands around his mouth, calling for his wife, Carrie. "Carrie, come over here! There's someone you'd love to see!"

A few moments later, Mrs. Adams came from the kitchen, carrying a sweet scent of pancakes with her. She had a pink and white checked apron tied around her neck, and a bit of white flour on the side of her cheek. She was still as cheery and bubbly as the last time I saw her, two years ago. "Oh, my." She covered her mouth. "Aerial Mason? Is that really you?"

Man, this felt like a reunion party already.

"Hi, Ms. Adams." I waved gently.

Ms. Adams gasped, pulling me in for a tight squeeze. "It really is you!" she beamed. "I never thought I'd ever see your face in this house ever again!"

I smiled awkwardly, as Ms. Adams fumbled with my hair. "Jesus, you've grown up so beautiful!" she gushed, holding my arm in her hands. "Have you been eating, though? You've lost so much weight! Here, I just made some pancakes in the kitchen!"

I laughed, shaking my head. "No thanks, Ms. Adams. I'm actually here because Clarice called me this morning."

Ms. Adams' eyes widened. "Oh, really?" she grinned. "You and my little pumpkin are friends again?"

I laughed bitterly, shrugging. "I guess so."

"Well she's just upstairs in her room. You still remember the directions, do you?" she asked.

I nodded, giving her a smile. "First door to the left."

She winked. "You got it."

I walked up the stairs, knocking the white bedroom door. "Clarice? I'm here." I said, as I pushed open the door.

I found Clarice applying some hot pink lip gloss in front of her vanity, which was overloaded with different makeup products. "Oh, hey." She said, keeping her lips pouted.

"Your room's certainly gotten a lot," I paused, taking in all the pink that was covering her room from the ceiling to the floor, "pinker, huh?"

Clarice shrugged, giving me a weak smile. "Well, Aubrey and Kelsey helped me redecorate my room after I joined the cheerleading team."

I nodded, taking a seat on her bed that was overflowed with pink throw pillows. How do you sleep with so much crap on your bed? "You like it like this?" I asked, eyeing a deadly, neon pink feathered pillow.

Clarice bit her lower lip, shrugging. "Not really, but I got used to it."

I sighed. "So, what did you call me here so early for on a Saturday morning?"

Clarice turned to me with a nervous smile on her face. "I called you here today for moral support."

I frowned, getting curious and slightly worried. "What are you talking about?"

Clarice took in a deep breath, slowly releasing it out. "I'm going to tell my parents that I'm pregnant. I want you to be there with me."

"Really?" I asked, surprised.

She nodded, giving me a hopeful look. "So, will you be there for me?"

I smiled. "Always."

"You're what?!" Clarice's father asked dangerously low.

We sat at the Adams' dinner table, where Clarice and I sat across from her parents.

The look on Mr. Adams' face was scary mad. His face turned bright red, and his hazel eyes that Clarice inherited where dark with rage. Mrs. Adams, on the other hand, looked as if she were about to pass out. Her face had turned pale the moment Clarice said she was knocked up.

"I-I'm pregnant." Clarice said again, making Mrs. Adams wince.

Mr. Adams slammed his fists against the dinner table, making the salt and pepper shakers clatter at the end of the table. "Unbelievable." Mr. Adams hissed under his breath, shaking his head back and forth quickly. "How long have you been pregnant?" he asked, spitting out the last word as if it were some foul language.

Clarice legs were shaking under the table, as she bit her lower lip nervously. "A little over a month now." She admitted, making her mother gasp.

Mr. Adams' eyes widened, as his ears turned red from fuming. "Clarice Jane Adams," he paused, staring at his daughter like a complete stranger, "you waited a full month before you told us?"

Clarice's eyes leaked with tears, as I patted her arm reassuringly. "She was scared, Mr. Adams." I told her parents gently, hoping to lift away some of the tension.

Mr. and Mrs. Adams' eyes snapped towards me, as if they've noticed me sitting at the table for the first time since Clarice has spoken.

"Aerial," Mrs. Adams gasped, "you knew all along?"

I shifted my bottom on the chair uncomfortably, nodding uneasily. "It's kind of the reason why Clarice and I are talking again."

Mr. Adams looked completely insensitive, as he licked his lips, running a hand through his bald head. "Aerial knew before we did?" he asked, looking at Clarice's face for answers. When she didn't reply, Mr. Adams shook his head, getting up from his chair. It scraped backward, creating an echoing screeching noise that would make someone's ear bleed.

We all watched as Mr. Adams disappeared through the front doors, and listened as his car drove away.

There was so much silence, that it was killing me. I watched as Clarice's eyes lingered onto her fingers, not daring to look at her broken mother, whose cheeks were tearstained.

"Who's the father of the baby?" her mother asked, not looking at her own daughter. "Is it that rude boy you brought home a few weeks ago?"

Clarice's breathing sharply hitched, as she licked her lips. "Yes." She croaked.

Clarice's mother pushed herself up, off the chair, as she began to exit the kitchen. "You are not my daughter anymore." Mrs. Adams' voice cracked, making me close my eyes. "My daughter would never make such a stupid decision."

I came back to Alex's house a little later than midnight. Part of the reason why I stayed out for so long was because Clarice became a mess, and was sobbing in her room the entire night. She finally fell asleep while we were watching our fourth movie that night. The other reason why was because I didn't want to face Alex. I hadn't spoken to him since that night, and I've been doing a pretty darn good job of avoiding him. Hayden even told me that Alex asked him to check up on me, which only made me snort and turn the other shoulder.

"I thought you were never going to come back." A voice startled me, as I locked the front door after opening it. I jumped, letting the keys slip out of my hands. I dropped to the ground, trying to find the keys in the dark.

Suddenly, the lights flickered on, as I snatched the keys from the floor. Hovering over me was Alex, who looked as if he hadn't slept in days.

Sure, I lived in his house for now, but I've barely spared him a glance this entire week. This was the first good look I've gotten of him since that night.

"I was just out a little later than expected." I mumbled, pushing past his shoulder.

Alex grumbled from behind. "When are you going to stop ignoring me?"

"I'll stop when I want to!" I snapped, glaring at him.

"You're living under my roof, and you'll talk to me when I want you to!" he shouted, making my clench my fists by my sides.

Did he really think he could control me just because I lived in his house? "I don't have to do anything I don't want to." I hissed, turning my back on him, as I began to walk up the staircases.

"If you're living here, then you will." He spat, making me stop in my tracks.

I closed my eyes tightly, as my hands trembled by my sides. "Then I'll leave." I said, staring him right in the eye. Alex's eyes widened with surprise, as he stared at me with a blank expression, like expected. "I'll leave by tomorrow morning, and that's a promise." I told him, trying to sound strong, but my voice just cracked at the end, giving off my weakness.

It took Alex a while to regain composure, but he finally stood up straighter, crossing his arms. "Fine." He tried to smirk, but it came off as a forced smile, making my heart ache with pain. "Go do what you want. I don't care."

I don't care.

I don't care.

Those three words broke me, as I dragged myself up the stairs. I bit my lips to stop them from quivering, as I closed my eyes tightly to keep them from crying.

Alex didn't care.

Why did it hurt me so much to know he didn't care?

Before the crack of dawn, I already had my stuff put together in my duffel bag, ready to go. I barely got an ounce of sleep last night, so I figured I just leave earlier. It would be early enough that Alex would still be asleep, so I wouldn't see him.

This was it. I was leaving, and I would have to go back home. I would have to go see my father again. I took in a deep breath, wondering how pissed off he would be at me for leaving and never returning any of his phone calls.

I closed my eyes tightly, taking a deep breath of air before walking away from Alex's house. I couldn't help but want him to come chasing after me, and tell me he was sorry. That he wanted me to stay.

The house was a complete mess when I got home. After weeks of not being here, the furniture was covered with trash, and there was a pile of dirty dishes and burnt toast in the sink.

I walked lightly towards my father's bedroom, noticing that he was knocked out on his bed. I entered his room, rolling his shoulder over to see if he was alright or not.

Suddenly, my father stirred, as my eyes widened.

What should I do? Run out and leave?

"Angel, is that you?" he asked me, letting out a tired grown.

I backed away from him, as he sat up, stretching out his arms. My heart was beating against my chest.

His eyes lingered over to me, as they opened with surprise. "Aerial." He paused, looking at me to see if I was real or not. "Baby, you're home."

He got up, and started to come closer to me, as I sank down in the corner of two walls. "Stop." I begged, covering my head with my hands. "Please, don't."

My dad stopped in his tracks, staring at me with hurt eyes. "I'm not going to hurt you. I just- I just miss you."

I glared at him, not believing a word he says. One minute, he was going to be nice to me, and then he was going to turn against me once he was drunk. "I'm home, but that doesn't mean I came home for you."

"Don't talk to me like that." He said sternly.

"I can't talk to you like that, but you can hit me?" I asked, backing out of his room. "Just leave me alone, dad."

CHAPTER 14

I was more than relieved when my father didn't bother me for the rest of the day. Occasionally, I would catch him passing by the bathroom just to check up on me. I was starting to feel guilty about telling him off earlier in the morning, but a part of me was proud of myself for finally standing up to him, no matter how scared I actually was on the inside.

When my father left for work after dinnertime that night, I decided to finally get out of my room and watch some TV in the living room. I thought I was going to stay home for the night in my pajamas with a bowl of popcorn on my lap, but just as I was about to put the bag of popcorn in the microwave, Hayden decided to call me.

"Hayden?" I asked, as I placed the phone to my ear, pacing around in my kitchen.

"Aerial? Are you busy tonight?" he asked.

"I was going to just have a movie night by myself, but I'm free if you want to do something." I said, picking up some empty cigar boxes on the couch. I frowned as I stared at the empty box.

I knew my father was an alcoholic, but I also thought I knew he gave up smoking ages ago, when mom was still here.

"Do you want to get dinner? There are some things we need to talk about." Hayden said, making me shudder. Had Alex told Hayden about what happened last night?

"Alright, I'll get dressed." I murmured, tossing the empty box of cigarettes in the trash basket.

"My car's getting a new paint job. Can you walk over to that old diner just a few blocks from your house?" Hayden asked.

"Are you talking about the one we went to last time for pancakes?" I asked, frowning, as I began to toss out a thick sweater and jeans from my dresser.

"That's the one. Hurry, okay? I'm almost there." Hayden said, as I wiggled myself into my skinny jeans.

"I'll try." I mumbled, as the other line went blank.

It took me ten minutes to walk to the diner, and from the glass windows, I could see Hayden waiting at one of the booths. As I entered the diner, a whiff of coffee and pancake batter filled of nose, making my stomach rumble.

I approached Hayden, sliding into the red leather seat across from him. He gave me a small smile, making me frown. He didn't look like his usual self today. He didn't have that cheery aura around him.

"Is something wrong?" I asked, giving him a worried look.

Hayden sighed, raising an eyebrow. "Shouldn't I be the one asking you that?"

I frowned, hoping that he wasn't talking about Alex. The last thing I needed right now was to have a conversation about him. "What do you mean?"

Before Hayden got to say anything, a perky waitress approached our table with a notepad and pen in each hand. "What can I get you guys tonight?" she smiled, her red lips stretching wide.

Hayden looked at me, signaling for me to order first. "I'll have the Fatty Breakfast Meal and a chocolate and vanilla milkshake."

The waitress giggled, as she nodded, jotting it down on her notepad. "What about you, sir?" she turned to Hayden.

"I'll have the same thing, without the eggs, though. And a strawberry smoothie." Hayden ordered.

The waitress ripped the sheet of paper from her notepad, holding it in her hands. "Coming right up." She gave us one last dazzling smile, before disappearing through the doors to the kitchen.

Hayden made sure no one was around us, before he spoke up again. "I want to know why you moved out of Alex's house."

I pursed my lips, crossing my arms stubbornly. "Why don't you ask him that?"

"Aerial." He warned.

I sighed, rolling my eyes. He really wasn't going to give up until I gave him an answer, was he? "Alex and I might've gotten into a fight the other night." I paused, letting out a deep breath of air. "Things just blew up last night."

"What did you guys fight about?" Hayden pushed.

I ran my hands through my brown hair, feeling frustrated. "His mother came home the other night, and he wasn't home. She told me how she was a single mother, and work was always in the way of Alex. That night, before she left, she made Alex some leftover dinner. When I told Alex his mother made it, he made a huge fuss about how he wouldn't eat it." I paused, groaning with stress. "He was being so arrogant and stubborn. I kept telling him how lucky he was to have a mother, and when he asked why I even cared, I told him. I told Alex that he was lucky enough to have one that wasn't dead."

Hayden's eyes widened, as his face went pale. "Oh, Aerial, I'm-"

I cut him off, nodding. "I know, Hayden. You're sorry. So was Alex."

Hayden cleared his throat. "Alex didn't know. If he did, he wouldn't have said it."

I scoffed, as the waitress came back with a tray of food in her palms. "That really makes no difference." I muttered, as she placed a large platter of food in front of me.

"He cares about you, you know?" Hayden said when the waitress went away.

I scoffed at the irony. "Oh, that's funny, because just last night, he told me how he didn't care if I left. He said he never cared." I said, trying to not make my voice sound shaky.

"He lied." Hayden flat out said, making me raise an eyebrow. "He's Alex. He doesn't want anyone to know if he cares about them."

"Then how did you know he cares about you?" I asked mockingly.

Hayden chuckled, and shrugged. "I just do. We've been with each other for years."

"Clarice taking me out for ice cream," I paused, licking the vanilla ice cream that was covering my spoon, "I could get used to this."

Clarice laughed weakly, shrugging. "It's just a way of me saying thanks."

I frowned, raising an eyebrow. "Thanks? For what?"

Clarice smiled, taking a bite out of the large banana fudge sundae that was settled in front of her. She specifically requested the waiter to give her five chocolate scoops with an uncut banana, drizzled in hot, chocolate fudge. Fine, right? But, when the waiter asked Clarice if she wanted any additional toppings, Clarice replied by asking if they could put pickles on it.

The waiter looked at her like she was out of her mind.

But anyways, Clarice got what she wanted.

When I asked her about it, she simply shrugged, and said that she was craving pickles.

"For being there when I told my parents the news." Clarice muttered. "Even though my dad probably scared you away, you still stayed with me through the whole night."

"It's what I'm supposed to do, right?" I asked.

Clarice twisted her lips. "I don't know. I mean, you didn't have to. Especially after everything I've done to you." She paused, poking at her ice cream. "I left when you needed me the most. But, when I need you right now, you're not running away."

I pursed my lips, staring down at my now mushy ice cream.

Suddenly, I wasn't in the mood to eat my treat anymore.

I sighed. What was I supposed to say to that?

"Do you ever miss her?" Clarice suddenly asked, startling me.

"Who?" I asked, even though I knew exactly who she was talking about.

Clarice looked uneasy, as she looked away from me. "Your mother."

I felt myself stop breathing, as I gulped. Talking about my mother never came easy to me. My throat always felt tightened up whenever I did. "All the time." I whispered.

"I could never imagine living without my mother." Clarice paused, giving me a small, sad smile. "You're so brave, Aerial."

My eyes reached Clarice's for a slight second, before we split apart. "Thanks." I muttered, barely meaning it. I wasn't brave. I was cracking on the inside.

"If you don't mind me asking," she paused, searching my face for answers, "how does your dad cope with it?"

He deals with my mother's death by taking it out on me.

"Honestly, Aerial." Clarice looked at me with a worried expression. "I'm here for you."

Licking my lips, I nodded. "I know." I whispered.

"My dad hasn't been the same since she died." I started off. Clarice frowned in confusion, because as far as she could remember, my father had always treated the both of us with so much love and care. "He started to drink. At first, it wasn't so bad. But, after a few months, he would come home completely drunk and wasted."

Clarice's eyes widened, her hazel orbs filled with regret and guilt. "He never hit you, did he?"

I gulped, as I tore my gaze away from hers. Suddenly, I heard her gasp, and I watched a tear slid down her cheeks. "Oh God." She muttered, clamping a hand over her lips. "I-I didn't know."

I nodded, licking my lips. "No one did."

"I-I wish I could've helped." She whispered, voice so fragile and genuine. "I was way too caught up with being popular. I didn't even realize-"

"It's fine." I cut her off.

Clarice frowned, twisting her lips. "He doesn't still, does he?"

I stared down at my hands, eyes dropping. "I wish he didn't." I muttered.

"Is that why you're staying over at Alex's house for now?" she asked.

"Yeah." I muttered. "But, I kind of moved out a few days ago."

Clarice blinked. "So, you're back with your dad?"

I nodded. "But, he hasn't done anything bad, yet."

"You're always welcomed to stay over at my place, you know?" she offered. "My parent's love you, and I do miss those sleep-overs we used to have when we were kids."

I let out the first laugh I've had in a long time. "I remember." I paused, smiling. "Thanks."

CHAPTER 15

The sound of glass shattering woke me up.

I jolted up from my bed, listening carefully, as another crash came from the kitchen. Getting out of my covers, I opened my door. I tiptoed to the kitchen, where the light was coming from.

Another crash.

I peeked from behind the wall, feeling my heart hammer against my chest.

What the hell was going on?

I watched as my dad take wine glasses from our cabinets, and smash them on the floor. He had a drunken grin spread across his face, as he picked up another glass, throwing it down on the floor with all his might.

My eyes widened, as I stepped out. "Dad, what are you doing? Stop!" I shouted, taking the few remaining wine glasses away from him.

His bloodshot eyes glared at me, as a bead of sweat dripped down from his forehead. "Give me it back." He glowered, stepping over the glass, making his way towards me.

I tried to move away from him, but his arm latched on to mine, pulling me forward. "Give me the glasses, now." His breath reeked of alcohol, making me wince.

He hasn't changed at all.

And to think after I've left for a few weeks, he would change. But apparently, he hasn't. Not a tiny bit has changed about him. He was still that demanding, violent, drunk father he once was, and always will be.

"Dad, please. You're hurting me." I mumbled, feeling my wrists burn under his tight grip.

My hands gave up, as I let go of the wine glasses. They crashed on the ground below us, making a deafening noise.

"You deserve to be punished for running away." My father slurred.

My eyes welled up with tears, as I tried to fight my way out of his grip. "I thought you changed!" I cried.

My father immediately let go of my wrists, pushing me down to the floor. I stared up at him with fear evident in my eyes.

Was he finally sober?

I hope he was. He's always less dangerous when he wasn't drunk out of his mind.

"I hate you." My father muttered, taking in a deep breath of air. "I hate looking at you. You look just like her."

My breath hitched, as I blinked away my tears.

He was talking about my mother.

I looked just like my mother.

"Why did she leave me? She could've chosen chemo." My father said, his voice becoming weaker and weaker. He was finally cracking; I could see the way his face was twisting into a hopeless frown.

"She didn't want to suffer." I croaked. "If you loved her, then you would understand why she didn't want to be on medication."

"Don't you dare question my love for Aspen!" my father lashed out, his palm slamming against my right cheek.

It was burning. My cheek felt like it was on fire.

I clutched my face, staring up at him with tears in my eyes.

He stared back at me with a blank expression, his mouth open, like he couldn't believe it himself that he actually physically slapped me.

But he did.

My own father just slapped me.

"Aerial, honey, I-"

No. This was the sweet side of my father. There was also the violent one. But, I couldn't live anymore with his two sides constantly switching back and forth. I couldn't come home anymore, scared to see if he was drunk or not.

"I'm leaving." I whispered, pushing myself up, as I backed away from him.

My father reached out for my arm, as I flinched under his touch. "You're not leaving, not again. You can't. I have no body." He said, his eyes pleading.

I should've left, right then and there. But, I didn't. One, because I would have no where to stay. And two, he was my dad. No matter what he did to me, or what happens, he was still my father at the end of the day. He had complete control and custody over me. He was the last thing I had that I could call family.

I pulled my wrists away from his hands, as I made my way to my room, locking the door behind me.

I watched as Aubrey strutted down the hallways the next morning, holding a stash of hot pink envelopes in her hands. Her friends walked behind her, as she handed everyone she passed by an envelope.

"You think she's having a party or something?" I asked, watching Aubrey give everyone fake smiles.

"It's her birthday this Friday." Clarice muttered.

"Oh, whatever, I'm going to class early to study for a test first period." I told Clarice, closing my locker. I didn't even take three steps when a chirpy voice stopped me in my tracks.

"Aerial, where are you going?" Aubrey asked, giving me an evil smile with a glint of amusement twinkling in her green eyes.

"Class." I muttered, trying my best not to sound rude or harsh.

Aubrey snickered, taking out an invite, and handing it to me. I stared at her hand with a blank expression. Was this supposed to be her way of inviting me?

"I would just love it if you could make it to my birthday party this Friday." Aubrey smiled, raising an eyebrow at me teasingly.

I stared behind her shoulder, locking my eyes with Clarice. She seemed confused at what Aubrey was doing. When Aubrey caught me staring back at Clarice, she smirked.

"It's okay, Aerial." She paused, turning to Clarice. "Clare Bear can come, too."

I crossed my arms, licking my lips. I was still unconvinced. "What's the catch, Aubrey?"

Aubrey smacked her glossy pink lips, shaking her head. "There's no catch, Aerial."

"Then why do you want the two of us at your party?" I asked challengingly. She better tell us now, before I find out later.

"It's my birthday, for crying out loud." She looked at me with an innocent expression. "I just want my two best friends to be there." She chucked an invitation towards me. She gave me a wink, before moving onto the next few people that were in the hallways.

I turned back to Clarice, who was staring at me with a frown on her face. "Can you believe her?" I scoffed, shaking my head. "Ridiculous."

Just as I was about to tear the invite in shreds, Clarice stopped me. "Wait, don't." she told me, taking the invite out of my hands.

I raised an eyebrow at the blonde. "You actually want to go to this stupid party?"

Clarice bit her lower lip, shrugging.

I rolled my eyes, sighing. "Holy shit, you're serious." I paused, as Clarice stared up at me with a small smile. "Why do you want to go?"

Clarice opened the invite, eyes scanning through the card. "I just want to fun, that's all."

"Fun?" I asked, wrinkling my nose. "Are you sure going to Aubrey Small's party is considered fun?"

Clarice gave me a blank look. "Look, I haven't had fun since I got pregnant, okay? Can we just go?"

I licked my lips, sighing. I shouldn't have said yes, but I did. "Fine. But, you can't drink, got it?"

Clarice grinned, nodding. "It's a deal."

"You got an invite, too?" I asked Hayden, staring at the hot pink envelope that was nearly falling out of his unzipped book bag.

Hayden stared over his shoulder, at the invite, before zipping his bag back up. "Yeah, Aubrey gave it to me earlier today."

I nodded." Same here."

Hayden raised an eyebrow, looking ultimately surprised. I mean, I would've been surprised, too, if I was Hayden. Aubrey hated my guts, and now she wants me to come to her beloved birthday party? It just didn't make sense. "She told me there wasn't a catch to me and Clarice being invited." I paused, letting out a bitter laugh. "I don't believe that for a minute."

Hayden grinned, as we got in his car that was parked in the school parking lot. "I don't, either. But, are you going to go?"

I shrugged, taking in a deep breath of air. "Clarice really wants me to go."

"Why? Don't they have some kind of bitch fight going on?" he asked, making me chuckle.

"I thought so, too." I muttered.

Hayden nodded, as he began to pull his car out of the parking lot. "Do you need to go home yet?"

I shook my head, staring at the time that was written on Hayden's dashboard. "Not until nine." Nine o'clock was when my father left for work. I didn't have to face him for the entire night, which I was thankful of.

"Great. Do you want to come over to Damian's house? A few of the guys are going to be there." Hayden asked, keeping his eyes focused on the road.

I secretly wondered if Alex was going to be there. It was going to extremely uncomfortable for me if Alex was there. We haven't spoken in an entire week, and I don't think either of us are planning to speak to each other any time soon.

"Are you up for it?" Hayden interrupted my thoughts.

I cleared my throat, pursing my lips. "Sure. I've got nothing better to do."

When we arrived at Damian's house, there were already a few cars parked on the driveway, and even a few on the side of the road. Hayden and I got out simultaneously, as we walked up to his front steps. We rang the doorbell, waiting for someone to come get the door.

A familiar blonde appeared by the door, looking a bit shocked to see me. But, she smiled at Hayden, letting the both of us inside. "Hi, Hayden." She grinned, placing her hands on Hayden's shoulder.

Now, I remember. She was with Natalia the other day when we were all at Alex's house. If I recall, her name was Phoebe. And if she was here, then Natalia must be, too. I knew right away that Natalia wouldn't be happy to see me, and I can say the same thing about her.

"Phoebe, it's good to see you." Hayden smirked, his eyes raking down her body. It was then I noticed that Phoebe was wearing a low-cut top, and denim cut offs. Didn't she know that it was nearly winter, and there was snow covering the ground?

What disgusted me more was that Hayden was actually flirting back with her, checking her out and leading her on. But, I guess it was just Hayden's natural instinct to flirt back with her. He's always been the flirty and goofy type.

I followed Phoebe and Hayden downstairs, where I could hear a bunch of various voices chattering and hooting.

"Guys, Hayden's here!" Phoebe announced, barely acknowledging me.

My eyes scanned the basement, noticing a few people I knew, but I couldn't recognize the majority. My eyes finally landed on Alex, who was slouching on the couch with Natalia sitting beside him, holding a cigarette between her two fingers. Her cat-like eyes immediately shot up to me, giving me a glare full of anger and hate.

"What the hell is she doing here?" Natalia spat at me, making Alex's eyes wander up to me. "She doesn't belong with us."

"There won't be a problem if you leave her alone." Damian stepped in, offering me a small smile. "Come sit next to me, Aerial."

I gave him a thankful smile, as I took the empty seat beside him on one of the separate couches. "Thanks." I muttered low enough, so no one could here.

Damian smiled back, nodding. "No problem. If you want a drink, there's a bunch upstairs in the kitchen."

I shook my head, giving him a small smile. "I'm fine, thanks."

Suddenly, a few of the guys got up, one of them holding a deck of cards in their hands. "Who wants to play?" one asked, shuffling the deck of cards.

Natalia scoffed, raising an eyebrow. "No one wants to play a stupid game of Go Fish with you idiots." She snapped.

"We aren't playing Go Fish." The guy grinned deviously. "I was thinking maybe we could all play a game of poker."

"Strip poker?" Ashton asked, wiggling his eyebrows.

A few of them chuckled. "Even better. Who's in?"

Everyone gathered onto the floor, into a fairly big circle. I was hesitant, as I sat back in my seat. "Are you coming?" Damian asked, pulling me up.

Natalia's head suddenly shot back at the both of us, smirking at me. "Come on, Aerial. I want to see you in that training bra of yours."

I blushed, feeling my cheeks get warm.

"Aerial doesn't wear a training bra." Hayden defended me, making Phoebe shoot a glare at me. "Just ask Alex. He would know."

My eyes widened, and I could feel my skin burning. Did Hayden really just say that?

I could feel everyone's eyes on me, as Damian pulled me into the circle. Alex was sitting on the opposite side of me, where he could get a perfect view of my flushed face. But, I didn't dare look at him. I wouldn't.

"Alright, let's get started. Texas Hold Em', okay?" the guy asked, already dealing out two cards per person.

Whoever didn't fold before the winner was announced had to take off one article of clothing that was on them.

After ten rounds, I was lucky enough to win two of them. I was also lucky enough to only have my shoes and sweater off. I thanked myself for wearing a tank top this morning, otherwise, I would be in my bra by now.

On the other hand, most of the guys had their shirts off, and a few were even down in their boxers. Phoebe was the one who had the least clothing on, though. She was down in her bra and panties, which I was almost sure that she was trying to lose on purpose, just to get down in her underwear.

"Okay, should we take a break?" Damian asked, grabbing a bottle of beer off the table beside us.

"Are we allowed to keep our clothes off?" Phoebe asked, batting her eyelashes.

A few of the guys laughed, as I stared at her pathetically. "Why not?" Damian smirked.

I put my shoes and my sweater back on, heading upstairs to see if I could find something that wasn't alcoholic. I rummaged through the fridge, finally pulling out a can of soda that was buried in the back of Damian's fridge.

"You're just a little angel, aren't you?" a sarcastic voice snarled at me from behind.

I turned around just as I was about pop open the can of soda, facing Natalia. She looked at me with hate, and fury burning in her eyes.

"I don't know what you're talking about." I mumbled, popping open the can, and taking a long sip.

Natalia's left eye twitched, as she clenched her jaw.

I don't know why she was always so angry at me. I never did anything to her, and she was just making things worse by snapping at me for no reason.

"You. You think you're all innocent and you try to walk around like a Virgin Mary." She spat at me, making me flinch.

"I never said I was innocent." I said lowly, settling down my can of soda on the kitchen counter. I crossed my arms, giving Natalia an impatient look. "Stop trying to assume things."

Natalia's face turned red with embarrassment and anger, as she reached in her pocket. I frowned for a second, wondering what she was doing. But, she finally pulled out a small bag with white powder in it. It wasn't what I thought it was, was it?

"If you aren't an innocent bitch like I think you are, snort this." She flung her hand towards me, holding the bag of cocaine out.

I gulped, biting my lips. My hands trembled as I reached up for the drugs. I knew I was going to regret this, but I just had to prove to Natalia that I wasn't a little prissy like she pinned me to be. I just wanted to stop being downgraded on, because she thought I had something going on with Alex. Which I didn't, but sometimes, I do wish I did.

"Are you going to take it any time soon?" Natalia stared at me challengingly, waving the bag in my face.

I took in a deep breath, before snatching the cocaine out of her palms. I gripped onto the bag tightly, hands shaking as I opened it.

"Just put a little up to your nose, and sniff." Natalia said in a dangerously low voice.

I shouldn't be doing this.

I shouldn't.

I was smarter than this.

"Aerial, what the fuck are you doing?!" an angry voice startled me, making me drop the entire bag. The white powder spilled all over the floor, making Natalia growl.

"You bitch! That cost me hundreds!" she shrieked.

Suddenly, a hand went flying towards my face, slapping me right where my father did last night.

My face went numb once again. My hand clutched my face, as Alex stared at me with widened eyes. I felt warm liquid on my face, as I looked down on my palms.

Blood.

Natalia's hand had struck my face so hard, that her nail dug in and scratched my face,

"You deserved this." She glowered at me, her eyes burning into mine with hate. "You're just a pathetic little-"

Two arms held Natalia back from my face. Alex pulled her away from me, as she began to scream and protest.

"Let me go, Alex! Let me teach that slut what-"

"Shut up, Natalia." Alex groaned.

My legs wobbled as I got up, tears threatening to spill down my face.

How could've I been so stupid?

I began to ran, my hair whipping behind me, as I ran out of Damian's house. I ran down his street, the wind brushing my tears back, as I struggled to breath.

A hand suddenly held onto my wrist, stopping me from walking. I felt my wrist burn from the bruise my father left yesterday. Immediately, I pulled my hand back, staring at Alex with fear.

"Don't hit me!" I begged, tears flowing from my eyes. "Please!"

Alex's expression turned into pain, as my chest ached inside. "I'm not going to hurt you." Alex said, frowning. "What's going on? You were about to do drugs back there!"

Tears streamed down my face, as I felt myself unable to speak. My throat was tightened up, and my mouth was dry.

"I thought you were smarter than that, Aerial." He paused, looking me in the eye with so much disappointment. "I thought you were smart enough to not be pressured by Natalia."

I felt myself slowly cracking.

My mother once told me that no matter how down you're feeling, someone out there in the world has it worse. But right now, I could care less.

"You're acting like it's my entire fault!" I finally snapped, feeling so much better. "Your girlfriend gave me the cocaine!"

Alex gritted his teeth together. "She's not my girlfriend. And, you could've said no."

I laughed bitterly through my tears. "Fuck it, Alex. Fuck you, your stupid girlfriend, and fuck everyone."

I turned around, as I began to walk away. I knew I was being very unladylike with my choice of words, but what was I supposed to do when I was being blamed for peer pressure, even after I got slapped and scratched?

CHAPTER 16

I was never the most patient person in the world. I never liked waiting for stuff to be finished, like waiting in line at the grocery store, or waiting for a test result. I also hate sitting in waiting rooms at the hospital, especially when I wasn't even waiting for my own appointment.

Clarice asked me to come along for her first prenatal appointment at the hospital today. Normally, I didn't like spending my Thursday afternoons waiting in the hospital, but she begged me to come along with her. When I asked why she didn't ask her parents to come, she told me how they still weren't supportive of her baby.

The door that Clarice went into an hour ago finally opened up, as the doctor escorted Clarice out. "All you have to do now is go to the receptionist to book your next appointment." Doctor Madison told Clarice, giving her a smile.

"Thanks." Clarice nodded, quickly walking over to the reception desk to make an appointment for the next month.

When she was finished, she came over to me. She gestured for me to get up, as I followed her to take the elevator down to the parking area.

"The doctor told me everything was alright, so far." Clarice said, as the elevator went down.

I nodded, staring down at my shoes, as the elevator doors opened. The two of us stepped out, as another couple with a stroller entered in after us.

"I asked her when the morning sickness will end." She unlocked her, as the two of us got inside. "She told me most morning sickness' end between ten to fifteen weeks."

I sighed, staring out the window. Clarice began to drive out of the hospital, as I rested my head against the glass window. "Great." I mumbled.

Clarice stared at me curiously from the corner of her eyes. She could tell there was something up, and she wouldn't back off until she got her answer. "What's up with you today, Aerial?" she paused, giving me a stern look. "And, don't you dare lie to me."

I licked my lips, crossing my arms stubbornly. "Nothing's wrong."

Clarice stared at my cheek as we came to a red light, frowning. "What happened to your cheek? That scratch wasn't there when I saw you yesterday."

I groaned, throwing my head back against the cushion. "I got slapped, okay? I got slapped, Clarice."

Clarice choked, as her car swiveled, making the car behind us honked its horn. Clarice pulled over to the side of the road, staring over at me with disbelief. "Who slapped you?" she cried.

I let out a deep breath of air, closing my eyes. "It was just Alex's psycho ex-girlfriend." I murmured.

Clarice's mouth dropped. "That bitch!" she hissed under her breath. "Okay, now she's going to have to deal with a pregnant woman!"

I let out a low laugh, shaking my head. "Don't worry about it, Clarice."

Clarice raised her eyebrow, shaking her head. "You're kidding." She snapped. "Don't worry about it? She slapped my best friend!"

My heart skipped a beat, as I did a double take to her.

Best friend?

I licked my dry lips, staring at her with a blank face.

Did she just call the two of us best friends?

Clarice stared at me awkwardly, clearing her throat. "Sorry, I-"

I cut her off, giving her a small smile. I was helping her through her pregnancy, and we've grown closer because of it. We reconnected, and I did consider her pretty close to me now. Maybe it was time I moved on. Maybe it was time I let go of that grudge I was holding against her. She was human, after all.

"No." I smiled. "Best friends. We're best friends."

A grin spread its way across Clarice's face, as she leapt in her seat. She held my arm, eyes glistening with so much happiness. This was the most happy I've seen her since she found out she was knocked up. And, I was pretty damn proud that I was the reason of it.

"Now," Clarice said, staring up her car again, "I think we should go celebrate with a Big Mac."

I frowned, staring at her with eyebrows rose. "Big Macs? Clarice you're pregnant. That stuff has no nutritional value."

Clarice scoffed, rolling her eyes. "Since when have I ever followed the rules, Aerial?"

I smiled at the thought of her always being the rebellious one out of the two of us. In junior high, Clarice was the one who always got the both of us in trouble. She was always the one who didn't do her homework, talked back to teachers, and punch anyone who was mean to me.

"Fine." I smiled, giving her a warningly look. "Just this once."

We got our Big Macs to go, and decided to eat them while we drove to the mall. "We need outfits for Aubrey's party tomorrow night." Clarice told me, as she munched away on her burger, which she bought three of. Being pregnant really boosted up her appetite. The cashier at McDonald's even gave her a strange look when she made the order.

"We're going to look gorgeous in our dresses." Clarice mumbled, while the burger was still in her mouth.

I choked on my burger, shaking my head at the blonde. "No way. You aren't putting me in a dress."

Clarice gave me a puppy dog look. "Why not? All the girls are wearing dresses."

I rolled my eyes, throwing away my wrapper. "I haven't worn a dress since eight grade graduation, and I don't plan on wearing one any soon." I paused. "Why can't I just wear pants with a nice shirt?"

Clarice glared at me, shaking her head. "No. If you're coming to that party, you're wearing a dress."

"But I don't even want to-"

"You better go. I'll make sure of it." Clarice gave me a stern look, indicating that she was dead serious.

I tried my best to ignore Alex, Damian, Hayden and anyone who was at Damian's house the other night the next morning at school. I could tell that they were trying to talk to me, but every time I saw them come close to me, I weaved my way around them, or turned the other hallway.

I knew I was wrong for ignoring them all as a whole, but I was just too embarrassed to face them. I knew Natalia had said something bad about me to everyone, and I knew that they would all believe her lies.

"Aerial." Hayden's voice echoed through my ears from behind.

I picked up my pace faster. Just a few more steps and I can disappear through the other hallway.

"Aerial, stop avoiding me!" Hayden snapped, pulling my shoulder back. He whirled me around, as I came face to face with him.

"I have to go study." I mumbled, not looking him in the eye.

Hayden sighed. "But, it's lunch time."

"And, I have a test the period after lunch." It wasn't necessarily a lie. I did actually have a Spanish test after lunch, but, I studied the night before. I knew everything on there was to know, but I needed a good excuse right now.

Hayden crossed his arms, giving me an impatient look. "Fine. You can ignore everyone else, but not me."

I scoffed, trying to pretend like I had no idea what he was rumbling on about. "I'm not ignoring any of you." I said, my voice higher than I wanted it to be.

Hayden rolled his eyes, and sarcastically remarked, "Yeah, and Alex isn't completely drooling over you."

My eyes widened, as I blushed. Way to make me look like an idiot, Hayden. Congratulations. "Shut up."

Hayden shrugged. "Okay, fine. But seriously, we need to talk."

I crossed my arms, giving him a fake smile. "Yes, sir?"

"I need to know why you did it." Hayden said seriously, giving me a worried look.

I frowned, genuinely confused this time. "What are you talking about?"

Hayden licked his lips, leaning closer to me. "Why did you snort the coke?" he said in a hushed voice, so that no one could hear us, even though we were in an empty hall.

My jaw dropped, as I pushed him away. Those lies Natalia's been feeding everyone are ridiculous. She knew I didn't do anything, and all that cocaine on Damian's floor was proof.

"I didn't!" I snapped, feeling my blood boiling in my veins.

Hayden stared at me, trying to read my face to see if I was lying or not. Didn't he know I was smart enough to not do it? Was his lack of faith in me really that low that he believed something that came out of Natalia's mouth?

"But, Natalia said-"

I cut him off, glaring at him. "Natalia said this, Natalia said that!" I shouted. "Who cares what she said?!"

Hayden stared at me with guilt in his eyes, as he shuffled his feet uncomfortably.

"You actually believed some lie about me that came from Natalia." I said in a low voice, feeling betrayed. "How could you?"

Hayden shook his head. "No, no. I believe you now, Aerial."

I clenched my fists, backing away from Hayden. "I don't give a shit."

I began to run away down the hall, towards the girl's bathroom. I could hear Hayden's voice calling after me, telling me to stop. But, I didn't.

Everyone was turning against me.

"Cheer up, Aerial." Clarice smiled, applying some a rosy pink lipstick onto my lips. "You look gorgeous."

Clarice finished up doing my makeup, as she spun me around, so that I was facing the mirror on her vanity. My jaw almost dropped at the girl that was in my reflection. I was wearing a short mint green dress that was tightened at the waist, but flowed down freely to just above the knees. Clarice had curled my brown hair into loose ringlets, and done my makeup naturally, which gave me a soft aura.

"I must say, I'm proud of my work." Clarice clapped her hands together, biting her lips from beaming.

I let out a breath of air, smiling with disbelief. "Oh my God, Clarice." I mumbled, touching the ends of my curls. "It's me."

Clarice gave me a teasing smile. "I knew there was an inner girl inside of you."

My head suddenly snapped towards her, as I give her a playful glare. I punched her shoulder gently, as she chuckled. "Alright, let's get started with you now." I muttered, holding up a straightened.

Clarice's eyes widened at the weapon in my hands, as she shook her head rapidly. "No, no!" she shouted, taking it out of my hands. "You'll end up burning me with that."

I pretended to look offended, as I crossed my arms. "Hey!"

Clarice bit back a laugh. "I've got everything covered for myself." She paused, plugging the straightened in an electrical outlet. "Just go sit and look pretty."

Two hours later, we pulled up to Aubrey's house. There were several of cars jam packed in her driveway, and Clarice had to make sure she didn't scrape anyone's car when she parked into the tiny spot.

We walked up to Aubrey's door, which was a French paneled door with glass windows. We rang the doorbell, and as soon as our fingers touched the bell, the door swung open. Aubrey was revealed, wearing a lilac purple dress, with crystals decorating the entire bust area. Her fiery red hair was pinned up with tight curls falling out, as she gave the two of us a smile. "You guys are late." She snickered. "But, I'm glad you guys made it here."

Clarice gave her a tight smile, and I caught Aubrey's eyes staring at the both of our dresses with envy. "Happy birthday, Aubs."

Aubrey twisted her lips, letting the two of us inside. "You can put my present on the table right there." She pointed to the table over at the right corner that was piling up with colorful wrapped presents.

"Will do." Clarice gave her a smile, making Aubrey fume with anger.

We walked towards the table of presents, setting ours down on the side. We both pitched in and got Aubrey a purse from her favorite boutique, according to Clarice.

"Did you see the way she looked at you?" Clarice asked me, walking over to a waiter, who was handing out little cupcakes.

She took a cupcake off the tray, giving a small smile to the waiter. "She was totally jealous of how good you look."

I blushed, shaking my head. "It's funny, because I thought she was looking at you."

Clarice rolled her eyes, giving me a little punch. "Okay, fine. She was looking at the both of us." She paused, staring at someone who was in the distance. "But, I know that Alex has all eyes on you."

I frowned, turning around. Standing at the top of the staircases with a group of people was Alex, who was wearing a black dress shirt, with a pair of dark jeans. His eye caught mine, as he quickly looked away, laughing at a joke Hayden said.

I licked my lips, turning back to Clarice. "Whatever." Smiling weakly. "I heard a few girls talking about a chocolate fondue fountain. Let's go find it."

Clarice raised an eyebrow, but laughed when I pulled her arm. We weaved our way through dancing girls wearing pastel dresses, and guys wearing tucked in shirts with dress pants. As we were trying to push our way out of the crowd, I found Clarice suddenly being pulled away from me.

I frowned, turning around. I stared up at Daniel's six foot figure, latching his hands around Clarice's arms protectively. He hovered over her, leaning closely to her face with anger in his eyes. "What are you wearing?" he hissed at the blonde, staring down at her mini pink dress that hugged all her curves.

Clarice stared at Daniel with disgust, pushing him away from her. "Get off of me, Daniel." She scrunched her face, fanning her nose. "Are you drunk?"

"No!" Daniel shouted, causing everyone around us to stop dancing. The music cut off, as I watched Aubrey try to find out what the chaos was going on about. "You're leaving with me."

Clarice struggled to get her wrists free from Daniel's strong grip. "You're hurting me." She cried.

I watched as Daniel's nails dug into Clarice's soft skin, making her wince.

I couldn't watch any further as my best friend got physically hurt by her douche bag of an ex-boyfriend. "Get off her." I hissed, ripping his large hands away from Clarice's wrists.

Daniel's eyes suddenly snapped towards me, his bloodshot eyes glaring at me with fury. "Who do you think you are, bitch?" he shouted, pushing my back.

I staggered, finding myself unable to keep balance. I fell over, landing straight on my bottom, as I heard a crowd gasp.

"Aerial!" Clarice cried, as Daniel hovered over me.

"I'm not afraid to hit a girl." Daniel grinned deviously. "I hope you know that for your own sake, Mason." He pulled my brown hair up, raising my face towards his. "People like you need to know your place in this world."

I watched as he raised a fist, getting ready to throw it at me. I heard Clarice scream, trying to get someone to help us.

I closed my eyes, getting ready for the immense pain, but the fists never came in contact to me. When I opened my eyes, Clarice was helping me up.

I watched as Daniel got tackled to the floor by Alex.

Alex's eyes were dark with hatred, as he threw punch after punch. He knocked his fist against Daniel's nose, creating a sickening crack that echoed through the room.

I watched the chaos go on right in front of my eyes, as Aubrey came rummaging through the crowd towards the fight with a group of jocks from the football team.

"Get them off each other!" she shrieked, as I watched a jock rip Alex off of Daniel uneasily. "They're going to get blood on my carpet!"

Alex shrugged the jock off, as he glared at him. "Don't touch me." He growled dangerously.

Daniel was lying with his back down on the floor, as blood spewed out from his nose. "You're dead, Montgomery." He spoke weakly to Alex.

Alex paid no attention to him, as his eyes met mine for the first time. I didn't look away like I usually would've. Instead, I kept close contact with him, reading all of the angry emotions that were running across his eyes. There was anger, hatred, frustration.

"All of you!" Aubrey cried, tears streaming down her cheeks. "Get out!"

And with that call, everyone scrammed.

Clarice held my arm carefully, as she helped me outside. "Oh my God, are you okay?" she asked worriedly.

I turned back to see if I could catch a glimpse of Alex, but he was gone.

"I'm fine." I whispered.

CHAPTER 17

Waking up early on Saturday morning's to get breakfast at the diner was one of my favorite things to do. I mean, who doesn't want to wake up to juicy and greasy bacon?

Surprisingly, there was quite an amount of people at the diner this morning. People usually come here in the mornings to get take out breakfast.

I sat in one of the empty booths by myself, waiting a fifteen minutes before the waitress came by with a thick stack of fresh pancakes, and extra bacon, upon my requests.

"Do you want some coffee with that?" she asked, voice relatively tired with matching bags evident under her eyes.

"I'm fine, thanks." I muttered.

She nodded, as the disappeared to the next table. I took the syrup that was in a bottle at the end of the table, and poured it all over my pancakes until they were dripping down the sides.

"Is that enough syrup for you?" a voice suddenly interrupted me.

I looked up, staring into Hayden's hazel eyes. He gave me a lopsided smile, as he slid in the empty seat across from me. "You don't mind if I sit down, right?" he asked, holding a mug of coffee, which I assumed he ordered.

"Not at all." I muttered, stuffing a strip of bacon into my mouth.

Hayden stared at me intently, while I made a point not to look at him. I kept my focus on my breakfast, no matter how uncomfortable I felt while he was staring at me.

"The rumors are true, aren't they?" he asked suddenly, making me cringe.

"Rumors, huh?" I asked, angrily poking into my pancakes. "So, you actually do listen to all that crap. Like the one where Natalia said I snorted crack." I laughed bitterly, giving him a glare. "That one's my favorite."

Hayden licked his lips, staring at me with guilt. "I'm sorry, Aerial. I was just caught up in everything. I forgot to talk to you about it first."

"Whatever." I mumbled.

Hayden pursed his lips. "I just wanted to make sure you were okay. Daniel didn't hurt you, did he?"

"No." I said.

"Good thing Alex was there to be your knight in shiny armor, huh?" he tried to crack a joke to lighten things up. I couldn't help but feel the corner of my lips twitch upwards. It was unbelievably hard to stay mad at Hayden.

"I see you smiling, Aerial." Hayden teased, poking my thumb. "I'm sorry."

I ignored him, shaking my head. I stuffed some bacon in my mouth, as Hayden pouted his lower lip out. "I'm really sorry. Like, really, really, really, sorry. Sorrier that I was when I accidentally drowned my goldfish when I was five. Sorrier than when I-"

I groaned, letting a grin crack across my face. "Okay, okay, fine! You're forgiven."

Hayden pumped his fist in the air, smiling wider that I was. "Yes!" he chanted, making a few people turn their heads towards us. He ignored them all, as he leaned closer towards me, grinning like an eager school boy. "So tell me, how romantic was it of Alex to beat up Daniel for you?"

I chuckled, staring at Hayden with eyebrows raised. I definitely missed him. "You sound like a girl right now, Hayden."

"What if I am?" he asked challengingly.

"Then I would be really scared." I smiled innocently, pinching his cheeks.

Hayden gasped, as he pulled back, giving me a look of shame. "Aerial!"

"You deserved it." I muttered, giving him an evil smile.

I asked Hayden to drop me off at Alex's house around nine that night. Hayden wiggled his eyebrows suggestively, but I strictly told him that I was going over to Alex's house to thank him for yesterday. If it weren't for him, Daniel could've punched me, and possibly broke my face.

I walked up Alex's front steps nervously, hands trembling as I clicked the doorbell. It didn't take long before the door flew open, revealing Alex. He was wearing a black t-shirt that wasn't too tight, but hugged him close enough so that you could see how thin but built he was and his jeans were dark and worn out.

He's eyes widened slightly when he saw that it was me standing on his front steps. His face was a mixture of confusion and surprise.

"What are you doing here?" he asked with a raspy voice, sounding like he just woke up minutes ago from a nap.

"I like the warm greeting." I sarcastically said. "Can I come in?"

Alex looked hesitant, which made my heart sank a little, but after a while of thinking, he stepped out of the way to let me in.

I heard Alex close the front door behind me, as I turned around to face him. "I came here to thank you, for putting Daniel in his place. If it weren't for you, Clarice could've gotten a miscarriage."

Alex stared at me with a blank face, his blue eyes boring into mine with intensity. "I did it for you."

I gulped, feeling my breathing stop. "Right," I muttered, staring down at the floor, "thanks for that, too."

"Is that all?" Alex asked, his voice sounding like he could care less what I had to say to him. It hurt me, but what was I supposed to do?

"Yeah." I whispered, giving him a forced smile. "I guess that's it."

Alex shrugged, pointing towards the front door. "Well, I'm going out in a few minutes. You might as well leave now."

I mouth parted open, as I stared at Alex with disbelief. So, this was it for us? I felt my heart slowly and painfully start to crack, as I nodded weakly. I bit my lip to stop the tears that were threatening to spill out any second. I glanced at him one last time, before brushing by his shoulder.

Just as my hand was about to touch the doorknob, I heard Alex call out my name. "Wait, Aerial." His soft tone took me by surprise, making me turn back around.

"Yeah?" I spoke, licking my lips nervously.

Alex bit his lips, before his eyes met mine. I wanted myself so badly to tear my gaze away and to not be sucked into his blazing blue eyes, but I just couldn't. I was lost inside them.

"I didn't mean it." He paused. "I didn't mean it when I said I never cared."

I held in my breath, staring at Alex, not knowing what to say. "I-I," I paused, feeling my throat going dry, "okay."

Alex's eyes went dull with disappointment. Suddenly, a smile spread across his lips, but it looked too forced and fake. It looked like he was trying his best to smile, but he just couldn't. "Great." He said huskily. "Let's just put everything aside us, and be friends, yeah?"

No. It's not what I want, and I know it's not what you want either. I don't want to leave without talking through about everything, and I don't want to leave as just your friend. Because truth be told, Alex, I like you. No, no. I don't just like you; I think I'm falling for you. Hard.

"Sure." I smiled weakly, feeling my eyes well up with tears. "I'll see you at school."

With that, I turned around, letting a tear fall down my cheek. I wanted so badly for him to come after me, and tell me that he was just joking. I wanted him to tell me that he was sorry, and he wanted us to be more than friends. But, he didn't. He didn't, because this was reality.

I approached the car Hayden was waiting in, getting in the passenger seat.

Hayden's eyes lit up with hope, as a grin stretched across his lips. "Is everything back to norm-"

He stopped talking once he was the tears slowly and painfully rolling down my cheeks. His grin fell, as he frowned. "Aerial, what happened in there?" he asked gently.

I shook my head, looking up at Hayden through my messy hair that fell in my face. I laughed bitterly, as my voice cracked. "He said just to forget about everything. And that we should be friends." I smacked my forehead with my palm, laughing like a lunatic. "Friends. Friends, Hayden. You hear me? He wants to be friends!"

Hayden placed his hand on my shoulder. "Calm down, Aerial." He soothed.

"The one guy I've only ever liked wants to be my friend." I croaked. "God, I must be going insane."

Hayden cursed under his breath, putting on my seatbelt for me. "You need rest. I'm going to bring you over to Clarice's house."

"I've been meaning to thank you for getting Daniel off of me at Aubrey's party the other day." Clarice said, as she sprayed some hairspray through her blonde curls. She turned to me when she was finished, giving me a genuine smile. "My baby might've been gone if he took me away that night."

"I was just doing what was best." I truthfully said, sitting on her hot pink rug.

Clarice smiled, while she turned back to her vanity to apply some mascara on her lashes that were already thick and long. "School starts soon. Should we start going now?"

I nodded, pushing myself up and off of her carpet. I've been sleeping over at Clarice's house the past weekend, only going home to get a few changes of clothing. I've ran into my dad once while I made a stop, but he never once acknowledged me. He acted like I wasn't even his daughter, and left me alone.

"My mom's letting me use her car today, so we don't have to walk." Clarice said, as we got into her mother's car.

Clarice turned on the radio station, and turned to a channel where it played a song that was overplayed and abused. "How do you listen to this crap?" I asked, listening to Kesha's robotic and computerized voice.

"It's catchy." Clarice laughed, rolling the windows down, letting the wind whip behind our heads.

Suddenly, Clarice's phone let out a ring from her bag. "I think I just got a text. Check it for me, will you?" she asked me, keeping her eyes steady on the road.

I reached in Clarice's purse, fishing out her phone. I read the name on the screen, frowning with confusion as I did a double take. "Why is Damian texting you?" I asked, holding up her phone.

Clarice blushed, biting her glossy lips. "I don't know."

Clicking open the message, my jaw dropped as I read it aloud. "When do you think we can hang out again?" I gasped. "What does Damian mean by 'again'?"

Clarice's cheeks went warm, as she shrugged innocently. "We might've hung out a few days earlier."

I smacked her shoulder, startling her. "Hey! I'm driving!" she hissed.

"You went on a date with Damian and you didn't tell me?!" I gawked.

"You don't even care about this stuff." She muttered.

"Yeah, but you're my pregnant best friend!" I snapped. "I'm supposed to know who you're dating."

Clarice gave me an apologetic look as we stopped at the school's parking lot. "I'm sorry. It's just so much has been happening to you, I didn't want to bother you."

I sighed. "You could've just mentioned that you were dating Damian."

"Sorry?" Clarice smiled hopefully. "I'll buy you ice cream again?"

I gave her a look, making her frown. "That ice cream better be drizzled in chocolate."

She clapped her hands happily, as a dazed look appeared in her eyes. "Anyways, since the cats out of the box now, I have to tell you how romantic Damian was on our first date!" she gushed.

I laughed, shaking my head. "Why do I have a feeling I'm going to regret ever reading that text?"

"Your problem." Clarice teased. "So, he just randomly texted me one night. And since then, we would text each other every day. One day, he just asked if I wanted to go to this new Italian restaurant that opened downtown. So of course, I said yes! I insisted to pay and everything but he was like no! Then I was like yes! Then he kept saying no! But, I said-"

"Okay! Okay!" I gave her a playful grin. "I get it. You guys lived happily ever after."

"Who lived happily ever after?" a voice suddenly interrupted the two of us.

We turned around to face Hayden, Alex, Damian and Ashton. I couldn't help but noticed that whenever they walked all together in a group together, they looked like they could belong in some kind of band. It was almost intimidating.

"Oh, just Damian and Clarice." I stared at Damian accusingly, as he smirked, pulling in Clarice to his arms.

"You finally told her?" he asked Clarice with a grin.

Clarice rolled her eyes. "She kind of read the text you sent this morning."

The two shared a kiss, as Hayden stared at them with eyes widened. "Wait," he paused, "the two of you are dating?"

Clarice pulled out of Damian's lips, raising her eyebrows at Hayden. "Am I that hideous?"

"No, no. It's just-" Hayden tried to think of what to say, "it's Damian. How could someone like him?"

Damian gave Hayden a light punch in the stomach, as everyone let out a laugh. "Shut up, bro." Damian grinned at Hayden. "Clarice has good taste in men."

"That's why Clare Bear's ex-boyfriend knocked her up, huh?" a nasally voice suddenly snarled, making all of us turn our heads.

Walking down the hall towards us was none other than Aubrey Small. Her red hair flew behind her as she walked, and her poison ivy green eyes had a glint of anger in them.

"Back off, Aubrey." Damian defended Clarice, pushing her gently behind him.

Aubrey rolled her eyes. "No, I don't think I will!" her voice high and pitchy. "You ruined my birthday party." She hissed at Clarice, pointing her finger at her.

"She didn't ruin anything." Alex stepped in. "It was Daniel, that stupid ass hat you decided to invite."

Aubrey glared angrily at Alex. "Listen, Alex. I have no problem with you now, even though you did get Daniel's blood on my carpet." She paused, shooting me a glare. "But, if you push my buttons-"

"I don't give a shit what you think about me." Alex glowered.

Aubrey held in a deep breath of air, as she twisted her lips with rage. "You know what?" she stared at us threateningly. "None of you are invited to my eighteenth birthday."

We all stared at each other to see if Aubrey was being serious. She was.

And when we realized she was, all of us let out a misfit of laughter. Was she serious? None of us wanted to go to one of her stupid, lame parties.

"T-That's hilarious!" Ashton cried, as he held his stomach from laughing so hard.

Aubrey clenched her jaw with fury, as steam came out of her ears. "We're out, girls." She snapped her fingers at the followers behind her, who were trying to contain their laughter, as well.

CHAPTER 18

"Aerial's birthday is next week!" Hayden hollered, as we all gathered at his house.

My head snapped towards him, as I frowned. I don't recall ever telling Hayden when my birthday was. "Did Clarice tell you?" I asked curiously.

Clarice shook her head, as she laid her head on Damian's shoulder. "I didn't tell him anything." She raised her hands up innocently.

"Alex told me." Hayden said, holding a can of beer in his hands.

Frowning, I looked over to Alex, who he had head dipped low. The only time I ever remember telling Alex was months ago, when we first met. How the hell did he remember that?

"You remembered?" I asked, clearly surprised.

Alex grumbled something under his breath, as he shot a glare over to Hayden. He shrugged, kicking his feet up to the empty seat beside him. "I'm not forgetful." He simply spoke.

"But I told you my birthday months ago." I pointed out.

Alex rolled his eyes, giving me a look. "Just be happy I even remembered."

Hayden chuckled, cutting the both of us off. "Would you two stop bickering like an old couple already?" I blushed, as Alex looked away from me. Hayden took the seat beside me, as he threw an arm around my shoulder. "So, what do you want to do for your big one- seven birthday?" Hayden eagerly asked.

I honestly didn't know.

I almost forgot that my birthday was coming up until Hayden brought it up moments ago. I guess more important things have been happening so far.

"I don't even know. I was just planning on staying home and having a Family Guy marathon, yeah?" I gave him a small smile.

Clarice piped up, shaking her head. "No way! I might've missed your past two birthdays, but I'm not going to miss another one."

I gave her a weak smile. "It's okay, guys. Turning seventeen isn't as big of a deal as eighteen, or twenty one."

"We have to do something." Damian paused, as a wicked smile spread across his red lips, rosy from kissing Clarice all day. "Say, Aerial. You've never been to a club, have you?"

I shook my head. "No, I haven't. I'm still underage."

Damian shrugged. "No problem. I have connections to this really awesome club downtown. The place always has a line waiting outside the door, but I know a few people who work there. We could get in."

Hayden's face lit up, as he jolted up from his seat. "Are you talking about the club where Natalia first met Alex?"

Damian nodded with a grin across his face, as Hayden hooted. "No way! That place is amazing!"

"It sure is." Alex mumbled sarcastically under his breath.

I stole a glance from him, pursing my lips.

Great. I was going to have my birthday party at the place where Alex met his ex-girlfriend that brutally slapped me after trying to convince me to snort cocaine.

"So, we're all agreeing on the club, right?" Damian asked, already taking his phone out of his pocket.

Everyone seemed so eager, and I didn't want to be the one to pop the balloon. "Sure." I forced a smile.

"Great." Damian grinned, pressing away on his phone. "I'm making plans right now."

Clarice giggled beside Damian, as she snuggled up against him. She pressed the side of her cheek against his chest, beaming. "This is going to be great!" she laughed. "I've never been to a club before."

Damian kissed the top of her head, placing a hand on her stomach. "No drinking for you, alright?"

Clarice pouted. "Okay."

"You won't be near a drink." I told her protectively.

A small smile slipped across her face. "I know, I know."

"Quit moving!" Clarice hissed at me, trying to curl my hair. "I'll end up burning you before the boys come."

The two of us were running a tad bit late. The boys were about to show up to Clarice's house any minute now, ready to pick us up to go to the club, while Clarice was trying to curl my hair to perfection.

Suddenly, the door bell rang. Clarice groaned, as she handed me the handle of the curling iron. "Hold this and don't move."

She tried to walk as fast as she could down the stairs in her heels. I heard the sound of the boy's voice, as I bit my lower lip.

"Where's the birthday girl?" I heard Hayden's smooth voice ask.

"She's still getting ready." Clarice spoke.

Moments later, Clarice bustled in the room. She took back the curling wand, quickly trying to finish up my look. Once she was done with my hair, she sprayed some cold mist all over it, making me wince. "What is that?" I asked.

"Hairspray, so your curls don't fall out." She said, pulling me up from the seat in front of her vanity. "What do you think?"

I stared at my reflection, my eyes going wide. Once again, Clarice never failed to make me look like an entirely different person. She made me look like I was some kind of royal-status heiress from the Beverly Hills. She chose an exotic red cocktail dress for me that wrapped me tight in all the right places.

"I'm so jealous of you." Clarice smiled, handing me a pair of nude pumps. "Your legs look like they could go on forever."

I smiled, opening my arms out wide to give her a hug. "Thanks, Clare Bear."

She laughed lightly. "Happy birthday, Aerial." She pulled away from me, a relieved smile on her glossy lips. "Now come on, we should get downstairs before the guys break something."

I chuckled. "Your mom would be pretty pissed if they broke her vase."

Clarice looked mortified. "Don't even go there."

I laughed one last time, as I stepped down the stairs.

"The birthday girl's finally here!" Hayden was the first to spot me, as he opened his arms wide to give me a tight squeeze. "Happy birthday! How does it feel to be seventeen?"

I grinned. "I don't feel any different from when I did a day ago."

Hayden picked up a sparkly bag that was by the door, as he handed it to me. "This is from all of us. We all pitched in for it."

I bit my lip from smiling, as I took out the tissue paper nicely, not wanting to rip any of it. When I finally got to the gift, I couldn't help but beam from happiness. "Are you kidding me?" I asked with disbelief, as Hayden nodded with a grin across his lips. "You guys got me an iPad?"

"Do you like it?" Damian asked nervously.

I scoffed, throwing my arms around him. "I love it! Thank you guys so much."

My eyes met Alex's, as his gaze tore away from mine, dropping to the floor. He told me that we should be friends from now on, but it doesn't even feel like we are.

"We should head out now." Damian said, reading the time on his watch. "It's around ten, and the clubs get real packed around eleven."

We all headed out, and got into the limo that they rented for me today. "You guys even got me a limo?" I asked when we settled in. "Quit spoiling me." I teased.

"It's your birthday." Clarice smiled, snuggling up against Damian's arms in the limo. "You get to be spoiled."

I was surprised when Alex decided to take the seat beside me in the limo. He didn't say a word, and had a blank stare in his eyes.

Hayden turned on the music that was built in the limo, pouring himself a drink from the built-in bar.

"Happy birthday." Alex muttered beside me.

I licked my lips, staring up at him. His blue eyes reached down to mine, as a small smile appeared on my face. "Thanks."

It took thirty minutes to get to the club downtown. Pulling up to the entrance of the club, I could tell that it was definitely a hot spot. There was a massive line outside the club, and there were many people trying to get their way in the club without waiting an hour. The five of us walked straight up to the line, as Damian gave the bouncer a man hug. "Damian! Man, it's been a while since you've been here." The bouncer chuckled.

"I'm here today with a birthday girl." He pulled me forward, as I blushed. "You think you could get us in?"

The bouncer laughed, giving me a wink. I looked up, giving him a weak smile. He moved out of the way, giving us space to go in. "Thanks, man." Hayden told the bouncer, as we all followed Damian into the club.

I heard people complaining in the background, and I almost felt bad for skipping them all. "It's fine." Hayden assured me, as we entered the club.

The club was lit up in all different kinds of colors, varying from yellow to purple. The music was blaring so loud that I could feel my heart racing. We all found ourselves a table, and Hayden was the most eager to get to the bar.

"Any one was drinks?" he grinned.

"Get us anything strong, to start off the night." Damian grinned. "Except Clarice, get her a soda."

I wanted to open my mouth to say something, like I didn't want a drink. I was strictly off limits with drinking, and the only time I've ever touched alcohol was when Alex tricked me into thinking I was drinking lemonade, not some spiked lemonade.

Clarice suddenly snapped her head over to mine, raising an eyebrow. "Aerial? You're okay with a drink, right?" she asked aloud, making Hayden stop before he went off to the bar.

Everyone stared at me curiously, except for Alex.

He had a worried expression on his face.

"Y-Yeah. I'm okay with it." I laughed nervously, immediately regretting it. "It's my birthday, right?"

Hayden nodded, as he disappeared through the darkness. Clarice stared at me with a frown, as she scooted over to where I was. "What the hell, Aerial? I thought you didn't want anything to do with alcohol, especially since your father-"

"Clarice, I don't want to be a party pooper, okay?" I smiled weakly.

Clarice licked her lips. "Don't feel like you're being pressured, okay?"

I hesitantly nodded, as Hayden returned with a tray of drinks. "Four Suicides and one Coke."

"Suicide?" Damian asked, examining his glass. "That's a new one."

Alex was the first to take a sip, immediately chugging the whole thing down in just a few gulps. "That's a strong one." He said, setting his empty glass down on the table.

"That makes me want one." Clarice said sarcastically, taking a sip from her soda.

Hayden was the next to try, coughing after a few sips. "Damn, this thing is crazy."

"What's in it?" Alex asked.

"The bartender told me it had a little bit of everything in it." Hayden said, drinking down another few sips.

Damian drank the whole thing, letting out a burp of delight. "I actually like it." He turned over to me, noticing that I haven't even taken a single sip. "Are you finishing that, Aerial?"

I gulped, licking my lips. I saw Alex give me a look, as Clarice raised an eyebrow at me. "Be careful." Alex muttered.

I pushed the cup towards my lips, as I took a large gulp. Immediately, the stingy alcohol began to burn my throat, as I coughed uncontrollably. Alex snatched the drink away from me, patting my back. When I stopped choking, I blushed furiously, as Damian gave me a cocky grin. "You're definitely a weak one, Aerial."

Clarice shot him a glare, making him shut up.

I sulked back in my seat, groaning. How ridiculous did I look coughing up my first drink on my birthday?

"How about we go dance?" Clarice suggested, as Damian pulled her up.

"I want to dance with the birthday girl first!" Hayden called out, dragging me out of my seat.

We all went off to the dance floor, except for Alex. He sank back in his seat, looking bored and miserable. I almost wanted the night to end, just because I didn't want to see him so unhappy.

"Keep doing that." Hayden said, as I swayed my hips.

I frowned, looking up at him. "What?"

Hayden chuckled. "I didn't mean it in a perverted way. I mean, just keep doing what you're doing. It's making Alex fume."

My eyes widened, but ultimately, I followed his instructions. Hayden pulled me close to him, as I moved my hips back and forth. "I wish you could see him right now. He looks so pissed."

I blushed, biting my lower lip. "Shut up, Hayden."

"You want to get him jealous, right?" he asked seriously.

"If I said yes, would it seem like I'm using you?" I asked, raising an eyebrow.

Hayden shrugged, shaking his head. "Not at all."

I laughed, as I kept on dancing with Hayden, following the rhythm of the music. "I'm surprised that you can actually dance that well." Hayden said, once the music ended.

I chuckled. "Shut it, Hayden. Now go dance with that girl in the blue dress." I pointed over to the petite brunette that had her eyes on Hayden for a while now. "She's been creeping up on you since we've gotten here."

Hayden smirked, giving me a hug. "I'll see you later."

I made my way over to the bar to get a drink, but nothing alcoholic. I didn't want to deal with being drunk, or choking like a maniac. "One Shirley Temple, please." I told the bartender.

Moments later, he reappeared with a bloody red drink in his hands, sliding it over the counter towards me. "Thanks." I muttered, taking a sip from the sweet drink.

"I hope that's not alcoholic." Alex suddenly spoke, sliding in the empty stood beside me. "I wouldn't want you to have a coughing fit, again."

I smiled, shaking my head. "Don't worry. It's just a Shirley Temple."

"Good." Alex said.

I looked up at him, forcing a smile. "Don't look so miserable." I laughed bitterly, slapping his shoulder. "It's my birthday."

Alex looked up at me with a glint in his eyes. "I could say the same about you, too."

I pursed my lips, staring down at my drink and away from him. "What do you mean?"

"You obviously don't want to be here, around sweaty dancing sluts and alcohol."

"I'm just new to this stuff, that's all." I shrugged.

Alex looked hesitant, like he was trying to say something, but he didn't know how to. "D-Do you maybe want to get out of here?"

"Ditch my own party?" I chuckled. "And go where?"

A small smile, the smile I haven't seen in ages, finally appeared on Alex's face. "I have just the place in mind."

Chapter 19

"Alex, are you sure it's safe here?" I asked, walking around barefoot down the rocky hill. I had taken off the heels Clarice let me borrow for tonight off a while ago. Trying to walk down on a bunch of boulders without tripping in heels would be extremely hard.

"Trust me." Alex turned back to me. He gave me a small smile, and held his hand out for me. "I'll catch you if you fall."

I licked my lips, staring at his outreached hand nervously. I was hesitant to take it, but I soon enveloped my small hand into his. "Okay." I breathed.

His long and lean fingers laced into mine, as we continued downhill. "What are you trying to show me anyways?" I asked, pushing a branch that was in my way.

"This." Alex said, letting go of my hand. I couldn't help but feel disappointed, but when I saw the scenery before my eyes, I gasped.

"Wow." I stared at the lake that was looked incredibly beautiful and sparkly under the light that came from the full moon that was out today. "This is incredible."

Alex smiled softly beside me, staring up at the stars that looked unusually bright tonight. I couldn't help but notice how vulnerable he looked. Under that arrogant persona, he was a beautiful human being. "It is, isn't it?"

I stared into his eyes, loving how they lit up even in the dark. "It sure is."

Alex turned towards me, looking right into my eyes. My cheeks flushed when he noticed that I was staring at him the entire time. He let out a small smirk, twirling a lock of my hair between his fingertips. "Are we talking about the lake or me here?" he teased.

My eyes widened, as I blushed. I turned away from him, as I pointed to the lake. "I was talking about the lake." I cleared my throat.

Alex chuckled, nodding. "Alright, Aerial, whatever you say."

I rolled my eyes playfully, as I laid myself down flat on the ground. I didn't care that I was going to ruin my hair, or my dress. I didn't care, because as long as I was with Alex, nothing mattered to me but him.

Alex lay down beside me, and I couldn't help but noticed how our arms were touching.

Suddenly, Alex turned to me. There was a glint in his blue eyes when I stared back at him. "Aerial," he started off, letting out a deep breath of air, "what happened between us?"

"What do you mean?" I smiled weakly, even though I knew exactly what he meant.

Alex licked his lips, staring at me with an uneasy expression. "I'm sorry for bringing up memories of your mother, I didn't know that she was-"

"Dead?" I finished for him, feeling my own voice crack.

Alex pursed his lips. "Yeah." He paused, sighing. "I guess I can't apologize for your mother's death, but I can apologize for bringing it up. I honestly didn't know."

I nodded, closing my eyes. "I know. It wasn't your fault."

"Yes, it was." Alex insisted. "And I'm sorry for letting you go so easily. I really didn't mean it when I said I didn't care about you."

I bit my lower lip, staring at his eyes, so genuine. "Really?"

"Yes, Aerial." He laughed weakly. "You mean the world to me."

My throat tightened up, as I held in my breath.

I meant to world to Alex Montgomery?

"What does that mean?" I whispered, as Alex hand went up to cup my cheek. He ran his thumb across my cheek, making shivers send down my spine.

"I like you, Aerial Mason." He laughed bitterly. "No matter how annoying and irritating you can be sometimes, you drive me fucking insane."

His voice was so soft and gentle. I've never heard him speak like this before, and it made my heart race against my chest. It was so scary, because I liked Alex, too.

A small smile appeared across my lips, as I stared into his eyes. Never have I ever been this close to him before, and it was driving me crazy.

I held in my breath, as Alex leaned closer and closer to me each second. When our noses brushed against each other, my eyes fluttered down. I could feel his warm breath on me, and slowly, I began to lean into him.

But, our lips never met.

Alex's stupid phone decided to ring just before we were about to.

Alex cursed under his breath, as the two of us opened our eyes. The ringing began to continue on, as an apologetic look flashed across Alex's baby blue eyes. He pulled away from me, much to my dismay. The two of us sat up, as Alex snatched the phone out of his pocket.

"What do you want?" Alex spoke through the phone with much irritation in his voice.

A small blush crept up my neck just thinking about how close the two of us were from kissing. And, I didn't even pull away from him or stop him. I leaned in, too.

"We're fine, Hayden. The club just got too noisy, so we left." Alex grumbled, rolling his eyes. "No Hayden! W-We didn't hook up." He lowered his voice.

I let out a soft laugh, as Alex buried his face with his hands. "Listen, I've got to go now, okay?" And with that, Alex hung up on Hayden, stuffing his phone back into his pocket.

"Sorry about that." He said, shaking his head. "Hayden always calls at the wrong moments."

I chuckled, giving him a small smile. "He's not drunk, is he?"

Alex shrugged, standing up. He held his hand out for me, as I took it. He pulled me up beside him, giving me a small smile. "Let's hope he's not. Hayden's a horny drunk."

I grinned, shaking the thought out of my head. I stared back up at Alex, who was staring down at me with a glint in his eyes. "What are you looking at?" I asked teasingly.

Alex smiled softly, brushing a lock of my brown curls behind my ears. "You."

My breath got caught in my throat as his fingers gently brushed against my cheek. For the slightest second, I actually thought he was going to kiss me. But, instead, he let out a disappointing sigh. "It's getting late." He started off, making me frown. "I should get you home."

I gulped, forcing a smile on my face. "Okay."

Alex hailed a cab from nearby, since he left his car over at Hayden's house so that we could take the limo to the club earlier tonight. I stared at the time on my phone, noticing that it was two hours past midnight, meaning that my father would probably come staggering home soon. I bit my lip nervously, wondering if he even remembered if it was my birthday or not.

The cab finally came to a stop on the corner of my street. I reached into the clutch Clarice lent me for tonight, pulling out two twenties.

But before I could hand it to the cab driver, Alex pushed my hand away gently, paying the cab fare himself.

"Keep the change." Alex muttered to the driver, before the two of us got out of the cab.

I watched as the yellow cab drove away, disappearing off into the night. I turned to Alex, giving him a small smile. "Thanks for tonight."

Alex smiled back, but it never reached his eyes. "Let me walk you home."

"No, you've already done enough." I paused, staring down the street, where I could see my living room light turned on. That meant that my dad must be home.

Alex licked his lips, shaking his head. "I want to. Come on." He said, tugging my arm.

I felt my spine go stiff as we walked closer and closer to my house. I could already picture my father's bloodshot eyes, greeting me with my birthday present, a drunken slap to the face.

"Are you okay?" Alex asked. That was when I noticed that my hands were trembling by my sides. "You aren't cold, are you?"

I shook my head rapidly, trying to cover up my worries with a smile. "No, I'm fine. I just get all shaky sometimes, no big deal." I rambled.

Alex raised an eyebrow, obviously having his suspicions.

When we stopped at the end of my driveway, I gave him a large, wide, fake grin. "Thanks for everything! I'll see you at school. Bye!" I quickly said, turning around.

"Aerial." He stopped me, making me curse under my breath.

I turned back around. "Yes?"

Alex stared at me with a curious spark in his eyes. "Is everything okay?" he asked with genuine concern.

"Yes." I lied. I felt guilty lying to Alex like that, but it was only for his own good. If he saw half the things my father did when he was drunk, he would run away from me.

Alex obviously didn't believe me. How could he see past me like that? It was incredibly annoying, yet I was so thankful that he was able to.

"Can I use your bathroom?" Alex raised an eyebrow, his voice almost challenging me.

I gulped, shaking my head. "M-my toilet, it broke."

"Then where do you pee?"

I breath got caught in my throat, as I licked my dry lips. "I-I go to Clarice's house."

"You go all the way to Clarice's house to pee?" Alex asked, not believing a word that's coming out of my mouth. "Let me see if I can fix that toilet for you."

My eyes went wide when Alex strode past me, heading straight for my door. When I turned back around, Alex already had his right hand on the doorknob. "Alex, don't!" I stopped him.

Alex obeyed me, turning around to me with hurt flashed across his face. "Why don't you want me to see your house?"

"It's complicated." I whispered.

Alex clenched his jaw. "Am I not good enough for your dad?"

I shook my head quickly. "You won't understand!"

"Then why don't you tell-"

Suddenly, the door flew open. Alex stepped back a few steps, as I rushed up to the door. My father appeared through the doorway, face flushed, eyes red.

"What the fuck is up with the ruckus out here?" he snarled, eyes landing on Alex and I.

I shot Alex a look, trying to signal for him to get out of here, but he didn't even look at me. His eyes were glued onto my drunken father.

"What? Not going to answer me?" my father smirked, pulling my wrist with all his force. He pulled me in the house, as my eyes wandered back over to Alex.

"Don't touch her like that." Alex stepped in, ripping my own father's hands off of mine.

I was thankful that I could feel my blood circulating in my arm again, but Alex made a big mistake by challenging my father.

"And who the hell are you?" my father snapped.

Alex glared at him, clenching his fists by his sides. "I'm Aerial's friend."

My father stared at Alex with a blank face for a while, before he started to laugh, uncontrollably. "Aerial? Aerial is pathetic. She hasn't had a friend since her mother decided to drop dead on the floor!"

Tears welled up in my eyes at my father's harsh words. How could he even say something like that about the woman he loves? "Shut up!" I cried, my voice coming out desperate and high pitched.

Alex held onto my protectively, as my father fumed. "That's no way to talk to your father, is it?" he hissed, hot, alcoholic breath fanning over my face.

"Just leave her alone." Alex warned.

My father's eyes grew large and angry, as he threw a beer bottle on the floor. It shattered all over, making my flinch. Alex squeezed my arm gently, letting me know that I was safe with him.

And I did feel safe with him.

"I want you to get out!" my father shouted.

"If I'm leaving, Aerial comes with me." Alex glared at him.

My father clenched his jaw, an evil laugh escaping his lips. "Fine! Take Aerial away. She's no use around here, anyways!"

He didn't mean that.

He didn't mean that.

He was just drunk. It's the alcohol that was talking, not dad.

"Come on, Aerial." Alex tugged my arm softly, as tears fell from my eyes. "Let's go get your stuff."

Alex dragged me to my room, as I stared back at my father. How was this monster once a perfect, loving father?

Alex pulled one of my old suitcases out of my closet, as he began to quickly fill up my bags for me. He stuffed whatever he could find in my drawers, until the suitcase over overloaded. I sat on my bed, burying my face in my palms.

"We're done here." Alex said, holding my suitcase for me. "Let's go, Aerial."

"Alex." I croaked, following him out of my room.

"Shh." He soothed, kissing the top of my head. "I'll take you back to my house, okay?"

I didn't say a word, as the two of us weaved past my father. I stared at him one last time in the eye, as a grin spread across his face. "Happy Birthday!" he called out, as Alex and I stepped outside.

Tears streamed down my face, as Alex held me protectively. He had a look and anger and frustration in his eyes, as he led me to the end of the street. He took his phone out, dialing the cab service, as I stared down at my feet.

My father didn't want me anymore.

My mother was gone.

I was left alone.

"Come on, Aerial." Alex muttered, gently pushing me into the yellow cab. "It's going to be okay."

Chapter 20

Alex gave me a spare change of clothing from his dresser after things settled down at his house. His white t-shirt he let me borrow reached just a few inches above my knees, and I had to tie the drawstrings on his sweatpants tightly so that it wouldn't fall off.

When I came downstairs, Alex was just stepping out his kitchen with two blue mugs in his hands. His hair looked slightly messy, as if he was running his hand through it the entire night. He set down the two mugs on the coffee table, handing me a soft blanket before taking a seat on the couch beside me. I gave him a small smile, as I wrapped the blanket around myself.

"I made you coffee." He finally said, breaking the tension in the air.

I let out a low laugh. "You do realize that it's three in the morning."

Alex clenched his jaw, shrugging. "Yeah, but I guess you're going to need to stay awake if you're going to tell me what the hell just happened back at your house."

"I don't have to explain anything to you." I shot him a look before dropping my gaze to my cold hands. Truthfully, I didn't want to be so harsh on Alex about it. But, he already knows more than he should.

"I don't get what game you're trying to play with me, Aerial." He snapped at me, his blue eyes full of fury and frustration. "You go ahead and tell Hayden, but you can't tell me? After everything that I just saw?"

My eyes widened, as my neck snapped up towards him. How the hell did Alex know that I told Hayden? I clenched my fists, biting my lower lip. "Hayden told you?" I asked in a low voice.

Alex stared at me long and hard, before he let out a deep breath of air. "No." he paused, as I unclenched my fists, frowning with confusion. "But, it was obvious that you had some kind of phobia against alcohol, and I also figured that my best friend knew things about you that I didn't. I just didn't know that you were so scared of alcohol because of your dad."

So, the cat was out of the box.

Alex officially knew that my father was a drunk, violent, alcoholic.

"Why did you tell Hayden instead of me?" he asked.

I gulped, staring at him, feeling so weak and vulnerable. "Hayden was there for me."

"But so was I!" Alex's eyes hardened. "Why did you keep something like that from me?"

"You were hiding the fact that your parents are divorced from me! You were hiding the fact that you were so hurt because your dad left you guys." I snapped, feeling my eyes well up. "You were just as wrong as I was."

"I didn't hide anything. You already knew about that stuff." His voice lowered.

"But I had to find it out from your mother! Not you! You never told me anything about it." My hands shook by my sides. I didn't want to call Alex out like that, but I had to. It was about time we talked about the tension between us.

Alex stared at me with a cold and hard expression, before I watch him release the scowl that was on his face. His features softened up, as he sighed. "I just wanted to be there for you. I feel like it's my entire fault, because if I had known earlier, I could've gotten you away from him."

Is that how Alex really feels? He really thinks that it was his fault for not knowing about my abusive father?

"It's not your fault." I paused. "It never was."

"But how do you handle the fact that the girl you like has been being abused the entire time you've known her?"

I felt my heart stop, as I held in my breath. Alex admitted that he liked me earlier today, but I was completely dazed during that time. But hearing him say it now, it was almost a wakeup call. I was like an alarm going off inside of me.

"Don't look at me like that." Alex's eyes softened. "I said that twice in one night. I want an answer back from you this time."

I bit my lower lip, as I watched Alex's eyes flicker to my lips. I felt myself turn red, as I tucked my brown locks behind my ear.

"You like me?" Alex licked his lips. "Yes or no?"

I've been waiting for this moment since the moment I locked eyes with Alex months ago.

"Yes." My voice came out high pitched and squeaky.

And just like that, Alex's lips were connected to mine. To moment he pressed his lips against mine, I kissed him back. I could feel him smiling against our lips, as I pressed myself against his closer.

My first kiss.

I've always had it all planned out, under the rain, one leg kicked up.

It sounds like a teenage girl's fantasy, but this was even better.

Kissing Alex, right here, right now, it was so much better.

This night might've been ruined by my father, but it was the best birthday I've had since my mother was here.

I woke up in Alex's guest bedroom, his arms wrapped around my waist, our legs tangled with each others.

I smiled at how innocent and peaceful he looked while he was asleep. There were no traces of any arrogant smirks or scowls.

"Checking me out?" Alex suddenly said, startling me. I stared back at his smirk with disbelief. With one giant push, he went tumbling on the ground below the bed. His eyes went wide, as he gave me a glare. "What the hell was that for?!"

I smiled innocently, staring down at his priceless expression. "I don't know, Alex. But, I don't remember you coming to bed with me when I fell asleep last night."

Alex rolled his eyes, as he stuck his hand out for me. "Help me up at least, will you?"

I gave in, as I held my hand out for him. But, to my surprise, I came crashing down on top of Alex, who was on the ground. My cheeks flamed up once I realized that my legs were on either side of him.

"I don't know about you, but I quite like this position." Alex smirked.

"You jerk!" I hissed, punching his chest. I don't know who got hurt more, because my hand was throbbing after I pulled my fists back from his hard chest.

"If you didn't like this position, then you would be off of me by now." Alex said teasingly.

I gasped, as I pushed myself off of him. I was so flustered, that I didn't realize that is leg was in the way. I tripped over him, toppling over him once again.

I just can't win, can I?

"And now you're even falling for me?" Alex grinned sarcastically. "You must like me a whole lot, Aerial Mason."

I clenched my jaw, but I couldn't help but blush. "How would you like it if my fist landed right here?" I asked, poking his left cheek.

"I'm fine with it." Alex paused. "As long as I have you to kiss it all better."

So this was what Alex was like with girls, huh?

I guess I could get used to the teasing.

I mean, two can play it that way, right?

I put on a smile across my lips, as I leaned in closer to him. He raised an eyebrow with surprise, as I inched my lips closer to him. Once he closed his eyes, I moved towards his ears. My lips brushed against his ears, as I felt him shudder. "How about no?" I whispered.

When I pulled back, Alex was glaring at me. "You're such a tease, Aerial."

"It takes one to know one." I smirked.

"So the doctor told me that in two more months, I'll get to know if it's a boy or a girl!" Clarice squealed, as she looked through a rack of baby clothing for boys.

I bit my lip, as she pulled out a knitted, pastel blue sweater. "But why are you looking through clothes for boys?" I raised an eyebrow. "What if you get a girl?"

Clarice put the sweater in her arms, fishing out a little pair of denim jeans. She pouted, giving me a bland look. "I can tell it's a boy, Aerial."

I laughed, shaking my head at the blonde. "Why do you want a boy so badly anyways?"

Clarice smiled faintly, as she tore her gaze away from the baby clothes. "In the future, I want a little girl. So if anyone hurts her, then her big brother can beat the shit out of them for her."

My smile faded, as I blinked. "You aren't still attached to Daniel, are you?"

Clarice rolled her eyes, snorting. "Please." She snarled. "I got over him ages ago."

I nudged her shoulder, giving her a playful smile. "Miss Clarice is all about Damian now, isn't she?"

Clarice winked, before turning her attention back to a stack of baby hats and scarves. "You know it." She grinned, picking up some matching accessories. "I'm just going to pay for these, and we'll go grab some lunch, okay?"

After Clarice paid for all of her new baby clothes, we headed over to the food court in the mall. The two of us got fried noodles from some fast food Japanese restaurant. I raised an eyebrow when Clarice got some ketchup, and squirted it all over her dish.

"It's actually really good." She muffled with noodles falling from her mouth.

I laughed, as I stirred some noodles onto a fork, putting it in my mouth. "So what's up with you? You completely ditched your own birthday party last night, and you don't even tell me where you went?"

I blushed, as I poked some chicken that was cut in my noodles. "I just left with Alex, that's all."

"And did what?" she raised an eyebrow suggestively.

I sighed, as I bit my lower lip. "He took me home, and he might've seen my very drunk father."

I could tell Clarice was trying her best not to cringe. I wasn't offended, or anything. Because truth be told, I was shivering myself.

"And what happened?" she asked quietly.

I let out a deep breath of air, shaking my head. "Dad said he didn't want me anymore." I paused, trying to hold back the tears. "He basically told me I was nothing."

Clarice gasped, as she stared at me with disbelief. "And what did Alex say?"

I could feel the upper corners of my lips twitching upwards just at the mention of his name. "He was amazing. He told me that I could stay over at his place, and he took care of me that night."

Clarice looked sad, as she stared down at her food moodily. "I just can't believe it."

"What?" I whispered.

Tears began to well up in her eyes, as she shut them tightly. Tears flowed down her cheeks, as she wiped them with the back of her hand. "Your dad was always so loving." She croaked, staring up at me with moist, blue eyes. "What the hell happened?"

I gave her a weak smile. "Life."

After I spent the day with Clarice that afternoon, I came back to Alex's house by dinnertime. When Clarice pulled up to Alex's driveway, I noticed that there were two extra cars parked there, and none of them were his.

"You'll be okay, right?" Clarice asked.

I nodded, as she leaned over her seat to give me a hug. "I'm going to be fine." I promised.

She smiled, as she unlocked the car for me. I got out, giving her one last wave, before she sped away.

When she was long gone, I stared at the extra cars that were parked with Alex's.

What was going on?

Alex had given me one of his spare keys last night, so I opened the front door myself. Immediately when I stepped inside, I heard yelling.

Lots and lots and yelling.

"Why are you even here?!" a woman screeched.

"Alex is my son too, and I want to take custody of him." A deep voice said sternly, making chills send down my spine.

"You walked out on mom and I years ago." Alex's voice hissed.

I stepped out from behind the wall, as I stared at the three that were gathered around the dinner table. There was Alex and his mother, then a man that resembled much of Alex, who sat at the head of the table.

My eyes shifted towards Alex's face, which was red from anger. His mother looked as if she had been crying for a while now, and the man that sat at the head of the table looked cold and harsh.

All eyes snapped towards me as I walked into the room, as the man at the head of the table stared at me with intensity. His eyes were demeaning and uninviting. "Who the hell is she?"

Alex's mother glared at the man. "Don't you dare talk to her like that."

"Well she is in my house." He spat.

"This isn't your fucking house!" Alex's eyes were full of hatred, as he stood up from his chair, slamming his fists against the dinner table.

The man at the head of the table scoffed, turning to Alex's mother. "Is this how you raised my son to be?"

Oh, he was Alex's father.

The one that left them years ago.

Alex turned to me, glowering with anger. "Go to my room, Aerial." He hissed.

I frowned, staring at Alex's mother's face, which was full of desperation. "But Alex-"

"Go!" he shouted, making me flinch.

I gulped, as I nodded meekly. I hurried upstairs, running to Alex's room, as I slammed the door shut. I pressed my back against the door, sliding down.

I don't know why, but I felt scared.

Not for me, but for Alex.

CHAPTER 21

I don't know how long I've been hiding in Alex's dark room. All I remembered was that I started to cover my ears once I heard the sound of glass shattering.

"You don't belong in this house!" Alex's mother screeched, as tears streamed down my face. I could almost picture a plate being thrown across the room, as Alex's father shouted back at her.

Hearing the sound of glass being intentionally broken made me remember my father being drunk weeks ago, throwing wine glasses all over the kitchen floor. I remember the hatred look in his eyes when I took the glasses away from him, trying to stop him from being violent.

I cradled myself by pressed my knees against my chest, and clamping my hands over my ears to muffle the noise.

I just wanted it all to stop.

I don't know how long it took until everything went silent.

It could've been hours of me crouching behind Alex's bed with fear, for all I know.

Suddenly, I saw a light peek from the door, as it slowly creaked open. I didn't dare look up, as I buried my head into my knees.

What if it was his father?

What if he wanted to hurt me?

"Aerial?" a soft voice asked. "Where are you?"

I was trembling with fear, as I pushed myself against the wall.

I suddenly felt a hand on my shoulder, as I flinched at the sudden touch. I nervously looked over to my right, staring at Alex. He looked like a mess, completely stressed out and tired.

"Aerial, have you been crying?" he asked me worriedly, wiping the tears away that were trailing down my cheeks.

He pulled me towards him, as he wrapped his arms around me protectively. I buried my face into his chest, as I began to sob. "It was so loud, Alex." I croaked. "It was so damn loud."

Alex sighed, as he rubbed circles on my back. "I'm sorry, Aerial." He soothed, kissing the top of my head. "He's gone now."

I gulped, as I squeezed my eyes shut. "He's not going to take you away from me, is he?"

Alex shook his head, holding my hands, and giving them an assuring squeeze. "I'm not going anywhere." He muttered into my head. "I'm staying right here, with you."

I pulled away from him, looking into his eyes with my blurry vision. I honestly didn't know what I would do without him. "Do you promise, Alex?" I asked.

Alex brushed a strand of my messy dark hair behind my ears, leaning in to give me a peck on my forehead. "I promise, Aerial."

We stayed like that for the entire night. He held me, as I rested my head on his shoulder. It just felt so right to be in his arms. I could stay in them forever, and I would be perfectly fine with it. Because whenever I was with Alex, everything felt right.

The next morning, I woke up before Alex did. There was a soft blanket around the two of us, which I don't remember having it the night before. I came to conclusions that his mother came in late last night to check up on us, and found us sleeping.

I quietly wiggled my way out of Alex's grip, trying my best not to wake him up. Even though we had a full night of sleep, he still looked worn out from last night.

I tip toed out of his room, and made my way downstairs. I could hear the sound of pans clattering, as I peered over the kitchen.

I found Alex's mother at the stove, flipping some pancakes and making scrambled eggs at the same time.

I stared at her for a long while, wondering how she was strong enough to get up and make breakfast after the rough night she had.

If it were me, I wouldn't even be able to get out of bed.

I must've made some kind of noise, because Alex's mother turned her head back around, as her eyes locked into mine. A tired smile appeared on her face, as she pointed to the ground below me.

"There's some glass near your left foot." She warned me. "Be careful."

I blushed, as I nodded. "Oh, thanks."

Alex's mother turned off the fire, as she placed an even amount of pancakes and eggs on two plates. "Do you know if Alex's is up yet?" she asked. "If not, I won't get him a plate, yet."

I shook my head. "He's still sleeping. He looks really tired."

Alex's mother almost looked guilty, as she nodded. "Okay. Thanks."

I watched as she saved some breakfast for Alex in the microwave. She handed me a plate of pancakes and eggs, which may I add, smelt delicious.

"Thanks, they smell great." I moaned, already taking a bite out of my fluffy pancake.

Alex's mother gave me a small smile, which looked too forced. I guess she was still affected by what happened to the night prior.

"I'm sorry you had to witness it all last night." She sighed.

I gave her a genuine smile, shaking my head. I didn't want to make her feel worse than she already felt. She was a single mother that was always working to support her and Alex. "Don't worry about it."

I finally looked up to take a good glance at Alex's mother. It was then I realized just how completely worn out she looked. The lady I once saw in pictures around this house was young, happy and fresh. But seeing her in person, now, she had dark bags under her eyes, and premature wrinkles on her forehead.

"I just can't give Alex enough, can I?" she muttered so quietly, as if she were talking to herself. "Maybe his father was right. Maybe if Alex went over to live with him, he could get more. His father has enough money in the world to swim in. Alex would be happy. He would be so happy."

I pursed my lips, gulping. I've always wanted a mother of my own, and seeing someone else's mother suffer was just too painful for me. "He loves you, you know?" I told her. "Even though he acts like he hates you for leaving all the time, he knows how hard you work for him. Money doesn't mean a thing to him."

His mother's blue eyes, identical to Alex's, stared up at me. She gave me a small smile, as she choked back a laugh. A tear fell from her baggy eyes, as she pressed a hand on my shoulder. "You're really something special, honey."

I didn't know what to say.

No one's ever called me special before.

I've always thought of myself as plain, average. Nowhere near special.

"What are you two doing down here this early?" Alex asked, coming down the stairs, running a hand through his messy hair. I bit back my lips, noticing how gorgeous he looked with his hair all over the place, and how his white v-neck he wore yesterday was all wrinkled.

"Early?" I scoffed. "It's already twelve, Alex. We skipped half of school today."

Alex rolled his eyes, carefully walking to the fridge to pull out a carton of milk. He drank the milk straight from the carton, as his mother shot him a glare. "Alex, where are your manners?"

"It's not my fault you aren't ever here to raise me properly." He snapped. "Just like dad said, right?"

I wanted to slap some sense into him. I bit my lower lip, as I glanced over to his mother, which looked like she had just crumpled. If only Alex knew how much she loved him.

"Alex." I said sternly.

"What? Aren't I speaking of the truth? She's always out-"

I clenched my jaw, as I pulled him out of the kitchen. "We'll be back in an hour." I told his mother, giving her an apologetic smile. "We're just going out for a walk."

When I stepped outside, I began to walk ahead of Alex. How could he have been so rude to his mother, even though he knew how much she worked for him?

"Aerial, I thought we were going to walk together." He smirked, holding my hand from walking any further.

I ripped my arm away from his, lifting my chin up high, my angry eyes burning into his. "Don't even start now, Alex."

His face fell, as the smirk slowly wiped off his conceited face. "Why are you so mad at me?"

"Because you treat your mother like crap!" I hissed, slapping a hand on his chest. "You don't even realize how much she loves you!"

Alex snorted. "You don't know a thing, Aerial."

I felt as if my heart just stopped as those words escaped his mouth. As soon as he realized just exactly what he said, his face went blank. Then, he looked as if he pitied me, as if he wanted to take it all back.

"Aerial, I didn't mean it." He said softly, holding me close.

I tore my gaze away from his, pushing him away from me. "Don't even try to fix what you just said." I had to bite my lip from bawling my eyes out. After everything I told him, he was still acting like a complete jerk. "You always say how much you hate your dad for being a complete dick, but you're acting just like him."

Alex's face wrenched, looking as if I just pierced a bullet through his heart. Suddenly, Alex pulled me forward by my hips, pressing his lips on mine. It wasn't passionate and slow like the other kiss he gave me a few nights before. The kiss he was giving me now was desperate and needy. I almost wanted to push him away, telling him that it wasn't the right time. But, I didn't. I pressed myself closer to him, kissing him back with everything I had inside me. He had his hands caught in my tangled hair, fingers running down my back, sending me cold shivers.

"Alex." I gasped against his lips. "Alex, stop."

He stared back with a distant look in his eyes before he finally snapped back to state. "I'm sorry." He sighed. "I really wasn't thinking when I said that to you."

Alex's face looked so defeated, looking so genuinely guilty and regretful. My hands shook, as I reached up to tuck that strand of hair that was falling over his eyes. His blue eyes reached down to mine, as a faint smile appeared across his rosy red lips. "I'm sorry." He said, again.

I gave him a small smile, nodding. I didn't want to hold a grudge against him, and I didn't want to add more problems in his life. "It's okay."

And just like that, I forgave Alex Montgomery.

CHAPTER 22

Hayden's Point of View

A gorgeous red head sat across the room from where I was, a dazed and distant look in her emerald green eyes. She always had this tough, overly confident exterior about her, but deep inside her sharp, cat-liked eyes, I knew that she was broken.

And who broke her, you may ask?

Me.

I was the boy that crushed and ruined who Aubrey Small once was. Aubrey used to be sweetest girl I knew, even crying when she accidentally stepped on an ant when we were younger. The two of knew each other when we were just kids, not even starting the first grade yet. I remember her coming over to my house everyday as a child, because our mothers were the best of friends. I still remember how she use to hide behind her mother's leg, cheeks turning the same color as her dark gingered hair.

The two of us grew up together, and I even knew her longer than I've known Alex. I've always loved her in a way more than a friend should, but I never thought she felt the same way. But in the seventh grade, Alex finally urged me to ask out one of my best friends, the girl of my dreams.

I can still remember how wide my smile was when she said yes.

We went out for two years, and I actually thought that she was the one that I wanted to spend the rest of my life with.

Aubrey Small was my everything.

That's why I'll never forget the day I completely betrayed her.

Just the summer before we started to go to the ninth grade, a few of Alex's and my older friends introduced us into the world of alcohol and weed. So, just a week before high school started, Daniel Reynolds' threw a big back to school party at his house. Aubrey was hesitant to come, because it was going to be her first party without parents and with beer and weed. I assured her that I would be by her side the entire time, watching out for her.

But things got caught up too quickly, and everything was moving just a little too fast.

Two hours after the party started, I was completely drunk and wasted. Aubrey was no longer by my side, and I was upstairs, shirtless with Tammy Pine.

The door suddenly barged open, as Aubrey stood by the doorway, eyes watery. I'll never forget the look in those beautiful, glassy green eyes, so full of hurt, betrayal and pain.

I caused all of those emotions.

Before I could roll off of Tammy and chase after my girl, she was already long gone. I remember rushing out of the room, trying to look for Aubrey. But by the time I searched the entire house, I knew she was gone. One stupid mistake, and my best friend and love of my life slipped out of my fingertips.

And on the first day of school, Aubrey Small came back a different person.

She was no longer that shy, innocent doll who got cheated on.

She was strong, cold and the girl who cheats.

She walked right by me on that very first day of school with another man beside her.

But despite how much I've hurt her, she never told a soul about that night. She never told a soul about how I cheated on her.

And ever since then, I've never been able to find myself in a steady relationship without thinking about how much I wanted my old Aubrey back.

"Hayden?" Alex pushed my shoulder, interrupting me from my thoughts.

I snapped out of trance, as I stared up at Alex. He was raising his eyebrows down at me curiously. Then, when he studied my face for a little longer, he knew what I was thinking about.

He knew that I was thinking about the girl I used to love so badly.

When I first told him years ago, he judged me. He shouted at me, telling me how much I fucked up, and how I would never be able to find another girl that would love me as much as Aubrey used to.

And I knew he was right.

"Okay, for this semester's final project, I want you to partner up!" Mrs. Norman, our home economics teacher, announced.

"Do we get to choose partners?" a girl in the front of the class asked.

Mrs. Normal rolled her eyes, shaking her head. "Hell no." she snapped. "The last time I allowed you all to pick partners, Hayden and Alex decided it would be funny to throw eggs at each other." She shot us a glare.

A few people in the class made groaning noises, as Mrs. Norman pulled out a clipboard from the drawer in her desk. "I've already assigned you all partners, so..."

"Charlotte and Alex."

"Janie and Elliot."

"Hayden and Aubrey."

My head immediately snapped up, as I stared at Mrs. Norman with wide eyes. Did she really just-?

"Excuse me?" Aubrey snarled, as her voice full of malice filled the room.

Mrs. Norman lowered her glasses to the bride of her nose, raising an eyebrow. "What's wrong Aubrey?" she asked.

Aubrey clenched her jaw, and she could tell that I was looking at her, but she wouldn't even dare to look me in the eyes.

She still hated me.

"I don't think you assigned me the right partner." She gritted through her teeth, those full, pink pouty lips of hers pressing together tightly.

"Who would you like me to assign you with then, Miss Small? Someone who will do all the work while you sit there filing your nails?" Mrs. Norman asked, as Aubrey gave her a glare. "Continuing on to the list, Trevor and Nina."

And for the first time in years, Aubrey's emerald green eyes locked into mine from across the room. At first, they were blank, as if she was trying to remember something. But, they soon turned cold and harsh, as she gave me a glare.

After Mrs. Norman was done with the list, she told us to get into our assigned groups. I watched as Aubrey wouldn't even get up from her chair, so I moved over to take the empty seat beside her. I could tell that she was trying her best to ignore me, much to my disappointment.

"This project will count as fifty percent of your final grade. So if you're planning to slack on this project, you can kiss your final average goodbye." She warned, raising an eyebrow at everyone. "Now that it's all clear, your project will be to cook or bake something that I have taught you during this semester. It can be that Baked Ziti we made two months ago, or even that red velvet cake from a month ago."

"Red velvet is your favorite kind of cake, right?" I whispered over to Aubrey.

I still remember from the time we were in the fifth grade, and Aubrey was turning ten years old. Her parents surprised her with a very large, heart shaped velvet cake. I still remember how many slices Aubrey ate that night.

At first, Aubrey looked surprised, even relieved to see that I remembered. But she replaced the look with a scowl on her face, as she crossed her arms. "No. It's not."

I frowned. "What? But you ate six slices on your tenth-"

"Shut up!" she hissed, giving me a glare. "Cake is for fat asses."

Aubrey was never like this before I hurt her.

"Okay." I muttered, scratching the back of my neck nervously. "You can come over to my house tonight so we can decide what we want to do, okay?"

The bell rang, as if on cue, as Aubrey gathered up all of her stuff. She stood up, before she stared down at me with cold eyes. "I'm only doing this for my grade." She muttered, walking off.

"Do you want to come over tonight?" Alex asked, his arms snaked around Aerial's waist. Aerial gnawed on her lower lip, trying to hide her bright pink cheeks with her curtain of brown hair. "A bunch of the guys will be over."

I was about to say yes, until I remembered that I had to do the home economics project with Aubrey tonight. I gulped, feeling nervous just thinking about her coming over to my house. She hasn't stepped foot in it since the eighth grade. "I-I can't." I rubbed my sweaty palms. "Home economics project, remember, Alex?"

Alex blinked with surprise. But he nodded, completely under-standing. He didn't question me at all, because he already knew the entire story.

"So, what's this home economics project about?" Aerial asked, turning to Alex.

Alex rolled his eyes immediately, shaking his head. "We have to bake or cook something for some stupid final project or whatever. Worst of all, in partners." He groaned.

Aerial raised an eyebrow curiously. "Who's your partner?"

"Charlotte." He shrugged. "She's probably going to do all the work anyways, so easy A for me."

Aerial chuckled. "Then I guess I don't have a reason to be jealous now, do I?"

Alex smirked, leaning over to peck Aerial on the cheek. A blush appeared on each side of her cheeks, as she rolled her eyes. "What about you, Hayden? Who are you partnered with?"

I flinched, as I stared down at my half eaten sandwich. "Aubrey." I muttered.

Aerial immediately laughed, as she covered her mouth with her hand. "Are you serious?" she choked. "I feel so bad for you! She's a complete bitch!"

I clenched my fists under the table. I shouldn't be mad at Aerial for hating Aubrey, especially after Aubrey's tormented her and Clarice since the freshman year, but I couldn't help myself. My blood was boiling in my veins.

"Don't say that about her." I growled, shoving my seat back. I stood up, as Aerial's eyes widened. She frowned, looking unsure of what she did wrong.

I regretted blowing up on her like that, but I just couldn't stop myself from being mad for some reason. Aerial had every right to hate Aubrey.

I shook my head, as I turned to walk out of the lunch room.

"Did I do something wrong?" I heard Aerial ask before I left.

My doorbell rang at nine later that night. I'd taken the time earlier to take a shower, and even spray some of that expensive cologne from my father's drawer. I raced downstairs once I heard the door open, and found my mother greeting Aubrey. I watched as my mother's jaw dropped, as she pulled in Aubrey for a tight hug.

My mouth literally dropped once I saw how beautiful she looked with her red hair cascading down her back in loose waves.

"Aubrey, honey, I haven't seen you in ages!" my mother squealed, wide smiles plastered all over her face.

For the first time in years, I saw a real smile from Aubrey Small. It wasn't one of those forced, sarcastic ones that never met your eyes, it was real. Her eyes glittered as a small laugh escaped her rosy red lips.

"I didn't expect it to be you when Hayden said he was going to have someone over!" my mother laughed. "He even took a shower for you!"

My cheeks turned red, as I appeared from behind the wall. I gave my mother a tight smile, as she clamped a hand over her lips. "Oops!" she teased. "I'll catch up with you later, Aubrey." My mother giggled, before disappearing off to her room.

I scratched the back of my neck, as I began to lead Aubrey over to the kitchen. "So, I've got the ingredients for basically every-thing we've learned in class, since my mother's a huge cooker and everything. And you know, she just likes to experiment and do-"

Aubrey interrupted me with a cough, as she crossed her arms, leaning on the counter. "Does she have ingredients for red velvet cake?"

A smile stretched onto my lips, as I nodded. "I'm pretty sure she does."

An hour later, we had the cake made, and ready to be baked in the oven. I've been trying to catch Aubrey's glance for a while now, but not once did she look over at me. I knew she was trying her best not to, as well.

"Okay, so we have to let it bake for another hour." I said, washing my hands that were covered in cake batter. "Do you want to go up to my room?"

Aubrey pursed her pouty lips, as she shrugged. "I don't think that's a good idea."

I felt my heart drop to the pit of my stomach, as I gave her a weak smile. "Come on. You haven't seen my room since the eighth grade." I saw her shoulders tensing up. "Aren't you curious about how it looks now?"

Aubrey clenched her jaw, staring down at the floor. "Fine, whatever." She muttered, following my way up to my room.

When she walked in, her face fell, as she gave me a glare. "There's nothing different about your room."

I bit my lower lip, shaking my head. A weak smile formed onto my lips, as I tried to lift the tension between us. "My covers are now blue."

I caught Aubrey's lips twitching up for a slight second, before that scowl appeared on her face again. "They were always blue, Hayden."

"I'm glad you remember." I said.

Something flashed across Aubrey's eyes, as she took in a deep breath of air. "It must be a coincidence, then." She mumbled, eyes roaming around my room. Her eyes finally stopped at the top of my nightstand, specifically the picture frame that was on it.

It was a picture from our eight grade prom, when I asked her to go with me. The two of us were laughing, my arms around her waist. She was wearing a cherry red dress that matched her fiery red hair, and I was wearing a black dress shirt with a matching red bow.

"You still have that?" she asked, voice shaky and unconfident, like it usually was.

I bit my lower lip, nodding. "Yeah."

Her face went pale, as she picked up the frame, running her fingers across the glass. "Why?"

My eyes studied her saddened green eyes. I held in my breath, noticing that it was the first time I've seen Aubrey Small display real emotion in literally three years.

"It's not something I'd like to forget, that's why." I whispered.

I watched as she flinched. She licked those full red lips of hers, as she set the picture frame back down. The oven from downstairs let out a beep, signaling that the cake was nearly finished baking.

"Let's go get that cake." She muttered.

I sighed with disappointment, as Aubrey headed downstairs. Before we reached the kitchen, she surprised me by turning around, locking her eyes into mine.

"Give me a copy of the picture, will you?" she asked.

CHAPTER 23

"What do you think is up with Hayden?" I asked, as Hayden walked into school the next morning, head help up high, grin wider than usual.

Alex shrugged, pretending as if he didn't know, but deep inside, I could see in his eyes that he knew exactly why Hayden was so happy today.

I frowned, curious as Hayden approached us. "Hey guys!"

"Hi." I mumbled, still trying to figure out what was happening. Just yesterday, he was so moody and snappy towards me, for calling Aubrey Small a bitch. Why was he so defensive yesterday? As far as I knew, Hayden hated her just as much as Clarice and I did. After all, she was the one who babbled to everyone that Clarice was pregnant, and was the girl who tormented me since freshman year.

Hayden seemed to notice my foul mood towards him, as his grin slipped off his face. He cleared his throat, shooting a look towards Alex. "Um, Aerial, can we talk for a minute?"

Alex rolled his eyes. "Why can't I stay?"

"I don't want you to give me a black eye when I profess my undying love for your girlfriend." Hayden sarcastically said, earning a glare from Alex. Alex let out a huff, as he pushed past Hayden's shoulder roughly, making him stumble back a few steps.

Once Alex disappeared down the hallway, turning to the corner, Hayden turned back to me with a weak smile on his face. "I wanted to say sorry about yesterday." He scratched the back of his head.

I sighed, nodding. I couldn't stay mad at Hayden forever, I mean, we were best friends. "It's fine. But are you going to tell me why you went all PMS on me when I called Aubrey a bitch?"

Hayden's cheeks turned bright red, as he cleared his scratchy throat. "Right." He muttered under his breath. "About that, you see-"

"Oh, gross." A voice suddenly snarled, as Aubrey stared at Hayden and I with disgust. "It's Voldemort and Chewbacca."

I glared at the red head, but Hayden dipped his head low, losing all of his confidence. He almost looked hurt by Aubrey's words.

Whoa, what?

"You guys make a great couple." She sarcastically smirked, as she walked away, her sky high heels clicking behind her.

When she left, I turned to Hayden, who looked like a puppy that just got slapped. "Hayden, what the hell is going on?" I asked sternly.

Hayden sighed, looking defeated, and unlike his usual cheery self. "There's something I need to tell you about Aubrey and I."

I gulped, already having a bad feeling in my stomach. "Okay." I paused, letting out a deep breath of air. "Talk."

"Well, Aubrey and I had a past…" he started off. He started by telling me how they were childhood best friends, which made me frown. What happened to them? And then he proceeded to tell me how he dated her for two years, until he cheated on her at a party. My mouth dropped with disbelief, but all the pain on Hayden's face told me that he wasn't joking around. After, he told me how he changed her, making her into the person she is today.

"I still love her." He finished.

I gulped, trying to take it all in. "Is that why you were so defensive about her yesterday?"

He nodded weakly, sighing. "She came over to my house for the home economics project last night. And everything was almost back to the way they were."

"That's why you were so hurt when she turned back into a bitch just moments ago." I concluded.

"I deserved it." Hayden shook his head.

"Hayden told you, huh?" Alex asked, as we stepped into his house after classes that day.

I nodded, giving him a weak smile. "I still despise Aubrey, but it changes how I think of her now."

Alex chuckled, wrapping his arms around my waist. "Well, I used to be pretty close to her, too. But after things fell out between Hayden and her, we stopped talking. And I started disliking her when I saw what a bitch she was to you."

I smiled, standing on the tip of my toes to brush my lips against his. "Is your mom home today?" I asked, as we pulled apart.

The house was awfully quiet when we came home, and we noticed that her car wasn't in the driveway. Alex shook his head, reading the time on his phone. "No, she left earlier today, after we went to school. She told me that she needed to go on another business trip today."

I bit my lower lip. "Oh."

Alex held my hand, giving me a light squeeze. "I talked to her last night, you know?"

I raised an eyebrow, clearly surprised. "Really? How come I didn't notice?"

"I went downstairs to talk to her after you fell asleep." He paused. "I finally noticed how stressed and tired she looked. I sat down at the dinner table across from her, where she had all these papers all over the table, doing work. It took me a while to say something, but the first words that came out of my mouth were, I'm sorry."

A couldn't help but smile. Alex was finally realizing how lucky he was to have a mother that loved him so much, and worked her ass off to put a roof on top of his head.

I let out a soft laugh, wrapped my arms around him, as I pressed my cheek against his chest. "That's really good, Alex." I paused. "It's actually amazing."

"I couldn't have done it without you knocking some sense into me, though." He chuckled, kissing the top of my head.

I rolled my eyes, but I couldn't help but feel a sudden warmth in my heart. "You're a loser." I teased, poking his hard chest with my index finger.

He grinned, showing that rare dimple on his left cheek. I almost wanted to stand on my tippy toes to reach up and his him right on that spot, but I held myself back.

"Aerial, can I ask you something?" he suddenly asked, making me stare up into those blue eyes of his.

"Okay." I said unsurely.

Alex let out a ragged breath, stroking my cheek with this thumb. He lit his lower lip, making my eyes cast down towards them.

"Do you ever miss your dad?" he asked me, voice as soft as feathers.

Do I ever miss my father?

Even though he may be the world's crappiest father out there, he was still my dad. He was still once the loving father that would take me to the boardwalk late at night and buy me ice cream and cotton candy. He might be a violent drunk now, but I still love him.

He's all I have left as family, and I'm all he has left.

We need each other.

"Yes." I finally mustered out, feeling a whole lot of tension lift off of my shoulders. "I miss him, a lot."

For the slightest second there, I thought Alex was going to judge me. I thought he was going to tell me what everyone else would if they knew about my father. For a second there, I thought Alex was going to tell me that I was incredibly stupid for missing someone who hurt me so much.

But, Alex never did.

Instead, he tucked a piece of my wavy brown locks behind my ear, and gave me a gentle smile. "I know you do." He whispered.

I frowned. "What do you mean?"

Alex pressed his forehead against mine, his eyes never leaving mine. "Even though you want to hate your father so much, you can't, because he's still your dad. You just can't help but care about him."

I gulped, as I licked my lips. Alex understood so well, because he was thinking about his own dad. "Alex-" I started off, feeling my voice become scratchy.

"The both of us live such dysfunctional lives." Alex cut me off, sighing.

Alex's eyes looked so defeated and saddened. I wanted to kiss him right then and there. I wanted to try to fix him by kissing him. But, I knew that even I couldn't fix this broken boy.

"I guess imperfect people like imperfect people, right?" I whispered.

Alex finally let out a low chuckle, his hot breath tickling my lips. I closed my eyes for a second, before I snapped back into reality.

"You're really something fucking special." He finally said, making the corners of my lips twitch upward. "You really are."

"Hi Mr. Adams, is Clarice home?" I asked, standing on the front steps of the Adams residence. Clarice's third monthly doctor's appointment was tomorrow, and I wanted to see if she needed company.

Mr. Adams shook his head, staring down at his gold watch that was latched across his left wrist. "I'm afraid not. She left to go to the movies an hour ago." He paused. "I was assuming that you were going to be with her."

I frowned, but then I suddenly remembered how Clarice said that she had a movie date with Damian tonight. She must've not told her parents yet about her new boyfriend. I don't blame her; after all, she is pregnant.

"Okay, thanks." I muttered. "Tell Mrs. Adams I said hi."

I got ready to head out, but Mr. Adams stopped me. "Wait, Aerial." He cleared his throat. "Do you mind coming in for a minute? There's something important my wife and I need to discuss with you."

I frowned with confusion, as I nodded. I followed Mr. Adams into their kitchen, where Mrs. Adams was stirring a wooden spoon into a metal pot.

What could they possibly want from me?

Mrs. Adams spotted me in her kitchen, as she squealed. "Oh, honey! It's great to see that you're alive!"

I raised an eyebrow. What on Earth was she talking about?

"Excuse me?" I asked with uncertainty.

Mrs. Adams turned the fire on her stove on low, as she took off her floral apron. She joined Mr. Adams and I at the kitchen's dinner table, pouring me a cup of tea. "Well, it's just we got worried when we got a phone call from your father last weekend."

I choked on my tea, as I covered my mouth with my palm. "What?" I asked with disbelief.

"He called us really late at night, asking if you were staying over at our house for the night. He said that you ran off with someone and told him that you were never coming back." Mr.

Adams sternly said, raising an eyebrow. "Is there something going on at home?"

I felt my throat dry up, as I took a large sip of tea. The hot liquid burned in my mouth, but I could barely feel my tongue being burnt, because I felt too numb.

"No." I lied right through my teeth. "Everything is fine at home."

Mrs. Adams sighed with relief, wiping the sweat that was forming across her forehead. "That's such a relief! We were getting worried, because your father hasn't been staying in contact with us ever since..." she paused, her face getting white and pale. "Your mother left us."

I was getting angry, and I could feel the blood boil in my veins. Moments like these were when I couldn't tell what expression I had on my face, or control what I wanted to say.

"She didn't leave anyone." I hissed.

Mrs. Adams eyes widened at my sudden outburst, as her face flushed into a cherry red color. "Oh, honey, that's not what I meant." She quickly said.

I rolled my eyes, as I pushed myself off my seat. I slammed my fists on the wooden dinner table, making the cups of tea shake.

"Right." I sarcastically muttered. "I'm going to leave now. Tell Clarice to give me a call."

I spent the rest of that night on top of a cliff, staring out at the stars and the moon right before my eyes. Everything just seemed so much better and brighter up there.

Eventually near midnight, I came back to Alex's house. All of the lights in the house were turned off, so I had to be extra careful, tip toeing my way up to Alex's room. When I snuck inside, I could faintly see Alex's figure under his bed from the moonlight coming from the windows. His hair fell in front of his face, and his pale skin seemed to glow.

I crawled in the sheets with him, wrapping the blankets around me. Alex stirred a little bit next to me, as I turned over to stare at him. His dark eyelashes were so full and thick, and his rosy red lips were parted just a little bit.

I knew that if Alex ever left me, I wouldn't be able to survive.

I needed him, probably more than he needs me.

"I love you, Alex." I whispered.

CHAPTER 24

B y the beginning of the fourth month of Clarice's pregnancy, her baby bump was starting to show. It was no longer a secret that Clarice was pregnant, because one glance at her stomach, and you could see the small bulge that was poking from her lean belly.

She stopped throwing up a week ago, but her cranky mood swings and strange cravings for carrots dipping in barbecue sauce were still there.

"I get to find out if it's a boy or girl in another month." Clarice beamed. "Oh my God, I hope I get a boy first."

I raised an eyebrow. "Why?"

Clarice smirked. "If I ever had a baby girl, her big brother can beat the shit out of anyone that hurts her."

I let out a snort of laughter, as I stared at Clarice with amusement. "Do you have any idea what you want to name your boy yet?"

Clarice twisted her lips, as she took a moment to think about it. She finally shrugged, letting out a defeated sigh. "No, not yet."

I gave her a weak smile. "You still have time."

Clarice let out a low laugh, rolling her eyes. "Not a lot of time. Can you believe it? Four months have passed already. I've been having a baby growing in my stomach for four months now."

I spaced off, thinking about everything that's happened in the past four months. First off, I met Hayden, who became my best friend and Alex, who became the man that I was sure that I was in love with. Then, I reconciled with Clarice after finding out that she was knocked up. And most of all, I finally left my father. I left that place that I once called home and the person I used to call my daddy.

"I guess a lot has happened these past four months, huh?" I let out a bitter laugh.

Clarice gave me a small smile, if she knew exactly what I was thinking. I remember when we were little, we were both convinced that we had twin telepathy. "For the better though, right? Everything happened for the better."

I raised an eyebrow. "Even getting pregnant?"

Clarice smiled, shrugging innocently. "I guess so. I mean, if I never got pregnant, then we would've never become friends again, right? And I would've never Damian and them all."

I smiled, lacing my arm through Clarice's. I let out a laugh, as I nodded, feeling a warmth in my heart. "Right, Clarice. You're so right."

Later that night, after I finished taking a shower, I crawled into bed with Alex. The cool comforter covered the two of us, as Alex's arms snaked around my waist, pulling my back into his bare chest. I couldn't help but feel my cheeks turn warm, and even though the room was dark, my cheeks were red enough for Alex to see.

"You're so cute when you blush." He smirked, his hot breath tickling my ear.

I gulped, as I bit down on my lower lip from smiling. I rolled my eyes, letting out an unattractive snort. "I was not blushing." I lied, turning around so that I faced him. I poked his hard chest with my index finger. "You, sir, need to put on a shirt."

Alex raised an eyebrow, lowering the blanket so that his entire bare stomach was exposed to me. I narrowed my eyes away, forcing myself not to look. "What, are you going to tell me that you don't like what you see?"

I pulled the covers over us, rolling my eyes. "You're an idiot, Alex." My voice came out croaky, my mind still focusing on the hard panels that were on his stomach.

Alex chuckled, as he pulled me in towards him. His hand rested on my back, sending shivers down my spine. My head was pressed against his chest, and I could hear his every heartbeat. I felt myself smiling when I realized that his heartbeat was as fast as mine.

"But you love me, don't you?" his voice came out teasingly.

I felt myself tense under his touch, as Alex stopped smirking. I looked up into his blue eyes, as he stared back at me, realizing exactly what he just said. Then, he looked like he wanted to take back his words, as if he regretted everything he just said.

"I-I didn't mean it like that." He uttered out quickly.

I felt my heart drop to the pit of my stomach, as I nodded weakly. His face fell, as I bit down on my lower lip to hold back the tears that were threatening to spill from my eyes.

I love him.

But he obviously didn't feel the same about me.

"Whatever." I whispered, feeling my voice being to drift off. "Just forget it."

Alex clenched his jaw, and I could feel his shoulders tensing up from our close proximity. I didn't dare to look at him, as he brushed a piece of my hair behind my ears. I thought that was it for the night, and that was how we were going to end it. But, right before my eyes began to flutter down, Alex's voice stopped me from falling asleep.

"Aerial." He whispered so gently.

"Yeah?" I muttered, sleepy and tired.

Alex hesitated for a moment, before he licked his lips. I heard him let out a long sigh, before he shook his head. His fingers began to tangle with my thick hair, running his hands through it. "Nothing." He muttered. I wanted to say something, but I was too tired to utter out a word. "Your hair is so soft." Alex said, making my eyes close.

The past few days, Hayden has been distant and more quiet than usual. Whenever I saw him during school, he looked exhausted and worn out. I knew that he was hurting because of Aubrey, and even Aubrey knew. Every time Aubrey walked by Hayden, her eyes lingered on him for a moment, eyes turning soft. But, whenever she saw me looking back at her, her eyes snapped away, and she scowled at me with hatred.

I arrived to school late today, and the hallways were completely deserted. As I was gathering my books out of my locker, I saw Aubrey coming down the hall with a bathroom pass in her hands.

Immediately, I stopped her in the halls.

She gave me a cold glare, as she tried to walk the other way. But, I stuck my arm out, shaking my head. "Aubrey, I need to talk to you."

The red head sucked in a deep breath of air, as she let out a sarcastic laugh. "What the hell makes you think I want to talk to you?"

I bit down on my tongue from snapping at her. I knew I couldn't, because I wanted to do this for Hayden. All I wanted was to see my best friend happy again, not sulking around over Aubrey.

"I know about you and Hayden." I said.

Her green eyes snapped up to mine. For a split second, they looked saddened, but immediately, they turned dark and angry. She clenched her jaw, giving me a harsh glare. "He told you?" she growled. "Great, now you know what kind of monster he is."

"He's not the same person he was years ago." I defended Hayden. "He's sorry."

Now that I take a closer look at Aubrey, I saw how broken she was. I saw what no one else could've seen about her. I saw how she looked on the inside.

"Everyone is sorry at one point in their lives." Aubrey hissed. "But it doesn't change the mistakes they made."

I wanted to tell her that she was wrong. I wanted her to become the sweet person Hayden promised she was, but I just couldn't. I couldn't tell her any of that, because she was completely right. Everything she just said was true, and I couldn't prove her wrong this time.

"Exactly." Aubrey whispered this time. Her voice was so weak yet soft. I never in a million years thought that Aubrey could talk without that nasally tone she always carried with her. "You know I'm right, Mason."

She pushed past my shoulders, as she began to walk back down the hallways. I turned around, watching as Aubrey's naturally red hair flew behind her.

She acts like she doesn't care, but she does.

"He still loves you, you know?" I called out.

Aubrey stopped in her tracks, as if she suddenly became frozen. Slowly with tense shoulders, she turned to face me. Her face had crumpled, yet she still composed herself. "I know."

And with that, Aubrey finally got her last word with me.

It was Christmas today.

The entire town had been covered with bright Christmas lights since the end of Thanksgiving, but I finally took the time to notice everything today. With everything going on lately, I just ignored the fact that one of the most celebrated holidays was coming up.

I sat by Alex's fireplace just a few hours after the crack of dawn, staring out at the window. The entire floor was buried and covered by thick sheets of snow, and Alex's entire neighborhood was decorated with light up reindeers and blown up, life size Santa Clauses.

Although, Alex's house wasn't decorated with an inch of Christmas ornaments, at all. In fact, if you stepped inside Alex's house during Christmas, you would've thought otherwise. I didn't mind, though. I got used to it after mom died. After she left, dad stopped celebrating Christmas. When mom was here, there used to be a big Christmas tree in the living room, covered with sparkly garlands and silver and gold ornaments. Presents used to be overflowing under the Christmas tree, and all of our relatives used to come over. There would always be a tradition Christmas dinner at the table, and gingerbread cookies for desert, or Christmas pudding.

"You woke up early today." Alex's voice stopped my trance, as I turned around to look at him.

His hair was still messy from sleeping for so long, and there was a big wrinkle on his t-shirt. I gave him a small smile, pointing out the window. "It's snowing."

Alex looked past my shoulder, nodding. "Merry Christmas."

I blinked, as I turned my head out the window. My eyes focused on two small children that were rummaging out the doors with thick winter coats on, and sleds in their hands.

"Merry Christmas." I whispered.

Alex gave me a small smile. "My family hasn't celebrated Christmas in years, but if you want, we could bake cookies and make dinner and all that crap."

I let out a chuckle, staring at Alex with amused eyes. "Mine haven't either." I sighed. "But, yeah. I'd love to."

Alex grinned, helping me up. He escorted me to the kitchen, as he began to take out all the necessities for cookies. We found flour, eggs, sugar and all that good stuff in a pantry.

"I've never made cookies before, so if these come out bad, you'll know why." Alex said, making me laugh.

We were in the process of whisking the eggs and mixing the ingredients. As I finished with the eggs, I carried the bowl towards the mixture of cookies dough. I wasn't paying attention when I accidently bumped heads with Alex. The bowl full of whisked eggs spilt onto Alex's shirt before I knew it. I stared at Alex with wide eyes.

"Is that how it's going to be?" he asked.

For a second, I thought he was seriously mad. But, suddenly, I felt a cold egg being cracked on the top of my head. The egg whites dripped down my hair, as I let out a gasp.

Alex smirked, giving me a teasing grin. "Egg looks god on you."

I glared at Alex, as I took a handful of flour, rubbing it all over his hair. His hair became powdery white, as Alex stared at me with shocked eyes.

Just when I thought I had won the game, Alex sprayed some orange yellow goop on me from a can. "What is that?!" I shrieked.

"Cheese in a can." He smirked, as he continued to spray it on me like party spray.

I let out a laugh, as I grabbed some milk and tossed it on him. He became drenched in white liquid, but it didn't take him long to find something to toss at me.

I didn't know how long our war lasted, but I knew that we got carried away.

"What the hell is going on?" a voice asked, startling both Alex and I.

I froze in shock with an egg in my hand, while Alex had a carton of milk in his. We both slowly turned around to see where the voice came from, and faced Alex's mother.

My cheeks turned bright red, as the egg slipped out of my hand. It landed on the floor with a thud, making me want to go hide in the corner.

Kill me, now.

"Oh, mom, what are you doing here?" Alex asked sheepishly, rubbing the back of his neck with his hands that were covered in flour.

"It's Christmas." His mother crossed his arm, raising an eyebrow between the two of us. "I thought I'd be nice if I came home to spend it with you two, but it seems as though you guys are fine without me."

I felt a pang of guilt in my stomach. "I'm sorry." I immediately said. "I'll clean it all up."

Alex's mother sighed, as she stopped me from picking up the goopy egg that was splattered all over the floor. "Don't worry about it. We'll clean it tomorrow." She turned to Alex, giving him an uneasy look. "Your father called last night."

Alex's jaw clenched, as his eyes hardened. "What did that bastard want?"

"He invited us to a Christmas dinner that he's having."

"Hell no, I'm not going." Alex declared. "And neither are you."

Alex's mother ran a hand through her hair, looking stressed. "I'm not your father's number one fan, but I think we should go to talk things out. His family is going to be there, so things can't get too crazy."

Alex's eyes widened, as he stared at his mother with shock. Suddenly, his eyes grew dark, as he glared at the messy countertop. "His wife and kids are going to be there?"

Alex's mother nodded weakly, sighing. "You know what? I'll just tell him we can't go, okay?"

Just as Alex's mother was about to walk away with a phone in her hand, Alex stopped her. "Wait, mom." He paused, letting out a deep breath of air. "We'll go."

CHAPTER 25

Alex wasn't exactly happy during the rest of the Christmas morning, until we had to go to his father's house for dinner. Alex's mother called us to tell us to get dressed, and I was debating on whether or not to wear something casual or formal. I knew Alex's father wasn't exactly on the average side when it came to money, in fact, he was higher than average.

"Don't worry too much about what you want to wear." Alex's mother poked her head into Alex's room, sporting a scoop neck, cherry red dress that went just past her knees. She was wearing a pair of elegant pearl earrings with a matching pearl necklace.

She looked rather beautiful.

I nodded, as I decided to wear a simple black dress that went just a few inches above the knee, and had laced sleeves a few inches past my elbows. I paired it with a pair of red ballet flats, since I knew I would be tripping all night if I decided to wear heels.

"That looks lovely." Alex's mother gave me a small smile. "Tell Alex I'll be waiting for you two in the car outside."

She stepped out of the room, as I quickly scrunched up my wavy curls that I took the time to do an hour ago. A few days before Christmas, Clarice presented me with a new tube of blood red lipstick. I swiped it across my lips, giving me quite an exotic look. I smiled at myself in the mirror, thinking of how proud Clarice would be if she saw how put together I looked without her help.

"Alex." I knocked on the bathroom door, where I had last seen him. "Your mother is waiting in the car."

I heard Alex muttered something I could understand. I knocked again, and this time, Alex swung open the door, looking annoyed and irritated.

He was wearing a buttoned down black shirt, tucked into a pair of black trousers. I licked my lips, loving the way he looked in a dress shirt.

"Can you help me put this tie on? I've been trying for the past half hour." He grumbled, a loose red tie hanging around his neck.

I bit back a laugh, as I nodded. I stood closer to Alex, as I began to wrap the tie around his neck. I felt his shoulders tense when my fingers brushed against his chest, as I held in a deep blush that matched the color of his tie.

"There," I breathed, pulling the tie tighter around him, "all done."

Alex gulped, as he nodded. "Thanks." His warm breath tickled my cheek, as I adverted my gaze down to my red flats.

"Let's go." I mumbled, already turning to head out of the bathroom. "We're already running late."

As I began to walk down the hallways, towards the stairs to go down, Alex called out my name softly. "Aerial, wait."

I turned around, raising an eyebrow. "Yeah?"

Alex let a small smile slip across his lips. "You look beautiful."

Two hours later, we arrived at Alex's father's house, which was all the way across town. It would've taken us a shorter time if there wasn't such traffic today.

Before we got in, Alex's mother turned to us from the driver's seat with a stern look across her features. "Before we go in, let's set some ground rules, okay?" she said with a firm tone.

Alex groaned, rolling his eyes. "Great." He muttered sarcastically.

"Absolutely no starting a fight with your father tonight and you must be polite to everyone," She sighed, "including his new wife."

"You've got to be kidding me." Alex muttered under his breath. "Isn't that slut like twenty?"

Alex's mother shot Alex a glare. "Watch your mouth." She snapped, before clearing her throat. "And she's twenty three, for your information."

Alex grumbled, as we got out of the car. My foot landed into a mushy pile of snow, as Alex's mother got a sparkly gift bag out of the back. "What did you get for their family?" I asked, eyeing the suspiciously large bag.

Alex's mother shrugged, fixing up the red tissue paper that stuck out. "Just a set of fine China plates." She paused. "And a few toys for the kids."

I nodded, as we walked up to the front porch of the house. We faced a French door with glass windows, as Alex jabbed the doorbell with his index finger.

Seconds later, Alex's father appeared by the doorway, opening the door for us to come in. He had a grin across his face, but I could tell that it was only from the empty glass of wine he had between his fingertips.

"Arlene," Alex's father gave Alex's mother a tight smile, shaking her hands, "thank you for coming tonight."

I could hear a bunch of chatter coming from what I assumed to be the living room. There was a bright light coming from down the hall, and I could hear various voices speaking at once, and glasses clinking against each other.

"Son, it's nice of you to come today." Alex's father patted Alex on the back.

Alex flinched at his touch, as he clenched his jaw. Alex gave him a cold look, before speaking. "I wish I could say the same about you, but I can't." he said in a low voice.

Alex's mother gasped, as she gave Alex a hard nudge on the elbow. "Alex, be polite." She reminded him, as Alex stared at the velvet carpeting below us.

"And I don't think we've been properly introduced yet." Alex's father turned to me, holding his large hand out for me to shake. "I'm Alex's father, as you already know. But, you can call me Roger."

I shook his hand, noticing how much of a tight and firm squeeze he had. I winced, as I pulled my hand away. "I'm Aerial, Alex's girlfriend."

Roger raised an eyebrow, turning to Alex with a curious expression, before facing me once again. "Say, how much do your parents make annually?"

I blinked, as Alex glared at Roger with much fury and hatred. I gulped, as I licked my dry lips. As I opened my mouth to tell him that my father didn't make much, Alex's mother cut in between us.

"Roger, where's your wife?" she asked, saving me. "I'd like to see her."

Roger let out a loud laugh, as he began to lead Alex's mother to the kitchen. I let out a breath of relief when I realized that I didn't have to be pressured into answering anything.

"Sorry about him." Alex muttered. "He's kind of a selfish dick that only cares about money."

I gave him a small smile with reassurance. "Don't worry about it." I paused, taking his hand into mine. At first, Alex felt tense, but as soon as I gave him a small squeeze, he relaxed. "Do you want to go to the living room? It sounds like all the guests are there."

Alex groaned. "I don't really want to, but-"

I dragged Alex to the living room, passing by mirrors with golden frames, and marble statues. I couldn't help but wonder just how loaded Alex's father was.

As we entered the living room, we were instantly hit with the aroma of strong perfume and thick red wine.

A server came towards us with a platter in his hands, offering us a glass of wine. I shook my head immediately, and when Alex noticed my foul reaction to the alcohol, he rejected, as well.

"You know, you don't have to stop drinking because of me." I pointed out to him.

"I'm not doing it for you, Aerial." He snapped.

I bit my lower lip, noticing how Alex wasn't in his happiest mood today. In fact, he was acting kind of stuck up and rude.

I was about to tell him off when I heard a girl squealing in our direction. My head snapped around, as I faced a tall and thin blonde with a sun kissed tan even in the winter. She was wearing a golden dress that was covered in sparkles from the deep, low cut in the chest to the hem that reached just below her butt.

"Alex, it's you, darling!" she beamed, wrapping her arms around Alex to give him a tight embrace.

I raised an eyebrow between them two, as Alex pulled away from her. She turned to me with a grin across her full lips, opening her arms for me. Before I got to react, she gave me a bone crushing hug, as I struggled to breathe due to the lack of oxygen and the fact that she smelt like she had poured an entire bottle of perfume on herself.

When we pulled away, the girl beamed, clapping her hands together. "I heard Alex got a new girlfriend, so I just had to come meet her!"

I raised an eyebrow, blinking. "I'm sorry, but do I know you?"

The blonde clamped a hand over her full lips, as she gasped. "Oh my gosh, I am so sorry! I totally forgot to introduce myself." She paused, sticking out her manicured hand for me to shake. "I'm Lucille Montgomery."

I frowned, as I shook her hand with a weak smile. "Montgomery? Are you Alex's sister?"

Lucille let out a high pitched laugh, shaking her head. "My God, you really think I'm that young?" she gushed, turning to Alex. "She's is a total keeper, Alex. But no, I'm not Alex's sister."

"Cousin?" I asked.

Lucille shook her blonde head of hair, giving me a bashful smile. "I'm Alex's step-mother."

My eyes widened, as I stared at her with disbelief.

This was the twenty three year old woman that was Roger Montgomery's wife? I choked back on my saliva, as Lucille patted me on the back roughly.

Oh God, was that even legal?

Roger had to be at least thirty years older than Lucille!

"Honey, are you okay?" she stared at me with a worried expression. "Let me go ask one of the waiters to get you a glass of water."

Lucille left us, leaving a trail of golden glitter behind her from her sparkly dress that was flaking. Once she was out of earshot, I turned to Alex with a gawk on my face.

"That's who your dad married?" I asked. "That's unbelievable!"

"Believe it." Alex muttered, shaking his head. "It's ridiculous, I know."

I gave him a small smile. "Well, at least it wasn't one of your secret girlfriends. You know how jealous I got when she ran up to you with a hug?"

Alex let out a short laugh, as I smiled. It was the first time I've seen him smile since we got here, and it was pretty good feeling that I was the one to make him smile.

The rest of the night was alright. Alex and I made sure to stay clear away from Lucille and Roger, and any of the teenage girls that were daughters of Roger's friends. They were all swooning over Alex, and giving me death glares when they saw that the two of us were holding hands.

They shot me glares with their freckled faces, and popped their bubble gum obnoxiously with their braced teeth.

It was finally the end of the night when everyone cleared out. Lucille was upstairs taking a shower, and the kids had fallen asleep hours ago.

The three of us were about to leave when Roger stopped us midway. He had an envelope in his hands, as he handed it to Alex. "Son, this is your Christmas present." He said. "Open it, now."

Alex stared at the bright red envelope curiously, as he tore off the envelope. Inside was a cheesy Christmas card with a snowman on the cover. When Alex lifted it open, his eyes widened.

"Dad," he paused, "plane tickets to France?"

Roger nodded, as Alex's mother gave him a glare. "What are you trying to do by sending my kid tickets to France, Roger?" she hissed.

Roger ignored Alex's mother, as he swung an arm around Alex. He patted him on the back, as he held the tickets out in front of him. "I recently bought a condo in France. Since you're going off to college soon, I figured that you should come live with me. I have a friend there who is the Dean of one of France's most prestigious universities. I could help you get in if you come to stay with me."

Alex's mother's eyes widened, as she gasped. "Roger, don't you even dare try to take my son away from me."

Roger glared at her, rolling his eyes. "Let Alex decide. He's eighteen, for crying out loud."

I was silent the entire time, still feeling numb.

I mean, how couldn't I feel broken and disappointed?

There was a possibility that Alex was going to leave me and go off to a different country.

"Alex." Alex's mother said in a warning tone. "Don't go."

I refused to look at Alex in the eye, even though I knew he was trying his best to get me to look at him. I just couldn't. The offer to France sounded great, but I was being selfish.

I didn't want to let go of my Alex.

The Alex that I love so much.

"I," Alex muttered, sighing, "I need to think about it."

I gulped.

No.

CHAPTER 26

I've been ignoring Alex for the past few days. It was hard, especially since we lived in the same house now, but I somehow managed to find a way to dodge out of his way.

I knew that I was being unreasonable by avoiding him, but I didn't want to face him. I didn't want to face him when he told me that he had accepted his dad's offer to France. I didn't want to face him when he says that he's moving to another country for four years.

So, needless to say, I was running away from my problems.

Maybe it wasn't the smartest decision, but it was all I could do at this point.

Alex wasn't dumb, though. He knew from the very moment when we exited his father's house that I was acting up. During the two hour drive back home, I kept looking out the window with ear buds plugged in so I would be able to avoid any conversation with him.

"Hello?" Clarice's manicured nails snapped in my face, as she gave me an irritated glare. "Earth to Aerial!"

Startled, I jolted up from my seat, snapping out of my thoughts. I face the blonde, who was raising her eyebrows at me. "Sorry, what did you say?" I muttered, stirring the untouched, chocolate milkshake in front of me.

Clarice frowned. "I asked if you were coming to Elliot Chamber's New Year's party, but it seems as if you have other things on your mind." She paused, leaning over the table, giving me a skeptical look. "Spill."

"It's nothing." I muttered, obviously lying.

Clarice shot me a glare, before taking her back hand, and slapping it against the side of my head. I winced, pulling myself away from her grip. "Ouch, Clarice!" I hissed, rubbing my aching head. "What the hell was that for?"

Clarice rolled my eyes. "How many times do I have to tell you that you can't lie for shit?" she cussed. "Now tell me before I spill my milkshake on your head."

I stared at her empty glass, raising an eyebrow challengingly. "You have no more milkshake, though."

Clarice eyed my full glass, giving me a sickening evil grin. "But you do." She snapped. "Now tell me."

I sighed, staring at her with frustrating. I ran a hand through my tangled hair that I hadn't bothered to run a brush through today. "I went to some Christmas dinner party that Alex's father hosted a week ago." I started off, as Clarice nodded slowly. "Things didn't go so well, at first. Did you know that his father is married to a twenty three year old?"

Clarice gasped, clamping a hand over her lips. "Are you serious?" she counted with her fingers. "Gross! She's only five years older than Alex! They could be siblings!"

I shrugged. "That's exactly what I thought. But anyways, pushing that aside, at the end of the dinner party, when the house cleared out, Alex's father gave him something." I gulped. "He gave Alex plane tickets to France."

"What about it? He wants to take Alex on a vacation?" Clarice asked.

I scoffed, shaking my head. "No." I muttered. "He wants to take Alex to live with him in France. He sugar coated everything, saying how he bought a fancy house there. He even told Alex that he has connections with one of the best universities there, and he could easily enroll him in."

Clarice's eyes widened, but she didn't look as panicked as I did when I found out. "What did Alex say to it?"

I shifted my eyes down to my cold hands, shrugging. "I don't know."

Clarice gave me a stank look. "What the hell do you mean you don't know?"

I bit my lower lip. "I haven't been exactly talking to him since that day."

Clarice's jaw dropped, as she gave me a disapproving glare. "You've been ignoring him?" she hissed. "What is wrong with you?!"

I grimaced under Clarice's looks of anger, as I dipped my head low. "I just don't want him to tell me that he's moving away."

Clarice's features softened, as she let out an exasperated sigh. "He told you he loves you, right?"

My heart instantly leapt, as my eyes snapped towards Clarice within a flash. When I didn't say a word, Clarice let out a long gasp. "Oh my God, no way." She whispered. "He hasn't, has he?"

I shook my head, wishing that Alex would say that he loves me already. I just wanted to know if he felt the same way I did about him. "No." I mumbled.

"Do you love him?" she asked.

I didn't even have to think this question over. Before I gave myself permission to speak, I said, "Yes."

"Then what the hell are you doing here getting milkshakes with me?" Clarice snapped. "You should be getting your man right now."

And before I knew it, I was out of the diner. Since Clarice and I had walked to the diner, I had to find myself back to Alex's house. But, that didn't stop me from running as fast as I could to find Alex. It was cold that day, and the wind was strong. I could feel my cheeks getting ruddy and frostbitten as my hair lashed behind my neck. I did my best to run through the piles of snow on the sidewalk, and dodging the sleek ice that hardened. I might've tripped a few times, but I didn't care.

I just wanted to tell Alex that I love him.

When I reached Alex's house, I pushed the doors open. I ran into the living room, where I had heard voices. I was preparing myself to run into Alex's arms, kissing him full on the lips, and telling him that I love him. But, I didn't expect to see his entire family standing in the living room with suitcases all over the room.

I stopped breathing once I saw his father.

I knew I looked like a complete mess, hair all over the place, sweaty and cheeks flushed red from running. But, I didn't care about my appearance right now. I just wanted to know what on

Earth was going on, and why Alex had suitcases lined up beside him.

"Alex?" I whispered in a voice so low, I doubt any of them could hear me clearly.

Alex's eyes were burning into mine for the entire time, eyes so blank and lifeless. "What's going on?" I asked.

Roger, Alex's father, came right up behind Alex, patting his back with his palms. I finally took the time to look at Alex's mother, whose eyes looked red from crying. "Alex here is coming with me to France."

Alex's mother let out a sob, as my eyes snapped towards Alex immediately. I stared at him with wide eyes, as my lips parted open with disbelief.

"Alex?" my voice came out breathless. "Alex, tell me he's lying."

Alex's eyes dropped from mine, as he stared at the floor below. With one shake on the head, my heart stopped. "He's not lying. " Alex spoke for the first time since I barged into the room. "I'm going with him to France."

My heart was beating against my chest so fast. I was afraid that if I wasn't going to calm down anytime soon, I would have a heart attack. Tears welled up in my eyes, as I watched Alex's eyes turned bright with worry through my blurry vision. My hands shook by my sides, as I nodded forcefully and weakly. "Okay." I whispered, barely believing the fact that I could speak.

Roger stepped in between us, carrying two of Alex's luggages in each hand. "I'll give you two a minute." He turned to Alex's mother. "Help me out, will you?"

Alex's mother looked so helpless, as she glared at Roger. She gulped, before taking the last suitcase in her hands, pulling the handle out to roll it on the floor. Before she left to the car, she turned to me with lifeless eyes. "I tried." She whispered.

Once Roger and Alex's mother were gone, I turned to Alex with tears flowing from my eyes uncontrollably. I had to bit my lower lip to prevent it from quivering. "Why didn't you tell me?" I asked, my eyes burning into his with sudden anger. "How come you never told me about this?!"

Alex's eyes shot towards me accusingly. "You've been avoiding me for an entire week! How the hell was I supposed to try to reach you?"

My heart sank to the pit of my stomach. "But it's not fair." I whispered. "You promised me that you would never leave me."

Alex's eyes stared at me with guilt and regret, before they turned dark again. "You don't even care, Aerial."

I took a step closer to him, pounding my fists against his chest angrily. "How could you even say that?!" I cried, slamming him with my fist. "I fucking love you!"

Alex's hands suddenly latched around my wrists, stopping me from hitting him. I let out a sob, as I glared up at him with hatred. "Let go!" I tried to pull away. "Let go of me!"

Alex's eyes bored into mine, as his grip tightened around my wrist. "What did you just say?"

"Let go!" I repeated, wanting to punch him just a few more times.

"Before that." He paused. "What did you say?"

Suddenly, I stopped trying to fight back with him, as my hands fell lifeless. My face turned to horror as I realized what I had said to Alex without knowing it. But, it was what I came here to tell him, right? I came here to tell him that I love him.

"I said I love you, you fucking idiot." I muttered, cheeks turning crimson red.

"How come you tell me that now?" Alex asked, eyes turning dark with anger. "If you love me, then you wouldn't have avoided me for so long."

"God!" I hissed. "I was ignoring you because I was afraid of this! I was afraid that you were going to tell me that you would leave me for some fancy ass school in France!"

Alex clenched his jaw, as he dropped my hands. My palms fell to my sides, as I couldn't help but feel my wrists burning from his touch. "You should've told me earlier." He mumbled, looking off to the side. "It's a bit too late now."

A tear slid down my right cheek. "You're actually going?"

Alex nodded, staring at me with heartbreaking eyes. "I have to." He muttered. "My father already enrolled me in the school this morning."

I felt my blood boiling in my veins. If I hadn't been ignoring him for so long, he could've actually stayed. I clenched my fists against my sides, digging my nails into my palms. I was so angry, I wanted to punch something. Anything, I just wanted to release all the anger I had inside of me.

"The stupid school is more important than me?" I managed to choke out.

Alex's eyes fell. "Of course not, babe." He wiped a tear from my cheek, pulling me in to him. His body felt so warm against mine, as I buried my face in his shoulder. "I love you."

I let out a sob. "Then why are you leaving me?"

Alex pulled away from me, placing his forehead against mine. He licked his lips, soothing out my tangled and unruly hair. "I'm going to come back one day, Aerial Mason. I'm going to come back a better person for you." He whispered, kissing the trail of tears on my cheeks. "I'm going to come back from France one day, and love you more than I love you now."

"I hate you so much, Alex. Don't leave me here." I begged.

Alex kissed the corner of my lips, making me arch my back. "I love you so much, Aerial." He ignored my pleading. "I want to hear you tell me that you love me one more time."

"This isn't going to be the last time." I whispered, as his lips finally met mine. Our lips moved in sync, as he had his arms tightly around my waist, trying to pull me in closer to him.

"Say it." He demanded against my lips. "Just one last time before I leave."

His lips moved away from mine, as he began to peck my earlobe. I gulped, as I felt my hands begin to tremble. "Alex, please don't go."

His lips left my ears, as he began to leave me a hot trail of kisses on my neck. He pulled down the sleeve of my sweater, exposing my bare shoulder. He began to suck on my collarbone, making me let out a gasp.

"I will you make you." He threatened, hands sliding down my back.

I closed my eyes, as he continued to kiss me everywhere. I wanted him to stop; I wanted him to tell me that he was going to stay with me forever. But, I knew I was being selfish. I was holding him back from doing big things.

"Alex, just tell me one thing." I moaned, as nibbled on my jaw line. "Do you want to go to France?"

"Mhmm." He mumbled, hands sliding into my shirt. His warm hands trailed up to my cold body, playing with the hem of my bra.

He needed to stop torturing me, right now.

"I love you." I finally said, while his hands tickled my ribcage.

Alex had stopped kissing me, but I was still pressed against him, and his warm hands were still holding me protectively.

"Now, give me one last kiss." I said. "And then you can leave."

Alex looked at me hesitantly, as I stared at his rosy red lips from kissing me so much. His head began to dip low, and soon, his lips were pressed against mine. It was the best kiss we've ever had together, and I almost didn't want it to end. It was absolutely intoxicating.

Before things got too attached and heated, I pushed him off.

"Okay, done." I whispered. "Your car is waiting outside."

Alex stared at me with surprised eyes. "Aerial, what-"

"Go." My voice broke, as I turned my head away from his. I didn't want him to see me cry. "Go to France. But, promise me you'll come back. Don't break this promise."

It was completely silent for a moment, until I heard Alex's footsteps leave the living room. Before he was completely gone, he whispered in a voice so low, "I won't. I promise."

When the front door closed, I broke down into uncontrollable tears.

CHAPTER 27

F ive Months Later

Winter had turned into spring, and spring had bloomed into summer.

I wasn't exactly enjoying the hot weather and sun outside like everyone else was. I was stuck in a hot and musky library, studying for finals that were due to take place next week. I've been in here for the past three hours, and my mind was about to explode. The words that were in the textbook had gone blurry, and my head was killing me.

My phone suddenly vibrated on the table, as I let out a frustrated groan. Reaching over, I clicked the green answer button, as I placed the phone beside my ear.

"What do you want Damian?" I snapped, reading the caller ID.

I heard rapid pants on the other line, as I suddenly sat up straighter in my seat. "Damian, what's going on?" I asked.

"Clarice!" he breathed with heavy rags. "Her water broke!"

My eyes widened, as I slammed the textbook closed. Pushing myself out of the chair, I began to sprint out of the library, forgetting to get my notes.

"Where are you right now?" I asked.

"We just got to the hospital." I suddenly heard a wail from the other line, then Clarice's voice screaming. "I don't care what you do! Just get me out of this fucking pain!"

I began to curse under my breath, as I hung up on Damian. My fingers trembled as I dialed Hayden's number.

Before Hayden even got a chance to greet me, I began to ramble on. "Hayden! I need you to pick me up from the local library right now! Clarice's water broke and she's about to give birth and Damian is stressing out and I need a car!"

"I'm on my way." Hayden said immediately, before hanging up.

Not even five minutes later, Hayden's car pulled up in front of me. I hurriedly got into his car, as I gave him the address to the hospital. I couldn't help but feel my heart racing against my chest, as I drummed my fingers against my kneecap.

"Crap, hurry up!" I hissed as we stopped at a never ending red light.

Hayden muttered under his breath. "I can't just run over a red light!"

The road was completely empty, and I didn't see a need for a red light in a situation like this. I stepped my foot over Hayden's, as the car went lurching forward.

"What the fuck are you doing?" Hayden shouted. "You're going to kill the both of us!"

I ignored him, as I continued to step on the pedal harder, steering the wheel. We got a few angry honkers in the way, but we managed to get to the hospital in one piece.

I ran out of the car with Hayden following me behind, as I approached the front desk looking like a mess. "I need to see Clarice Adams."

The nurse eyed Hayden and I, before clicking some buttons on her computer. "She's in the emergency room right now. I can only let you in if you are family."

"I'm her sister!" I immediately said, as I pulled Hayden beside me. "And this is her step-brother."

She eyed us skeptically, before giving us her room number. When the last number came out of her mouth, I dashed away from her, as I hauled into the elevator.

When I reached the room that Clarice was in, I found Damian sitting outside on the waiting chairs, with a hospital gown on and a hair cap.

When he looked up and saw us, he let out long breath of air. "I couldn't watch." He muttered with shame.

I wanted to slap him. "Are you stupid? She's relying on your ass right now! Get in there!"

A nurse came out of the room Clarice was in, as I stopped her. "Excuse me miss, my sister is in there. Can I go see how she's doing?" I put on a fake smile.

The nurse nodded, as she disappeared into a storage room to give Hayden and I matching green hospital gowns and caps. "You are required to wear these, and please remain calm when you enter the room." She whispered.

I nodded, as I threw on the hospital gown over my clothes. I patched up my messy hair into a bun, securing the hair cap on.

Damian and Hayden followed me from behind, as we entered the room. Clarice looked like she was in misery as a doctor and another nurse stood beside her.

"The stupid pain killers aren't working!" she complained, shooting the doctor a glare.

I ran over beside Clarice, whose cheeks were flushed red, and there was sweat dripping down her forehead. "Clarice, remember what we read in those pregnancy books, breath in and out slowly." I tried to soothe her.

She followed my instructions, as she sucked in a deep breath of air, before releasing it. "I can see the head of the baby!" the doctor called out. "Keep pushing!"

I held onto Clarice's hand, as her grip tightened around mine.

"It's coming!" the nurse smiled, wiping a tear that had fallen from her eyes. "You're doing great!"

Clarice bit her lower lip, as she tried to push even more. Suddenly, the nurse let out a wail of excitement, as the doctor held the baby in his arms. The nurse went over to get the baby a clean blanket, wrapping it securely around it.

"It's a boy." The doctor whispered, handing the baby to Clarice.

Clarice's eyes welled up with tears, as she let out a laugh. The baby boy's skin was red, but despite that, he was absolutely adorable. He had the exact same green eyes as Clarice. "He's so beautiful." She whispered, gently cradling the baby as it began to scream.

Damian and Hayden stepped closer to us to get a better view of the baby. "What are you going to name it?" Hayden asked, this index finger brushing against the baby's soft cheeks.

Clarice looked up at me, as her eyes locked into mine. "Aiden Mason Adams."

My eyes widened with surprise. "Mason? You're naming him after me?"

Clarice nodded, as she stared down at baby Aiden. "You're my sister, Aerial."

The doctor let out a cough, clearing his throat. "You have some family members waiting outside to see you. Only three people are allowed to visit at one time, so I'm afraid your friends will have to leave for now."

"Will they be able to come back and visit?" Clarice asked, smiling at Damian, whose face was still pale and white.

"Of course." The doctor smiled.

Hayden and I left the hospital afterwards, ripping off our ridiculous looking hospital gowns. But, Damian told us that he was going to stay behind for just a little longer.

"Baby Aiden is beautiful, isn't he?" Hayden asked, eyes still mesmerized from the trip to the hospital early this morning.

I nodded, unable to hold back my smile from being so wide. I haven't felt this happy for smiled so much since Alex left. It felt pretty good to finally feel happiness again, yet there was still a part of me, wishing that he would've been with me. "He sure is."

Hayden noticed my expression, because he let out a low laugh. "Alex is missing out, isn't he?"

"He is." I agreed, my eyes casting down to the pavement below me.

"He misses you a lot, you know?" he suddenly said.

I looked up at Hayden, whose brown hair has grown through-out the months. They were reaching just above his eyes, long enough so that he could toss his hair.

"I doubt it. He's probably having the time of his life at a French university with hot French girls walking around in their French bikinis." I sarcastically said.

Hayden shook his head. "No. I just called him a few nights ago. He tells me how much he wants to see you again." He paused. "He asked me why you never tried to get in contact with him."

I stared down at my dwindling fingers, which had chipped blue polish. "I don't know." I shrugged pathetically. "If I'm going to see him, it's going to be in person. Not through Skype."

Hayden nodded understandingly. "I get it."

I left school early today to go see Clarice, who was still re-covering in the hospital. I knew it wasn't the smartest idea to do, considering the fact that I have finals in just a week, but I weighed my options, and figured that if anything, I would just do a crash course.

"Hey." I smiled at Clarice, who was sitting up from her bed with some hospital food in front of her on a tray.

Clarice gave me a tight smile, poking her scrambled eggs with a plastic fork. "Oh God, I don't think any of this is edible." She muttered with disgust, pushing her green looking eggs away.

I let out a low laugh, picking up some cherry flavored jelly that at least looked edible. "Try some of-"

Before I got to finish, Clarice's hand went flying towards the fork, smacking the jelly onto the floor. She glared at it evilly, as she shook her head. "That," she pointed to the floor, "is horrible."

I chuckled, as I pulled out a turkey sandwich from my bag. Clarice's eyes immediately widened and sparkled, as I reached for my sandwich, unwrapping it quickly. "Oh my God! Yes, food!" she chanted, taking a bite as she munched unattractively.

"Have your parents come by yet?" I asked her.

Clarice nodded, swallowing her massive bite of sandwich. "Yeah." She said. "Mom started bawling when she saw Aiden."

I grinned. "Well, he is pretty damn cute."

Clarice's smile suddenly faltered, as she placed her half eaten sandwich on the tray. She gulped, as she stared up at me with defeated eyes. "Daniel came by a few hours after you left."

My eyes widened, as my ears perked up. "What?" I asked with disbelief. "He didn't hurt you, did he?"

Clarice shook her head. "He just wanted to see Aiden." She paused. "You know he's in military school now, right?"

I raised an eyebrow, my mouth dropping. "No way." I muttered. "What did he say to you?"

"He was actually really nice. He didn't exactly seem too nice when I told him that Damian and I were together, but he didn't flip out, either." Clarice stared down at her pale fingers. "He even wants to help support the baby financially."

I bit my lower lip, my mind blank and unsure. I didn't really trust Daniel with baby Aiden just yet. It had only been a little over half a year when he completely went ballistic on Clarice at Aubrey's party. "And what did you say to that?" I asked.

"I told him that I didn't need his money." Clarice gave me a weak smile. "But since he is the legal father, he's allowed to see

Aiden once in a while. But he probably won't have much time, since he's going to join the military and all."

I felt more relieved when Clarice said that. Some part of me knew that Daniel hasn't fully recovered from his anger problems. God forbid that one day he snaps, and he was around baby Aiden. Who knows what he could do?

My phone suddenly vibrated in my pocket, as I frowned at the screen. It was from a number that I've never seen before. I quickly flashed Clarice the screen to see if she could recognize the number, but she shrugged, shaking her head.

I told her I would be back in a few minutes, as I stepped outside of her room. Clicking the answer button, I pressed the phone against my ears.

"Hello?" I spoke, my voice unsure and confused.

There was a long pause on the other line, but I could faintly hear someone slowly breathing. I held in my breath, having the idea of exactly who it was. I closed my eyes, as the familiar sweet voice filled my ears.

"Hi Aerial."

"Hi Alex." I whispered so low, I wasn't sure if he would be able to hear me from the other line.

I bit my lower lip, as took in a deep breath of air. This was the first time I've heard Alex's voice in literally half a year. I got chills just from thinking of how unreal it was that I was on a phone call with him right now.

"What are you doing right now?" Alex asked.

I began to walk to the room where baby Aiden was placed in with a bunch of other newly born babies. I spotted him in a blue crib with a baby blue blanket wrapped around him tightly.

A small smile appeared across my lips, as I tapped my fingers gently against the glass to say hi to him.

"I'm at the hospital, visiting Aiden." I said, as baby Aiden's eyes opened up. He looked around with confusion written all over his face, until his eyes fell on me. I watched from behind the glass as he let out a giggle, making me smile.

"Right." Alex said. "Clarice gave birth yesterday. How was it?"

I turned my face away from Aiden, leaning against the glass. "It was great." I said truthfully.

"I wish I could've been there."

I bit my lower lip, as I scratched the back of my neck nervously. "When are you going to be back?" my voice shook, almost afraid of the answer.

There was a slight pause on the other line, until Alex finally answered me. "I don't know. I'll probably be back after I graduate."

My voice got caught in my throat, as I held in my breath. After he graduates? That will take at least another three and a half years.

"Why can't you come back now? It's almost summer, you know." I whispered.

"I know, but my dad isn't willing to let me go back just yet." Alex suddenly said, as his voice became smooth. "I really miss you."

I clutched on my phone tighter, as I felt a ball rise up my throat. Tears welled up in my eyes, as I let them drip down my cheeks. "I know." My voice cracked.

"I love you, Aerial." Alex said seriously. "When I come back, I'm going to love you more than I ever have."

I let out a bitter laugh, closing my eyes. "A lot can change in three and a half years."

Alex paused on the other line, before he cleared his throat. "What do you mean? Like meet new people?"

"There's a possibility." I sighed. "By the time you come back, I'll be in college, too."

"But, there can still be a you and me, right?" Alex asked, voice unsure and shaky.

Silence.

It was so quiet, it could've killed me.

"We'll see what happens." I said softly. "But for now, I think its best if we move on."

"Aerial-"

"Call me when you come back in three years." I cut him off.

My heart was breaking on the inside, but I knew what I did was the best for the both of us. He left me, and now it was time for me to leave him.

"I'll be waiting for you." Alex said.

CHAPTER 28

Three Years Later

"This is hideous." Clarice sighed, staring at her reflection in the mirror. She was wearing a large wedding gown that was tight from the waist up, but the bottom puffed up drastically. It looked more of a Disney princess costume than a potential wedding dress. Clarice pouted as she stared at the atrocious looking wedding dress, before she stripped out of it. "I swear, I'm never going to be able to find the perfect dress."

"Don't say that." I assured her, as I handed her the seventh wedding down that she was going to try on today. "You'll find one, for sure. This place is huge."

Clarice pursed her lips, before she put on the next wedding dress. I had to admit that it wasn't the worst dress out there, but I knew that it wasn't extravagant enough to please Clarice. It was just a bit too dull and plain for someone as unique as Clarice. Clarice came to the wedding dress boutique today, in the hopes of finding a wedding dress that showed off her curves, had a sweetheart neckline, and had crystals all over the bust.

"I hate this dress." Her negative comment confirmed my predictions. She groaned, before she took a seat on the couches beside me, leaning back and closing her eyes. "Who knew wedding preparations were going to be so hard? I mean, I still have to meet up with the florist to get the centerpieces, and then I have to find my bridesmaid's dresses, and do cake tasting."

I gave her a weak smile. "Hey, the last one doesn't sound too bad."

She gave me a bland look, before she let out a long sigh. "But, when it's all over, Damian and I are going to a relaxing honeymoon vacation in the Bahamas."

"And while you guys will be enjoying the sun, I'll be studying for my midterms." I groaned. Clarice suddenly turned to me with a weak smile on her face, a mischievous glint in her eyes. I slapped the palm of my hand to my forehead, as I gave her a dull look. "What do you want?" I asked.

"Well," Clarice gave me a puppy dog look, "since Damian and I are going to be gone for a whole week, we needed someone to babysit Aiden."

My eyes widened, as I shook my head. "No, Clarice." As much as I loved spending time with Aiden, I couldn't flunk on my midterms. "I can't!"

"I know it's going to be a lot of work, but I can get my friend Liam to help you out!" Clarice promised, giving me a hopeful smile.

Oh, I know where this was going.

Clarice has been trying to set me up with one of her friends that are in her college classes for the past two years now. Apparently, Liam is some kind of heir to an oil company in South America. As Clarice would say, Liam is a "real catch".

"No, Clarice." I sighed.

Clarice huffed, as she crossed her arms stubbornly. "Why not?" she pouted. "You haven't been with anyone since Alex! It's time to move on."

I glared at her, as I rolled my eyes. "I'll move on when I want to move on, Clarice. God, I can't believe you're even bringing him up."

Clarice gave me a guilty look, as she sighed. "Look, I'm sorry, okay? I just don't want my best friend to grow old because of some guy that broke her heart in high school."

I stared down at my palms, thinking back to all the times Alex held my hand. It seemed like just yesterday that he was still beside me, holding me, and kissing me. But, in reality, he's gone. He's been gone for three years already. But, it didn't seem that way, because the look in his blue eyes, and the sound of his sweet voice was still so fresh in my mind.

Truth be told, I still love him.

But, yet, I still can't help but hate him so much. He's ruined every chance that I came close to moving on from him. Every-thing a guy asked for my number, I couldn't help but wish that it was Alex who I would be able to call. It just sucks how much I hate that I love him.

"Okay." I finally said, letting out a ragged breath of air. "I'll go on a date with Liam."

Clarice's eyes went wide, as she blinked. Her expression told me that she wasn't sure if I was being sarcastic or not. After a moment of silence, and her studying my face closely, she concluded that I was, in fact, completely serious.

She let out a laugh of disbelief, before she whipped out her phone from her purse. "Alright, I'm on it right now." She muttered, sneaking glances at me once in a while.

On the next Friday night, Clarice gave Liam the information to my dorm room on my university's campus. It was a little past eight o'clock, and I was dressed in a simple strapless black dress that went mid thigh, and a pair of red heels just to jazz up my outfit. Throughout the years, Clarice forced me to learn how to walk in heels, snapping at me that if I was going to be the maid of honor at her wedding, I would have to wear heels.

There was a sudden knock on my door. My roommate, Carmen, had already gone out with her boyfriend for the night, so it was just me in the room. I opened the door, and standing by the doorway with a boutique of red roses was who I assumed to be Liam.

"Hi, are you Aerial?" he smiled, holding his hand out for me to shake.

I nodded, as I gave him a small smile. I took his hand, and to my surprise, he held it up to his lips, giving me a peck on the back side of my hand.

"Nice to meet you, Liam." I forced a smile, trying to make my voice not sound uncomfortable or shaky. I mean, after all, this was the first date I've been on in three years.

Liam handed me the bouquet of flowers, as I took them willingly. "Thanks." I smiled, plucking on one of the cherry red petals. "These look really nice."

I put the flowers on my desk, before I grabbed me red clutch bag, and followed Liam outside. "So, where are we going tonight?" I asked him.

"A restaurant with the finest wine they sell in the country." Liam smiled.

I opened my mouth, trying to tell him that I didn't drink, at all, but I didn't want to make a bad first impression. After all, first impressions never go away, now do they?

"That sounds great." I put on a smile, as Liam opened the door of his expensive looking car for me. I slid inside, the cold leather seats touching my bare thighs.

As Liam starting driving, I couldn't help but notice that there was an awkward silence between us. I snuck a glance over at him, noticing that he didn't seem the slightest bit uncomfortable. In fact, he had a calm smile on his lips, as his fingers drummed lightly to the beat of the music that was coming from the radio.

I took the time to notice that he had curly blonde hair, and bright blue eyes. But, I also noticed that his blue eyes were nothing compared to Alex's. My mind flashed back to how Alex's eyes used to glow whenever he looked at me.

My heart clenched with pain, as I tore my gaze away from Liam.

This is exactly what I meant when I said that Alex ruined every chance of a relationship I ever had. Every man that I was affiliated with was compared to Alex mentally in my mind, and Alex was always better than them.

It was like I could never move on from him.

"We're here." Liam's voice suddenly interrupted me out of my thoughts, as he parked in front of a restaurant that looked absolutely spectacular from the exterior designing. There was a fountain in the center with a marble statue just a few feet from the front door. Lights were decorated all over the place, as Liam held the door for me to go inside.

"Thanks." I whispered.

The waiter seemed to recognize Liam immediately, as he quickly escorted the two of us to a private seating in the back of the room. It was a tiny square table with silky table cloth, and a single lit candle in the center. I noticed two wine glasses and a bottle of red wine off to the corner, as the waiter popped open the champagne to give us each a glass.

Before he poured any liquid into mine, I stopped him. "I'm fine, thank you."

The waiter nodded, as he handed us two menus. As soon as he left, Liam turned to me with a curious frown on his perfect features. "What's wrong? You don't like red wine?" he asked worriedly. "Because I'm pretty sure they have different kinds of-"

I let out a low laugh, shaking my head. "I just don't drink, Liam." I assured him. "I'm fine with water, anyways."

Liam looked relieved, as he nodded. "That's good." He flipped through his menu, as he stopped on a certain page. "Do you want to try some Rigatoni con la Pajata?"

My head snapped towards him, as I frowned with confusion. "What?" I asked.

Liam laughed, taking a sip of his red wine. "It's pasta. Try it, it's really good."

I nodded in agreement, considering the fact that I couldn't even pronounce any of the other items that were on the menu. When the waiter came back, Liam ordered two Rigatoni con la Pajata's for us, and spoke to the waiter in fluent Italian.

When the waiter left once again, Liam turned to me with a cocky smile on his face. "So, Clarice tells me that you haven't been on a date in three years?"

My cheeks turned bright red, as I made a mental note to kill her afterwards. "Yeah." I muttered. "It's kind of embarrassing, though."

Liam chuckled, as he leaned closer to the table. "Why, though?" he took a piece of my brown hair, twirling it with his fingertips. I gulped, as I shifted uncomfortably in my seat. I reminded myself that Liam was only trying to be nice. "You're far too beautiful to be single for three years."

I gave him a weak smile. "Thanks." I wasn't ready yet to get into my life story, so I decided to shift the attention to Liam. "So, tell me about you. What year of college are you in?"

Liam's face seemed to light up when I decided to talk about him. "Well, I'm in my last year. I'm graduating a year early, because I completed all of my courses already. It wasn't easy trying to get all of my extra classes fit into three years, but my dad has connections, you know? After all, my father is the founder and owner of Sun's Oil all over South America."

Somewhere along the lines of, "Then my father became a millionaire." I began to doze off. All Liam was telling me was how filthy rich he and his father were, and how he could buy whatever he wanted, whenever he wanted.

I was almost relieved when the food came, not because I was starving, but because Liam finally shut up.

"So, I hear that you went on a date with the son of some owner's oil company?" Hayden asked me the next morning.

I was at his apartment, one he rented after he moved out of his parent's house for college. I laid flat on my fact on his bed, fumbling around with a Rubik's Cube that I found under his bed. I also found a half eaten slice of pizza there, as well, but I decided to just leave it there.

"Did Clarice tell you?" I asked, cursing when I had an entire side completed with the exception of one square.

"Well, Clarice told Damian, and Damian told me." Hayden chuckled, stuffing a few fries in his mouth. "So how was it?"

I shuddered, as I turned towards him. "It was horrible." I muttered. "All he was talking about for the entire night was how much his father makes annually."

Hayden laughed, kicking his feet up to his desk. "Was it a lot?"

I glared at him, as I tossed one of his pillows on the bed at his chest. "That doesn't matter!" I snapped.

Hayden grinned, wiggling his eyebrows. He wheeled his chair towards me, as I gave him a glare. "So, Clarice and Damian are getting married in three months?"

I nodded. "Yes, sir. I went dress shopping with her last week."

"And how was it? Did she find a dress?" Hayden asked.

I shook my head. "Nope. Every dress she tried on, she called disgusting."

Hayden let out a chuckle, as he dipped his fries into a goopy pool of red ketchup. "Tell me when you guys are going to the cake tasting thing. You know how I love my free cake."

I laughed, as I gave him a light push on the shoulder. "How are you and Aubrey?"

Hayden and Aubrey officially reunited their long awaiting relationship during the last year of high school. It took Hayden a lot of convincing for Aubrey to finally forgive and forget Hayden, but Hayden tells me that it was all worth it.

I couldn't disagree with him, either, because ever since Aubrey and Hayden began to date again, I got a new friend. Aubrey, Clarice and I would all go shopping and just hang around together. We all forgave each other, and became pretty darn close over the years. Clarice even named Aubrey as one of her bridesmaids. The other one was one of her close friends from college, and another was her cousin, whom I've met quite a few times.

"We're doing great." Hayden smiled. "I think she finally trusts me again."

"Don't break the trust." I gave him a look, before giving him a playful grin. "I don't want her to be a bitch again."

Hayden laughed, and opened his mouth to say something. But, before he got to, his laptop let out a ring.

Our heads snapped towards the loud alarm, as Hayden got up to check his screen. He frowned with confusion, before he turned to me, biting his lips. "It's Alex. He's calling me on Skype."

I stared at the screen with a blank expression, before I let out a deep breath of air. I gave Hayden a weak smile, shrugging. "Answer it, I don't care."

Hayden stared at me carefully, before he answered the web-cam chat on Skype. Immediately, Alex's face popped up on the screen.

I held in my breath, as I stared at how much he had grown throughout the three years. Even though the webcam was a bit dark and blurry, I could tell that his jaw line had gotten much defined. He was wearing a white v-neck t-shirt, and I could see that his muscles have gotten slightly bigger. I almost smiled when I noticed that his hair was still the same, and his eyes were still as bright as ever.

"Hey Alex." Hayden said cautiously.

Alex gave Hayden a tired smile, and that's when I noticed the bags under his eyes. "Hey man."

Since Alex didn't seem alarm, I assumed that he couldn't see me yet. After all, I was pretty much hiding myself under Hayden's covers.

"Isn't it really late in France right now?" Hayden asked, frowning. "Why are you calling me for?"

Alex let out a chuckle that made my heart stop. "Am I inter-rupting something?" he teased. "I see someone on your bed. Is Aubrey there?"

Hayden bit his lower lips, as he turned back to look at me. I tried to tell him not to tell Alex that I was here, but Hayden mouthed, "I'm sorry."

"It's not Aubrey." Hayden sighed. "It's Aerial."

The webcam on the other side got extremely quiet, as I held my breath, waiting for Alex to say something.

Anything.

"Really?" Alex asked, voice unsteady. "Can I see her?"

My eyes widened, as the pace of my heart sped up. Was I really ready for this?

"Uh, sure." Hayden scratched the back of his neck. "Aerial, Alex wants to see you."

I cursed under my breath, as I slowly, and painfully, got up from Hayden's bed. I tip toed over to Hayden's webcam. I bit my lower lip, as I let out a nervous breath of air.

"Hi, Alex." I managed to choke out.

CHAPTER 29

Alex's Point of View

My eyes scanned the airport terminal, searching for a specific brunette who had the most gorgeous hazel eyes I've ever seen. But, all I saw was families giving each other bone crushing hugs with suitcases rolling behind them.

I bit on my lips, as I stared at the time written on my phone. I had just gotten off the airplane from France, and Aerial promised me last night that she was going to be waiting for me an hour earlier than the time my flight arrived.

"Alex?" a soft voice suddenly asked from behind.

I recognized the smooth voice immediately, as I turned around. My eyes locked in Aerial's, who looked more beautiful than the last time I saw her years ago. Her eyes shined bright, and her cheeks were pink and dewy. She had even taken the thought to apply some cherry red lipstick onto those luscious lips of hers. I almost wanted to wrap her into my arms, and kiss her as hard as I could.

She let out a soft laugh, as she approached me. She laugh sent shivers down my spine, as I stood frozen in my place, still not believing the fact that the girl I was still in love with was standing nearly inches away from me.

"Are you okay?" she asked, taking her fingers, and poking my left cheek. "You look a bit pale. Have they been feeding you well in France?"

Her voice almost sounded teasing, as I finally let out a small chuckle. Her hand was still on my cheek, as I cupped my hand over hers. Immediately, her cheeks turned red, as I pulled her finger away shyly.

"They have, actually." I smirked. "They serve the world's finest snails."

She gave me a sly smile, before bursting into a misfit of laughter. "I bet you miss having Big Macs." She paused, giving me an unsure look. "Do they even have McDonald's in France?"

I gave her a look of amusement, as I finally realized exactly how much I've missed her throughout these years. Aerial was one of the biggest nerds back in high school, yet she still manages to asks the simplest questions. "Of course, Aerial." I laughed. "I went to France, not the dinosaur era."

She blushed, as she tucked a piece of loose hair behind her ears. "Oh." She muttered. "I knew that."

I grinned, before looking around the airport. "Is Hayden and Damian here? Or is it just you?"

She gave me a bland look, before the corner of her lips twitched up into a small smile. "Why? Am I not good enough for you?"

My blue eyes focused into her hazel ones, as I gave her a small smile. "You're perfect for me." I whispered.

Aerial's eyes widened, as her cheeks turned crimson red. She cleared her throat, as she dwindled with her fingers nervously. "Right." She let out a deep breath of air, shifting her gaze to the floor. "Hayden went with Damian to do the cake testing, and Aubrey and Clarice went to find bridesmaid's dresses."

"Why didn't you go with them?" I asked, giving her a smirk.

She gave her a glare, before she gave me a light punch on my shoulder. "I had to come get your ass. Now come on, I want to see if we can make it in time to go do cake testing."

"When does it start?" I asked, as I picked up my suitcase, following Aerial out of the airport.

"In ten minutes." She simply said, as we entered the airport's parking lot.

I frowned. "But, how are we going to make it in time?"

Aerial gave me a smile. "We'll manage."

I had to admit that I completely underestimated Aerial as a driver. She may look like one of those safe drivers, who are always fussing at everyone if they go a mile over the speed limit. But, she was a hell of a dangerous driver.

"How the hell did you even pass your driver's test?" I asked, horror plastered on my face as she went twenty miles well over the speed limit.

She laughed, as she rolled the windows down. The wind immediately entered the car, tossing Aerial's long, wavy hair behind her head. "I'm not horrible. I mean, you should see how Hayden drives."

I chuckled, remembering the last time I was in Hayden's car. He was the worst driver I've ever met to this day. I solely remember him even going as far as letting go of the steering wheel to get a bag of chips from the back seat of his car.

The two of us were lucky that we didn't die that day.

"We're here." Aerial finally said, as we parked in front of a bakery that's been in town ever since I was a little kid. I remember that this place was known for making the state's best cake.

We entered the bakery, as a whiff of sweet cookies and cupcakes filled my nose. My stomach immediately grumbled, as I realized that I hadn't eaten anything during my plane trip back.

"Alex!" Hayden suddenly called out, as I felt a pair of strong arms around me.

I scrunched up my nose with disgust, as I pushed Hayden off. He had a wide grin across his face, and I couldn't help but smile. "You're still an idiot, Hayden." I said, giving him a shove on the shoulder.

Hayden ignored my sarcastic insult, as he grinned, patting my on the back. "Man, I've missed you!"

I finally let out a chuckle. I was about to open my mouth to say something back, but Damian's voice interrupted us.

"Montgomery!" Damian grinned, opening his arms out to give me a friendly pat on the back. "Man, I was wondering when you were going to come!"

I pulled away from Damian, giving him a smirk. "Congrats on you and Clarice, man."

"Thanks." Damian chuckled, as I pounded my fist against his, something we always did back in high school.

Suddenly, a round man wearing a white chef's hat came from the back of the bakery. His hair was just turning a salt and pepper shade, and he had a thick mustache.

"Damian," the baker smiled warmly at Aerial and I, "who are you buddies?"

Damian stepped right in, putting an arm around Aerial and I. Aerial, who was on the other side of Damian, turned flush red, as she hid behind her curtain of hair. "This is my wife's maid of honor, Aerial." Damian ruffled up Aerial's hair, much to her dismay. "And this is Alex, one of my groomsmen."

"Hey." I shook the baker's hand as he stuck it out for Aerial and I to shake. "Nice to meet you, sir."

The baker snorted, letting out a raspy laugh. "Don't call me that, bud. You and Aerial can call me Dave." He paused, staring at the time on his golden Rolex watch. "How about we start the cake tasting now, eh? I have some of my best samples in the kitchen."

"That sounds great!" Hayden piped up.

We all laughed, as we followed Dave towards the back of the bakery. Lined up neatly on a kitchen counter were plates of little cakes that had been cut up into smaller portions.

"Try this one first." Dave said, handing us each a plastic fork, as we poked it into a slice of cake that looked dark on the inside.

Hayden was the first to give a reaction, as he scrunched up his face. He forced it down his throat, before giving it a thumbs down. "This is so," he tasted his tongue, "bitter."

Dave laughed. "It's dark chocolate cake. It's primarily more popular to the elders."

"I think we all agree that we pass on this one, right?" Damian asked all of us for our opinions.

Aerial and I nodded, as we moved onto the next platter of cakes. It had white frosting on the outside, and it looked chunky and rough on the inside. I took one bite, as I carefully tasted it. "Is this carrot cake?" I asked.

Dave nodded. "Sure is."

"Not bad." Aerial muttered, licking the cream off her spoon.

I smirked with amusement at her, as her eyes finally reached mine. Her tongue was still touching the tip of her spoon, as she pulled away quickly, a deep blush forming on each of her temples.

"What are you looking at?" she muttered towards me.

I grinned, as I stepped closer to her. She let out a surprised gasp when each of my hands found their way to her hips. I pulled her closer, completely forgetting that we were still testing out cakes. I dipped my finger into some of the white cream from the carrot cake, as I dabbed it onto her nose.

She let out a shriek, as she shot me a glare. "What the hell?" she bit back her laughter.

"You look cute like that." I said without thinking it over.

Aerial's eyes went wide and innocent, the same way she used to look in high school. Her lips parted open, only to tempt me even more.

"Hey, you two can flirt later, but no making a mess in my kitchen, alright?" Dave asked teasingly, noticing the blob of white frosting on Aerial's nose.

Immediately, Aerial stepped away from me, her back hitting the counter. She looked flustered, as she cleared her throat.

"Guys, come try this!" Damian called out, on the other side of the counter already. "I think we have a winner."

Aerial's eyes shifted towards mine for a split second, before she went over to Damian and Hayden. "I'm coming." She whispered.

After the cake testing, Aerial called it a day and went home. Damian, Hayden and I were all over at Damian's new apartment, which he shared with Clarice.

"Aiden, don't be shy, okay?" Damian whispered towards his son, who had a finger in his mouth. His hair was naturally platinum blonde, like Clarice's, and his eyes were big and wide. "Say hi to Uncle Alex."

I was sitting on Damian's couch when Aiden ran up to me full of giggles. "Hi Uncle Alex!" he chirped, as a laugh escaped my lips.

Aiden's speech was incredibly well for a three year old, like himself. "Hey buddy." I grinned.

"Daddy says that you're my uncle, right?" he managed to say without mumbling too much.

I saw from the corner of my eye Damian smiling when Aiden called him his father. "Your dad is right." I shook his little hand.

Aiden stared up at me with wide green eyes, before he bursts into giggles. "Does that mean you're married to Auntie Aerial?" he asked innocently.

The entire room became quiet, as my face went blank. I stared down at the little three year old that was by my knees, a grin across his face.

Damian let out a cough, as he scooped up Aiden in his arms. "Aiden, I think it's time for you to take a nap." He muttered.

Aiden frowned, kicking his feet. "Wait, daddy! I want to play Lego's with Uncle Alex!"

"You guys can play later." Damian assured. "Uncle Alex won't be leaving any time soon."

"Is that true?" Aiden asked, smiling. "Do you promise to play Lego's with me?"

I nodded, giving the little man a smile. "I promise, Aiden."

Damian disappeared with Aiden in his arms, as I heard him trying to shush Aiden down for him to sleep. I was left alone in the living room with Hayden, who seemed to have his eyes on me the entire time.

"So, how are you and Aubs?" I asked, plastering on a grin across my face that never met my eyes.

Hayden gave me a blank stare. "Do you still love her, man?"

I gulped, but I just pretended like I didn't know what and who Hayden was talking about. "What do you mean?" I nervously chuckled, downing a can of beer.

Hayden rolled his eyes, grabbing the can away from my hands. "Aerial, you dick. I'm talking about Aerial."

I stared at my best friend, whom I've known since I was in the first grade, for a long while. I finally let out a long breath of air, as I ran a hand through my dark hair. "Of course I still love her."

Hayden didn't say anything after that. We were always the best of friends, and we could tell each other anything straight out, but this time, Hayden had nothing to say. Neither did I.

We waited for Damian to come back, who eventually did a few minutes later. "Sorry about Aiden." He breathed, as he planked himself down on his sofa. "He tends to run his mouth some-times."

I let out a broken laugh, shaking my head. "It's fine. He's great, actually."

"Do you have any idea what color tie we should be wearing at the wedding yet?" Hayden asked, grabbing his can of beer from the coffee table.

Damian smirked, nodding. "Red."

I frowned. "What? Red?"

Damian nodded. "Clarice texted me earlier today, telling me how she and Aubrey found some red bridesmaids dresses that apparently look 'hot' yet 'appropriate'."

Hayden chuckled, a grin spreading across his lips. "I can't wait to see Aubrey in it."

CHAPTER 30

Aerial's Point of View

"The zipper won't go up!" Aubrey cried, as she tugged on the zipper that was stuck on the back of Clarice's wedding dress.

Clarice's eyes widened, as all of us bridesmaids began to rush over to where Aubrey was kneeling down. We all tried to pull the zipper up, but it wouldn't budge, at all.

"Are you kidding me?" Clarice panicked, as she glanced over her shoulder at the back of her dress. "I didn't gain any weight! I made sure that I kept a perfect figure for this day!"

One of Clarice's other bridesmaids, Alice, who was one of her close friends from college, pulled out a package of pins. "We'll have to use this, for now. The guests are already arriving!" Alice said, as she hurried over to Clarice, as she carefully clipped the pins on the back of her dress, until it looked zipped up.

Clarice sighed with relief, as she stared up at the clock above us. "Crap, crap, crap! It starts in fifteen minutes." She gasped, as she looked over at her three bridesmaids. "Can you guys go check to see if the guy's are ready yet?"

Alice, Aubrey and Clarice's closest cousin, Brennan, all rushed out of the room. I was about to go leave with them to find the guys, but Clarice stopped me. "Aerial, can you stay behind?" Clarice asked hopefully.

I smiled, as I nodded. "It's your wedding day, Clarice. You don't need to ask me for anything." I teased, as I reached over to wipe away a small smudge of rosy red lipstick that was on the corner of her lips.

Clarice rolled her eyes, as she spun around in her chair, facing the mirror. She studied herself for a long time, before she let out a deep breath of air. "I can't believe I'm actually getting married today." She paused, before glancing over at me in the mirror. "Thanks for being my maid of honor, Aerial."

I let out a soft laugh, as I smiled. "We've been through a lot together, haven't we?"

Clarice nodded, as her eyes began to get watery. I gave her a warning look, as I reached over to hand her a tissue. "Clarice, no tears, okay?" I laughed, as Clarice gently dabbed her eyes. "You didn't pay that makeup artist a hundred bucks for nothing."

The blonde chuckled, as she shook her head. "Sorry, Aerial. I was just thinking about how hard it was to get to where I am today."

I smiled, opening my mouth to tell her how much she meant to me, but before a word escaped my lips, the girls came running back into the dressing room. "The guys are all ready!" Brennan smiled.

"And may I add, Hayden looks hot in a tuxedo." Aubrey smiled dreamily, twirling a piece of her red curls.

We all laughed, as a small figure suddenly appeared from behind Aubrey's legs. I grinned, kneeling down, as Aiden came running into my arms.

"Auntie Aerial!" Aiden squealed, as I picked him up.

"Aiden!" I smiled, fixing his short, tousled blonde hair that he managed to get messy. "You look so handsome in a suit!" Aiden looked like the cutest boy alive in his little black tuxedo. He had a single red bow that was a bit lopsided, as I straightened it out for him.

Aiden's eyes suddenly became wide, as he stared at Clarice with glossy green eyes. "Mommy, you look like a princess." He gawked.

All of us girls laughed, as I passed Aiden over to Clarice. Clarice took her baby boy into her arms, as she grinned down at him. "Thank you, baby." She giggled. "Are you excited to be the ring bearer?"

Aiden nodded eagerly, as Clarice's wedding planner suddenly came into the dressing room. She had a clipboard and pen in her hands, and she had a headpiece around her ears. "Girls, I need you to get ready! You girls are going out first with the groomsmen." she called us bridesmaids out. "Clarice, your father is waiting in the lobby to escort you down the aisle."

We all gave Clarice one final hug, before we all scattered out to the lobby, where all the guy's were standing in their tuxedos. I smoothed out red bridesmaid dress that was strapless with a sweetheart neckline, and had a flare bottom that reached just at the knees.

"I would've gone for more of a cocktail dress for you guys, but I don't think it would've been appropriate for church." Clarice simple shrugged, while I laughed.

All of us bridesmaids had a bouquet for red and white roses in our hands, as we laced our arms around the groomsmen. I wasn't quite sure who I would've walked down the aisle with, but Alex smiled own at me, holding his arm out for me to take.

I blushed, as I bit my lower lip, lacing my arm around his. Brennan and Alice took the other two groomsmen's arms, as the doors opened.

All of the guests were standing up from their seats in formal attire, as Hayden and Aubrey were the first to make their way down the aisle.

"You look beautiful." Alex whispered in my ear, just as it was out turn to walk down the aisle. I couldn't help but smile, as flashes went off of people taking our pictures. I wasn't thinking about tripping or how I looked. All I was thinking about was how I wished that one day, I would be walking down this aisle with Alex, again, except, I wanted to be wearing a white dress the next time around.

As Alex and I reached the end of the aisle, we parted away, as I went over to stand by the bridesmaids, and he went over to stand with the groomsmen.

After all of us came out, it was time for the ring bearer and flower girl. Aiden looked so cute, grinning like a pro as he walked down the aisle. The little girl who was the flower girl was one of Damian's little cousins, and she looked a shy as she tossed rose petals.

Finally, everyone went silent, as Clarice and her father stepped onto the aisle. She looked a bit timid at first, but she smiled when her eyes met Damian's. Mrs. Adams began to cry when Mr. Adams escorted Clarice down the aisle.

"Dearly beloved, we gather here today…"

After the ceremony was over, we all went to the back of the church, where there was a garden. Tables and refreshments were set up, and music began to play as people all gathered to the center of the rose garden to dance.

"Wait!" Clarice settled everyone down, as they all turned to look at her. Clarice grinned, as she held up her bouquet of flowers. "Are you all ready for this?" she asked, turning around, as she closed her eyes.

All of the women and girls gathered behind her, opening their arms to catch the bouquet of flowers. In one swift motion, Clarice tossed it behind her, towards us, as girls started to jump for it.

I hadn't even noticed that I was the one to catch it until Clarice let out a squeal, running up to me while holding her dress up. "Aerial! You caught it!" she gushed, as I stared down at the bouquet that had coincidentally fallen into my arms.

I stared at it with a blank expression, as I looked up to catch the eye of Alex. He had his hands in his trouser's pockets, as he smiled back at me.

I bit my lower lip, staring down at the bouquet, as Clarice giggled beside me. "I guess you're the next to get married, huh?" she poked my shoulder, before Damian pulled her away to dance.

I placed the bouquet down on a table, as I went over to get a glass of cranberry juice from the refreshments table. As I filled it with ice and juice, I felt a light tap on my shoulders. I turned around, as Alex smiled down at me, picking up the bottle of cranberry juice I had just poured.

"Still don't drink, huh?" he asked, pouring himself a glass, as well.

I smiled softly, secretly satisfied that that he remembered all this time. "Nope. I don't planning on soon, either."

Alex smiled down at me, revealing that one dimple on his left cheek. "That's good."

A slow beat song suddenly blasted through the speakers, as all of the couples gathered on the dance floor. I immediately recognized the song as Lego House by Ed Sheeran. I smiled at the song choice, as I peered over to watch the couples dance. In the center were Clarice and Damian, having their first dance together as a wedded couple. I stared at how the two moved swiftly yet slowly to the soft beat of the tune.

I suddenly felt a hand cupping over mine, as a soft gasp escaped my lips. I stared up at Alex, feeling a familiar tingle at our hands touching, as he offered me a gentle smile. "Do you want to dance with me?"

I blinked up at him, trying to figure out if I had heard him correctly or not. When Alex suddenly frowned, waiting for my response, I snapped out of my thoughts. Clearing my throat as a hot blush crept up my neck, I nodded.

Alex's warm hand held me protectively yet gently towards the dance floor, as he placed his both hands firmly around my waist. I felt stiff and tense at first, but as soon as Alex got me to loosen up, I laced my arms around his neck.

I closed my eyes, humming to the song, as I swayed my hips back and forth slowly. I could feel Alex pulling me closer to him, as if I would fall and break if he didn't hold me tightly enough.

"I love this song." I whispered.

Alex smiled softly down at me, as his blue eyes got lost into mine.

I'm out of touch, I'm out of love, I'll pick you up when you're getting down. And out of all these things I've done, I think I love you better now.

He stared at me for a long moment, as his eyes intensely bored into mine. I held in my breath the entire time, until I casted my gaze over to the ground. "So, uh, are you just here to visit, or are you staying for good?"

He licked his lips, and I could slowly feel his weight being pressed against me, as he leaned closer. I gulped nervously when our faces were just inches from each other. "I don't know, Mason." He whispered, calling me by my last name, like he used to four years ago. "Do you want me to stay?"

I bit on my lower lips, as Alex's eyes shifted down towards them. My cheeks turned crimson red, as I pursed my lips. "Would it really make a difference if I stated my opinion?"

"Yes." Alex's breath tickled my upper lip.

I gulped. There was no point in back up now. "But, you did promise me four years ago that you would come back and stay."

"I said I would come back for you." Alex paused, as the grip of his hands around my waist suddenly tightened. "Let's say you were to not want me anymore. Would I have a reason to stay?"

"Yeah." I leaned into him boldly. I've never felt so brave and courageous around Alex before, and I could almost feel my heart beating out of my chest. "You could fight for me."

He looked at me with intense blue eyes, but he didn't say a word. I knew he wanted to, because I could read it all in his eyes.

I closed my eyes, as I felt my heart sink to the pit of my stomach. I couldn't believe that I was saying this, but I wanted him to tell me that he was going to always going to try to fight for me, no matter what. I dug my fingernails in my palms, wishing that he would love me as much as I loved him.

"Unless," I suddenly whispered, as my eyes stared up pitifully up towards his, "you don't think I'm worth fighting for."

Alex bit his lips, as his eyes suddenly hardened. I gulped, holding my breath, not ever taking my eyes ever away from his. Because I knew that if I looked away, I would lose him, forever.

"Is that what you really think?" Alex asked, his fingers suddenly flying up to my cheeks as he lightly traced figures onto my crimson red temples.

My heart was racing against my chest, as I stared down at the green grass below my feet. "I don't know." I whispered. "You aren't exactly giving me an answer right now."

Alex clenched his jaw, as I finally got a close look of how much he had grown throughout the years. His jaw muscles have gotten more prominent and defined. I licked my lips, as I resisted the urge to just press my lips against his.

"I liked you ever since I met you." He leaned in close to my ear, his hot breath whispering against my earlobe. I shuddered, as Alex continued to intimidate me. "And I have loved you since

I first realized that I could've lost you. What makes you think that I would stop fighting for you now?"

My breathing became slow and heavy, as I closed my eyes. I pressed my head against Alex's shoulder, as I slowly felt myself going weak.

"I waited four years, Aerial Mason." His lips brushed against my earlobe, snapping me awake. "I'm not usually a patient person. I don't want to wait anymore."

"A-Alex." My voice came out staggered and breathless.

Alex suddenly pulled me away from him, tilting my chin up with his fingertips. He made me look into those ocean blue eyes of his, as he stared at me intently. "Tell me that you love me, Aerial." He said lowly. "I waited too long for this. I don't care if you're lying or not, just tell me that you love me."

Alex was holding my hands, as I squeezed my palms against his. I let out a low laugh, dropping my head to the ground. "You're insane, Alex." I whispered.

"Just say it." He demanded.

I closed my eyes, and in a voice so low, I wasn't sure if he could hear, I told him. "I love you, Alex Montgomery."

And I wasn't lying.

EPILOGUE

"**S**hould I make chicken breast or steak?" I asked holding up two packages of meat. I groaned, as I ran a hand through my hair stressfully. "Whatever, I'll just make both." Alex stared at me with a frown. My hands shook as I unwrapped the packages of meat, separating the chicken and the steak in two separate trays.

"You don't have to be so nervous." Alex said, as I ignored him. Alex and I had gotten our own apartment shortly after Clarice's wedding. I was still in college, but Alex had graduated in France a year before I did, and was now working for one of the top business corporations in town. "It's just your dad coming over to visit."

I shot him a glare, as I began to lightly season the meats. "I also haven't spoken or seen him in four years, Alex." I muttered, shaking the ground pepper onto the steak angrily. "Did you also know that he's coming over with his new fiancé?"

Alex's features softened, as he licked his lips. He came over to me, wrapping his warm arms around my waist from behind, as I set the pepper down on the counter with a sigh. "I just noticed that you haven't been sleeping ever since your dad gave you that call." He kissed my cheek, as I closed my eyes, feeling tired and stressed. "I'm just worried about you."

"I'm sorry." I felt weak in his arms, and I was sure that if Alex wasn't holding me up, I would've fallen. "It's just everything has to be perfect."

Alex spun me around so that I was facing him. His hand flew up to tuck a strand of my messy hair, which I hadn't bothered to comb or run a brush through in days. His lips leaned towards my ears, as I felt his hot breath tickling my earlobe. "You're as perfect as it gets." He whispered, sending shivers down my spine. "How about you take a nap, and I grill the meat?"

I let out a soft laugh, resting my head against his shoulder. Alex's hands were running down my back, soothing me while making me tired and sleepy. "Alex," I muttered, "you and I both know that you can't cook for your life."

"True." Alex's soft chuckle filled my ears, as my eyes fluttered close. "I can start on those oven roasted potatoes if you want."

"Are you sure?" my eyes opened, as I stared up at Alex. "I mean, I could help if you want. After all-"

Alex cut me off by pressing his lips against mine gently. My eyes immediately shut closed, as I kissed him back with all the energy I had inside of me. Alex's grip around my waist tightened, as his nibbled on my lower lip. My arms knotted around his neck tightly, because I was afraid that if I didn't hold on tight enough, I would've fallen.

"Let's get you to bed." Alex muttered, carrying me bridal style to our bedroom that we shared. He placed me on our bed, tucking me in.

"Wake me up in an hour." I slurred.

Alex's kissed my forehead, before releasing my hand that he was holding the entire time. "Sure, babe."

"Wake up." I heard Alex say as he gently shook my shoulders. "Your dad is on his way."

My eyes snapped open, as I threw the sheets off of me. I stared at Alex with wide eyes, as panic began to come over me. "Alex, what time is it?" I asked, voice staggering.

Alex pressed both of his hands on my shoulders to calm me down, as my heart hammered against my chest. "It's seven, Aerial. Your dad will be here in thirty-"

"Seven?!" I screeched. "I still haven't made the meat yet! Oh my God Alex, get me out of-"

"Aerial." Alex held my down from fidgeting. "Aerial, babe, relax. I made everything for you. All you need to do now is get dressed."

My shoulders sagged, as I stared at Alex with my lips parted. "You did what?" I asked with disbelief, as I blinked. "Alex, you aren't lying are you?"

Alex let out a low chuckle, as he pressed his lips against my right cheek. "No, I'm not." He whispered, his eyes lingering into mine for a while before he cleared his throat. "Come on, you need to fix that bird's nest of yours."

My eyes widened, as my cheeks turned bright red. My hands immediately flew up to my hair, as I tried to run my fingers through the tangled mess insecurely.

"I'm kidding, Aerial." He smiled lightly. "Now hurry up. You've got thirty minutes."

I shot him a glare, as he got up from our bed to exit the room. Before he left, though, I called his name out. "Alex, wait." I said, as Alex turned around with a frown. "Thanks."

Alex let out a low chuckle, before winking at me with a smirk. "You can thank me later."

I smiled, as I watched Alex leave and close the door behind him. I blushed when I caught myself smiling even after minutes after Alex had left. I buried my face into my arms, before I quickly made a dash into the shower to wash out my unruly hair and cleanse myself.

After, I blow dried my hair, leaving my brown locks naturally wavy. I went over to my dresser, picking out black dress with laced quarter sleeves, and an open back. I carefully picked out a pair of red heels and a matching red lipstick to match it.

When I was finally finished, the doorbell rang. Quickly, I made my way down the stairs, noticing that Alex was already greeting my father. I held in my breath, as I smoothed out my dress.

"Mr. Mason, it's nice to see you again." Alex shook my father's hand.

I sighed with relief once I realized that my father wasn't drunk, and he didn't look like a mess. "Alex," my father gave Alex a hearty shake, "it's nice to see you, as well."

I stood behind Alex, as I bit my lower lip. My father's eyes suddenly casted towards me, as I gulped. His expression was blank and unclear once his eyes met mine, but a smile slowly spread across his lips, as he made his way around Alex.

"Aerial, honey." He breathed with disbelief. "I thought I'd never see you again."

I gulped back the tears, as I gave my father a tight smile. "I could say the same about you."

My father held my gaze me a while, before he cleared his throat. A woman stepped from behind him. She was small and petite, and had chestnut brown hair that went just past her chin. She had a few wrinkles, but gave off the aura of youth and freshness. The thing that caught my eye was the bump that was pushing out from her stomach.

"Aerial, Alex, this is my fiancé, Caroline." My father threw an arm around the petite woman, as she grinned at the two of us.

"It's so good to finally meet you guys!" she gushed. "You have no idea how much your father blabs on and on about you guys!"

I wasn't really listening to what Caroline was saying, though. I was too busy staring at her baby bump. It wasn't until Alex nudged my elbow that I finally snapped out of my gaze with Caroline's stomach. Alex cleared his throat, saving me. "Aerial and I made dinner, if you would just like to sit down at the table."

Caroline beamed, as she smiled. "I'm starving! Being pregnant for six months does give you quite an appetite!"

I gulped, as I stared at Alex. Well, that confirms my suspicions. Caroline was pregnant, and whoever was in that stomach of hers was going to be my baby sibling.

"Aerial, are you okay?" Alex asked, once the adults were out of earshot and at the dinner table. "You look kind of pale."

I sucked in a deep breath of air, before flashing Alex a smile. "I'm fine." I paused, staring at my father and Caroline, who were laughing. "Let's go serve dinner."

Alex gave me a curious look, before he followed my lead towards the kitchen. We got out the meats and potatoes, and carried it out to our dinner table.

"This smells great." My father complimented us, as he took a bite out of steak.

Caroline rolled her eyes, taking a big bite from her food. "It doesn't just smell great, it tastes great!"

My father laughed, as my eyes wandered over his face for a moment longer. I haven't seen him so happy in ages. A bitter chill sent down my spine as I realized that I was never the one to make him happy.

"That's a great compliment, guys." My father turned back his attention to Alex and I. "Caroline is always having these crazy cravings and she never likes to eat anything I make."

Alex and I laughed, as I finally took my first bite out of the steak that Alex made. To my surprise, I actually thought it tasted fantastic. I stared at Alex curiously, since I knew that he was never the best cook out there. He couldn't even make cereal without messing it up.

"Alex, you made this?" I whispered.

Alex let out a low chuckle, glancing at me. "I might've gotten some help."

I frowned. "From who?"

Alex grinned. "Hayden might've come over earlier today while you were sleeping."

"Man, I'm tired." Alex groaned, as his back hit our bed later that night.

After my father and Caroline left, Alex and I spent the rest of the night cleaning the kitchen and washing all of the dishes. I was surprised that the night went so well for all of us. When Alex brought out the wine after dinner, my father didn't even want to take a sip. When I asked later on, right before he left how his alcohol addiction was going, he told me that shortly after I left home, he went and got help. He then cupped my hands, and told me that he wants to see me again.

I changed out of my dress, and threw on one of Alex's t-shirts. Alex's eyes hungrily lay on my body once I slipped my dress off, and he groaned with frustration once I pulled his t-shirt over my head. "I love the way you look in my shirts." Alex paused. "But, I'd prefer if you had nothing on, at all."

My cheeks turned bright red, as I turned the lights off. Taking a pillow, I threw it towards Alex, as I heard it land on his chest with a thud. "You're such a pervert, Alex." I laughed, as I cuddled into Alex's bare chest under the sheets. "I see you've been picking up habits from Hayden?"

Alex's cold hands went in my shirt, as his hands wrapped around my bare stomach. I held in my breath, as shivers sent down my spine from the cold temperature of his hands.

"I can't help it if you're just that beautiful." He whispered, lips brushing against my ear teasingly.

I let out a low laugh, turning around so that I could see his eyes. "Alex, stop it."

"You're going to have to get used to it if we're going to be together for the rest of our lives." Alex mumbled.

I stared up at him, noticing that his eyes were closed. Did he mean that, or was he just mumbling in his sleep?

"You have no idea what you're saying, Alex." I sighed.

"I know exactly what I'm saying." Alex interjected. "I want to be with you forever, Aerial."

A soft smile appeared on my face, as I pressed my lips against his for a faint second, before pulling away. "Go to sleep, Alex."

"Aerial, we're going to get married one day. Maybe not now, maybe not until a few years. But promise me that you'll marry me one day?" Alex slurred, his breathing starting to get heavier and heavier.

I stared at his face for a moment longer, before I let out a soft laugh. "I promise I'll marry you one day."

I suddenly felt a pull, as my chest came crashing into Alex's. I stared up, as Alex gave me a small smile. "I love you."

"I love you too, Alex."